Lia

D0537839

REBECCA GETHIN

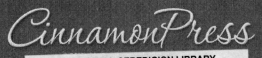

To Miranda and Toby

Partisans

He hacks at a snowdrift:
She skims the pine needles
That drop into their soup,
Scattering on the snowcrust
Ideograms of 'peace'
And 'love', suchlike ideals.

Michael Longley *The Ghost Orchid* 1995

1

Sea light bouncing off the walls dazzled Petronella back to the time her mother had brought her here when she was eight years old. Avenues, lined with palm trees, led down to the harbour and the blue of the Mediterranean beyond. In the other direction loomed the mountains, their ragged outlines swathed in cloud as if storms were lurching towards the thin rim of coastline.

She stood still beside a lamppost in the morning hubbub of Porto Romolo—cars and mopeds jerking their way through the stop-start of the streets, a hurly-rush of people on the pavements. Above the din, she heard the chink of espresso cups as the scent of coffee drifted from crowded bars.

On impulse, she turned down a deserted alleyway beside a church. When it tipped her out into a little shady piazza, the place fitted a space in her memory like the central chunk in a jigsaw puzzle. A whole picture materialised with that piece. Here, her mother had bought her a strawberry and chocolate ice cream and she had sat on the rim of the fountain, swinging her legs. The ice cream melted in the heat, running down the cone, which turned soft inside her palm. It was so large she couldn't eat it fast enough. Gradually, the cone wilted and began to list to one side. The whole thing turned into a disappointing sludge, ice cream leaking down the back of her hand in runnels.

As her mother was wiping the corners of Petronella's mouth with a handkerchief, a voice called 'Maddalena, Maddalena!' A beautiful woman with glossy black hair, wearing a white skirt and yellow high-heeled shoes, rushed up and hugged her mother, kissing her on both cheeks. Petronella had never seen shoes that colour, or heels that high. How did she stay upright? 'This is Renata—almost my sister, almost your aunt, *mia cara,*' her mother said. The two women chatted to each other in Italian and the language trickled by like water over stones, full of half-heard consonants and flattened vowels. She caught a few words, then more, then whole exchanges which she understood without thinking and felt comfortable in the flow of their conversation, the stream slowly getting deeper so that she was able to paddle in it and see sun shining on the ripples, and fish darting about like shadows.

Standing now beside the marble fountain and admiring the bunches of roses and carnations being sold on the market stalls, Petronella sensed the stickiness of that ice cream between her fingers. Scooters were parked higgledy-piggledy along the streets. As men kicked them into action, the beetle-backed mopeds rolled from side to side, till they gathered speed into balance. But it was the memory of feeling so close to her mother that came to her most strongly—how happy, for a brief moment, her mother had been here. Alex, her father, hadn't been with them, she couldn't remember why.

She climbed a run of steps and headed up a narrow street that she thought might lead to where Renata of the yellow stilettos had lived. After a couple of turns she was lost in a maze of alleyways, but eventually found herself in a cobbled piazza with a church at one end and some pavement cafés at the other. Swifts were mewing overhead like clockwork birds.

A church bell struck the time and she recognised the sound reverberating like a gong: another quarter of an hour being sliced from the future. She turned into the unobtrusive doorway. Even the church's name was familiar —San Pietro. After the bright sun, her eyes took a moment to adapt to the darkness. Unusually, the stone walls were bare of decoration. The nave rose into a high, unadorned dome.

Tears prickled her eyes without her understanding why. She wandered aimlessly past the side chapels, where votive candles in red containers were flickering and sorrowful plaster saints permanently prayed. When she reached the chapel of San Antonio, she stood still. He seemed a much younger saint than the others, a kindly youth with tonsured hair, holding a smiling toddler Jesus. He wore a traditional brown Franciscan robe. Recollection fizzed through her body.

From somewhere in her memory a film of the past was being projected on to the bare walls. A priest sailed past in his black robe. He looked like a rook with its feathers askew and she noticed his face was round and sweaty. Her mother spoke to him in an undertone and he listened with his head cocked and his eyes focussed on the ground, as if he could see something there. She told Petronella to wait —'I expect you to be here when I come back'—and walked into a wooden box that looked like a huge wardrobe, and closed the door. The priest also entered the wardrobe, but through a different door which creaked as he opened and closed it behind him.

Petronella heard voices speaking from inside the box, but couldn't hear what they said. Left alone, she sat there in the gloom, staring at Saint Anthony carrying the chubby infant. In the candle-light she had wanted to stretch out and stroke the plaster child, to feel his soft-looking hair, his warm skin. She was meant to have had a new baby brother. He'd never arrived.

Whenever the door opened at the far end of the church, a shaft of light illuminated the face of the Christ child. His eyes almost moved once. A woman approached, lit a candle and started murmuring. Petronella thought it would look better if she prayed too, so she wriggled onto her knees. She moved too quickly and knocked her knee on the leg of the wooden chair in front of her and made it clatter. She felt less out-of-place being holy in the side chapel breathing in the thick air of incense, its mixture of fallen leaves and her father's shirts, making her want to sneeze. The darkness around wasn't so frightening once her eyes became accustomed to the gloom. Every sound in the church created a muffled echo that resonated high into the dome. She imagined heaven to be like this with the sounds of angels passing by.

After what seemed a long time, Maddalena reappeared, her face puffy. She put on her dark glasses in the dark church and marched her daughter out into the daylight.

Petronella couldn't remember where her mother had taken her after that. She emerged into the sun-shot piazza, knowing she had made the right decision to return to Porto Romolo—to help her in her task of translating Maddalena's account. She had grasped hold of a thread that was purposefully towing her along. She couldn't let go now that it had been set in motion. No sooner had she arrived here than she seemed to have been sucked into an airlock of the past. As far back as she could remember she'd always felt unsure about what was happening in the present, that something other was taking place—but, over time, she had learned to live with it. That old feeling came back to her anew and the shock crept into the roots of her hair.

2

Determined to find light, valerian shoots sprouted between the flagstones from the white roots that swarmed underground. Alex would have sliced those off or, at least, got her to do it. Opening the front door with her key, Petronella half expected his voice to call out, 'At last, you're here! What kept you? Was the traffic bad?' She was uncertain how she would react. Hug him with relief, or feel a pang of disappointment? She didn't miss him as much as she should. It made her fearful, that he would guess what she was thinking from the look on her face.

Bad enough having to face the remains of his life in the house—the dear and drear furniture in the same old places, the draught through the letterbox, the well-maintained roof holding out the rain and keeping a lid on the household gods. She caught sight of herself in the hall mirror where she'd watched herself grow up—didn't like the looks of the middle-aged woman reflected back at her, curly hair greying, cheeks flushed with broken veins, her face marked by frown and laugh lines—but she recognised the child she had been by her aquiline nose and wide eyes. Next to it was the clock that her father used to wind every morning; she remembered its heart-broken chime, measuring out her childhood. A part of herself was stuck in this house. Without having to think, she knew where everything was kept, like the sellotape and string in the kitchen drawer, the scissors on a hook.

What struck her now was the absence of smell. As a child, when she came home from school the house had been filled with some aroma wafting out of the kitchen where her mother was cooking sorrow, which she stirred into whatever dish she was preparing for tea. Standing in the hallway forty years after her mother's death, Petronella's heart clenched, as if it were Maddalena who had only just died.

The house remembers me, she thought; it gave birth to me. I grew up in these rooms. There was something like a smirk in the way the door clicked shut, the way the light-switch was slow to respond in the sitting room. There, in an alcove, stood Alex's mahogany desk, which had belonged to his father. On the top was a silver-framed photograph of Maddalena in her wedding dress. Petronella picked it up to wipe the dust off and, in doing so, noticed the neat writing on the back—*Maddalena October 1945*. Beside this, was one of herself holding her son when he was a baby. Printed on the back—*Petronella and Matthew June 1978*.

Nobody had been in Dale View since Alex had been moved into the old people's home on the outskirts of Wikeley and she'd rushed by to fetch some things for him. He'd managed his household affairs himself and she'd had his mail re-directed to the new address. It was partly designed to give him the feeling he'd soon be going back home but then he died unexpectedly, soon after he had settled in—of pneumonia, they said. He was physically frail by then, but Petronella guessed his real malaise was due to being parted from his own bits and bobs.

Knowing she must sort through the desk for accounts and other documents, Petronella opened the desk lid. Scraps of paper, bills and receipts, had been left higgledy-piggledy. She gasped out loud; Alex had always given the impression of being so organised. But he had not kept any order for some time, had left confusion behind the neat face of the desk. Expecting to find birth certificates, bills, deeds and contracts stacked in apple-pie order, she was dismayed to find that everything was a complete mess in the drawers. They were stuffed with half-full stamp albums, out-of-date catalogues for wireless parts, old radio magazines. Perhaps he had had that condition when you become incapable of throwing anything out. There had always been things about him she'd never understood, neither his pinpoint accuracy with a wireless nor his fumbling with any kind of emotion.

She pulled open a little drawer between the pigeonholes inside the desk, which contained an assortment of old sixpences, fuses, valves. Her attention was drawn to a small brass key. She picked it up and savoured the chunky feel of it. Attached was a creased label on which she deciphered the name *Maddalena*.

Petronella ran upstairs to look in the corner of her father's room where she had remembered that there used to be a wooden blanket chest. She had never been allowed to rummage inside, but had a suspicion it contained her mother's possessions.

She slid the key into the lock and wobbled it about until it turned with a little clunk as if something was prised apart. From inside, wafted a strong smell of camphor mothballs. She recognised the fabrics of her mother's clothes. Some of her best things had been preserved, neatly folded. On the top rested a black felt hat with a little veil like Greta Garbo used to wear. There were silk scarves of various colours and some scarlet retro shoes that Petronella thought she would have loved to wear in the seventies.

Under the hat was a tapestried purse with some Italian coins. There was a photo album she remembered from its shining gilt-edged pages. The blue leather had faded only slightly and a tassel dangled from the spine. Inside were photos of herself as a child, and underneath each one her mother had written the month and the year.

She looked at one of herself, aged six according to the date. She recognised precisely where it had been taken by the particular shadows that advanced up Dale View's lawn in the afternoons. She felt a pang for the child looking straight out of the photo with a determined jutting of her jaw that gave an impression of challenging the observer behind the lens: 'It shouldn't be like this, it's up to you to sort things out for me.' Petronella recognised how it felt to be that child, could still feel her vulnerability beneath defensive layers of adulthood.

Another much older, burgundy-coloured leather album contained sepia pictures she'd not seen before. One particularly struck her: a group of people were laughing together; underneath was written *Meraldo 1914*. There were two photos of Grandfather Gianni, and Uncle Cristiano, neither of whom she had ever met, but whose faces she remembered from photos on Granny Rose's mantelpiece.

At the bottom of the chest there was a cardboard shoe box containing old postcards addressed to her mother and tied up with a red ribbon—also a card wallet containing identification with her signature, *Maddalena Petrini*, the date 1944, the words *Partigiani* and *Gruppi di Difesa delle Donne*. Petronella guessed this was an identity tag from when her mother had been a partisan during the war. Hadn't Alex mentioned her mother being involved in the Italian Resistance? But Maddalena had never talked about it. And Petronella hadn't paid attention to the little that he'd told her. Now, she wished that she had listened and asked questions. What exactly was a partisan? And what had they done?

Underneath the box was an exercise book, its pages full of writing and drawings, some quoted verses, a recipe or two. She must have brought the notebook with her when she came to Wikeley from Italy, then forgot where she had put it for safe keeping. Petronella recognised words and phrases here and there, but hadn't read or spoken any Italian for a while. *Carissima*... As Petronella riffled through the pages she heard her mother's voice whispering. She wasn't sure what she was expecting to find in the chest, and Maddalena was always capable of surprising her. Petronella opened a page at random and with the help of a dictionary worked her way through the last few lines:

> 'You'll learn,' she said. 'Looks like we'll both have to, doesn't it?' That night I cried myself to sleep. The straw sacks must have been full of lice because I was soon itching. It was the smell of sweaty men that frightened me as much as the sound of their breathing, their restive discomfort. We were lying so close together I was anxious...

The elaborately looped neat script was definitely Maddalena's. All curlicues and flourishes: almost illegible, like a code. She had spoken English with no detectable accent, but one thing she could never disguise was her handwriting.

Petronella scanned the page. Maybe she was mistaken. It could just be the traditional kind of writing all school children were taught to use. Handwriting was important in those days—the copperplate style that anyone schooled in calligraphy would have used. Her mother had formed letters like that. Perhaps, she thought, this was simply handwriting practice. And yet her skin was prickling.

Translating this took some minutes as her Italian was rusty even though she had grown up with it. She turned over the page:

> ...lest one of them kick me in the face as he turned over. It was cold. I don't think I could have got through the night without the slight warmth from Renata but, all the same, I could feel fits of shivering from time to time. I couldn't work out if it was her or me. We held each other's fingers all night.

The beige cover of the exercise book was well thumbed and speckled with age, like liver spots on an old man's skin. The ruled pages were worn and dog-eared. When she flicked back to search for clues Petronella looked at the verse written inside the flap of the front cover:

Ho io appreso quell che s'io ridico
A molti fia sapor di forte agrume;
E s'io al vero son timido amico
Temo di pereder viver tra coloro
Che questo tempo chiameranno antico.

It wasn't contemporary Italian. Maddalena had added, 'Paradiso Canto XVII' underneath it—so it was something from Dante's *The Divine Comedy*. Her mother had learned screeds of Dante off by heart as a schoolgirl. Petronella went downstairs to search the bookshelves for a dual-language version. She flicked through the pages of *Paradiso* and found the translation:

I have learned things which, if I report them
Will leave many people with a very sour taste;
But if I am a very timid friend of the truth
I fear losing my chance to live among those
Who will call these days the old days.

Something contracted inside the pit of her stomach. Why exactly had Maddalena chosen this passage? What awful thing had she experienced that would sour other people were they to know? Petronella re-read the phrase 'if I am a very timid friend of the truth'.

The ink was faded, making the words difficult to decipher, and the pages were so thin that Petronella thought they might tear. What had happened in the 'old days'? She opened a page near the end and a phrase leaped out at her:

I didn't even have his blood on my hands.

Whose blood? What was she talking about? This couldn't be true. Surely not. Seeing her mother's handwriting brought Maddalena loud and clear into her mind, as if she could have touched her skin, heard her voice calling from the kitchen, 'Is that you, *mia cara*?'

She couldn't tell if it was a story or some sort of diary, written in ink, but on different occasions; the central spread was a detailed sketch map with further additions and names inserted later in another pen, or in pencil.

Something slipped to the floor. She groped about in the gloom and found a piece of paper. Folded inside was a small black and white photo that had been left out of the album and kept flat between the pages of the old exercise book.

The photo was of a man whose face seemed familiar. He was probably some relation of theirs, a cousin perhaps. It wasn't Maddalena's brother, Cristiano, who was sent to fight in Greece—Petronella knew his face from her grandmother's picture of him. This man was older. He was wearing shorts and a cartridge belt, almost like a soldier's uniform. Sunlight was shining in his eyes making him squint a little. His shadow darkened the ground. He reminded Petronella of Matt. Nothing was written on the back. Who might know his identity? Taking the photo towards the light of the window she studied it, trying to see more.

She was curious to know what was being said or what was going on around him to produce that look. The camera had locked him inside a secret, letting through only this chink of light to illuminate some story she knew nothing about.

Petronella examined the piece of paper in which the photo was folded and saw it was a scribbled letter in Italian. She couldn't work out what it said at first. After a time, looking up words in the dictionary, she managed to decipher the faded lettering.

Canea Prison March 20th

My dearest—

Forgive me for risking all our plans. We would have been happy living the rest of our lives together. By tomorrow, I think I may be dead, and certainly by the time you read this. I want you to feel certain that I have loved you with all my heart. You brought out the best part of me and that cannot be destroyed, whatever they do. Don't let people forget what happened to us. One day, write about it. I think perhaps you will.

Right now, for my sake, you must walk away from this and not look back.

V~~~

The signature was indecipherable. Who was it that had loved Maddalena? And what had happened to him? And in what year had this been written?

The clues might be in the exercise book. She would have to translate it. And all in Italian. It would take some time. There was only herself and her forgotten Italian to rely on. There was no one else to ask for help.

3

A Truthful Account

These events culminated at Revalla in April 1945. I write to exonerate anyone else who was involved. My death may not bring an end. So I leave this memoir.

During the first night I spent with the partisans the sound of the river flowing between rocks seemed to have followed me all the way up the steep slope. At first, I thought I was hearing the rustle of my own fear as it shifted through my body. Later, the constant whispering gave me a handhold to grasp whenever I woke from fitful sleep that night in the pitch black. It wouldn't leave me entirely to my worst imaginings. The suffocating air seemed to be pressing down on us like an invisible roof. It reeked of sweaty clothes and perspiring bodies seldom washed, of the mildewy straw and rotting sacks, of men's urine and their stale cigarettes, of their tobacco-stained breath. It made me feel that my life was ruined, that all my hopes were ended. The noise of mucus rattling in their throats and the incessant coughing from one or other of the men jolted me awake whenever I dropped off. I thought of my mother alone at home, thinking I'd been arrested or had run away, wondering if she should lock the front door or leave it open in case I returned, as sleepless as me in this dark night—worrying about my father wherever he was, and my brother wherever he was. Leaving her without having been able to tell her what had happened was a physical pain.

Listening to the river, I went over how it was that I had arrived here and how I could have avoided it. My thoughts were dragged back to another sleepless night, six years before, when the world was teetering on a brink while ordinary people kept their eyes on the ground, living day by day. Had we known what to look out for we might have recognised the signs. We assumed we were entitled to hope and that we could plan our futures as we liked.

That particular evening in 1938—the one I think of as the start of everything—seemed perfectly ordinary. I remember the details of what happened so clearly, even before the Blackshirts arrived to take my father away.

He said goodnight to me. Sitting beside my pillow, he hugged me for a long time and then he kissed my forehead. He smelt of starch and tobacco, mixed with his own lemony scent. When he stood up he said, 'Even if you don't win the Dante prize you'll have a treat. Because you'll be the best. No doubt about it.' He went to the door and turned off the light.

'Pappa?'

'Yes, Maddalena?'

'Oh, nothing. Good night!'

'Sleep well, *carissima*.'

I watched him leave the room and heard him walk across the landing and go into my parents' bedroom where he had a desk. I didn't know what he was writing. Letters or poems. I heard the little bell on his typewriter tinkle when he reached the end of each line. The light shone under my door. If I had known I was not to see him again for a long time, I wouldn't have just said goodnight. I would have gone downstairs myself to save him, and lied to the Blackshirts when they came to arrest him. I'd have said he was away for a long time, that there was no point waiting. If I had known, I would have lied. There were things I wanted to ask that evening, but I didn't.

I was dozing when the sound of banging on the front door woke me. Because my mother was rolling out pasta on the kitchen table and her hands were floury, it would have been difficult for her to answer it. Cristiano was doing his homework at the table. She called out to Pappa to see who it was. He was already running down the stairs as I slipped round my door. The knocking went on and on as if they were trying to waken the dead. My heart thumped in time to the noise. Pappa opened the door and three policemen marched straight in.

'You are under arrest,' one of them said.

'What am I supposed to have done?'

'You must come with us now,' said another voice. 'We have to question you.'

'Why? What about?'

'We ask the questions!'

I watched from the top of the stairs as my father took his hat and coat and let them take him.

My voice was stuck with shock. He just had time to kiss my mother on the mouth, stroking her cheek with a finger and fling an arm round Cristiano who stood behind her. Pappa said, 'I'll be back later. Don't worry.' She stood by the front door as they pushed him into a motor that was parked outside the apartment. There were faces watching from the windows opposite. Minutes after they'd driven off the telephone rang. I heard her voice, 'I don't know what's going on, Signora. So kind of you to call.' I ran downstairs to her. She telephoned my uncle who took a long time to answer. 'Luciano, it's me, Rosa. I need your help. They've just taken Gianni away.'

I didn't hear what he said in reply, but could make out a distant tinny-sounding crackle from the other end of the line.

My mother said, 'No, nothing… What can we do now? Could you go down there and find out what's happening?' She clasped the earpiece tightly.

'So, what's the best thing? Can you speak to someone high up? Think of someone. Please.' My mother was crying behind her hand. I saw tears seep out between her fingers. He spoke to her for a long time. She finally said, 'Yes, all right. Yes, I'll let you know as soon as anything happens here.' Afterwards, she told me to go back to bed. I cried into my pillow. The hall light was left on all night.

Pappa hadn't reappeared by morning. Just before my brother and I should have been leaving the house to go to school, two Blackshirts returned and, without asking for my mother's permission, barged into the front room and started searching. Cristiano and I watched from the doorway. He turned away when they yanked open the drawers of the sideboard and found a pile of papers. If only Cristiano or my mother had thought of burning them. One of the policemen said, 'This'll clinch it.' And, without speaking to us, they left.

A judge called my father a 'subversive' and sentenced him to a year's exile in a remote village in the malaria-ridden south for, 're-education in patriotism.' We discovered later that he was one of the lucky ones because he wasn't shot. He was even able to take a few things with him. My mother put some clothes, a pen and a notebook, a volume of poetry, his pipe and shaving equipment in a suitcase and visited him in his cell to say goodbye. The next day he was to go south by train, accompanied by and probably handcuffed to a guard.

We could only imagine his departure. We didn't see him off but my mother waited outside the station for most of the morning. From the timetable she could see there were various trains to Rome as she assumed they would catch a connection from there to the South. But he did not appear. Later, the station-master told her that my father and a guard had boarded the last train to Rome that day. We didn't hear from him for weeks after they had taken him away. Every day we hoped for a letter, but none arrived. We hoped that no news was good news. From then on, my mother was always waiting. She spent much of the next few years waiting for her husband or her children.

4

As a child, Petronella felt she was waiting—that her mother was on the point of telling her something important. The feeling made her ache in the centre of her body. Whatever Maddalena wasn't saying could only be spoken in her mother tongue. Petronella thought that was the reason why, when they were alone at bath-time or bedtime, Maddalena would say a phrase in Italian for Petronella to repeat. Maddalena would mouth the words for her to remind her of the correct endings. She watched the shape of her mother's lips, the way her tongue touched her teeth. She tried to get it right by doing the same. Suspense clawed her insides. She would understand this important thing only if she could speak the language well enough. But Petronella feared she might not grasp its significance when the moment came.

In those days, Wikeley people didn't trust foreigners. Her mother's almost-perfect English accent was only a partial disguise—her handwriting gave her away. If Petronella took a note from her mother to school, the teacher tutted when she couldn't decipher the looped shape of the words. Everyone knew she wasn't English. The sitting room's bright upholstery in butter yellow and pale lilac stripes and most especially the sheen on the floor-length curtains, so unlike anyone else's at that time, made Petronella feel ashamed. Tasteless, they called it.

While queuing in the high street shops, Maddalena complained aloud that she couldn't buy flour to make her own pasta, that the potatoes were the wrong sort to make gnocchi, that the shops didn't stock olives and the coffee was insipid. She said it was all Alex's fault they had to live in a god-forsaken hole. She went to huge lengths to buy lemons and sometimes she could buy garlic when she went to Leeds. She read Elizabeth David avidly even though she couldn't purchase the exotic ingredients.

One day after school two of her friends came for tea. A long overdue return invitation. Maddalena greeted them in the hall. She had put on a blue dress, tightly belted at the waist and, inexplicably, was wearing her dark glasses in the house. Petronella was aghast. Her mother looked as if she had just come back from the hairdresser's. Her nails were scarlet, the same colour as her lipstick. She smelled of shampoo and hair spray.

'Hello, darlings, please come in and make yourselves at home.'

Petronella stiffened. Maddalena hugged her, then held her face in her hands.

'*Carissima,* what has happened to your hair? Come, let me fix it for you. It needs a good brush.'

'Not now, Mummy! Not now.'

'As you wish, *mia cara*. Be as scruffy as you like.'

'Could we have a picnic in the garden, you know—some marmite sandwiches or something just to eat outside, Mummy?'

'Oh, I think it too cold today! You must have your tea at the dining table. Be civilised about it. You need to think of your guests. They don't want to freeze in the garden and eat horrible bendy sandwiches. Now go and wash your hands, darlings, and then your tea will be ready.'

Petronella had hoped the picnic idea might avert the disaster that had already begun to unfold. When they were all sitting round the properly laid table Petronella could smell the perfumed scent of her mother's make-up, saw her pores under the foundation, the indentations of her lips under the lipstick. Petronella was certain that her schoolfriends' mothers didn't wander barefoot in their nighties round the frosty-white lawn after midnight—something had woken her the night before and when she'd lifted the leaf-patterned curtain she discovered her own mother talking to herself like a mad woman, under the moon gleaming like a slice of garlic.

Maddalena flourished a pizza on a plate in front of them. None of the other mothers served pizza, laced with garlic. When Petronella went out for tea at her friends' comfortably drab houses, their mothers produced ordinary things to eat like marmite or fish-paste sandwiches, corned beef or jelly containing bits of tinned fruit. For lunch there would be a pile of meat, gravy and vegetables all together on the one plate. That was normal. But her mother would never serve more than one kind of food at a time. Spaghetti for first, meat came second, then one vegetable after another. The same plate and the same knife and fork were used for different courses. Almost disgusting.

That day, Maddalena also produced her special lemon biscuits but this time she'd included soft cheese. Her friends tasted them but left the remains on the sides of their plates, and Petronella squirmed, knowing that tomorrow in the cloakroom her friends would be telling everyone how her family was mad, eating such weird foreign food. Sometimes it seemed that people at her school stopped talking and watched her whenever she came into a room. The words *wop* and *eyetie*, the sneer in the tone made her flinch—never said to her face, always behind her back, so that she could never be sure where it came from.

Petronella cast a sideways look across at her friends, but could not read their thoughts. Their faces seemed blank and disclosed nothing. She was the one who ought to suggest they do something after tea, but what should they all do?

There was never anything to do in this house. Except watch Maddalena. She polished the furniture so that you couldn't see the boredom but it was there all the time, little motes of it, revolving in rays of sunshine, waiting to cling to hair and clothes, land on flat surfaces. And Petronella breathed it in and breathed it out. It made her bones ache.

The dust was never allowed to settle—it kept moving in the air, invisible until the sun came out. They were like dead questions she wasn't able to ask. Her grandfather, for one. She'd grown up under the shadow of her grandfather's disappearance during the war. She knew to miss him even though she hadn't met him. In her grandmother's house there was a picture of Gianni in a silver frame, resolutely looking out into the room, as if he'd once had a future to look forward to. It sickened her that she hadn't known Gianni; he sounded nice, affectionate.

Granny Rose lived in Wikeley, too, and her house was in a row called Middleton Villas. All the walls had patterned wallpaper but a few of the joins didn't match—a piece of stem overlapped another or a flower sprouted from the wrong place. Petronella was alert to little imperfections in the sequence of things. Sometimes, if she arrived after school, Rose gave her apple sandwiches, Iced Gems, triangular chocolate Viennas and a glass of milk. Often they baked something together and Petronella stirred the ingredients in a large mixing bowl. They made Melting Moments and Cheery Buns, as she called them, which had glacé cherries in them. Then they sat down at the table again; granny made herself a pot of tea, gave Petronella another glass of milk and they ate what they'd baked, straight from the oven. The cherries in the Cheeries were sometimes too hot to bite.

Petronella noticed how her grandmother's lips moved when she thought no one was looking, though nothing louder than a whisper came out of her mouth. It was becoming a habit of hers. When she did this, she seemed to light up as if she were a candle, one of those big, round church candles where the wick sinks down below the wax edges.

So Petronella asked, 'Granny, why do you move your lips as if you are talking to someone when there's no one there?'

'Oh, but there is someone and I am talking to him.' She looked away.

'Granny, there really isn't anyone here and I saw you talking like that a moment ago.' Petronella spoke gently but firmly, just in case Granny Rose was coming down with something.

'Ah, well, just because you can't see them doesn't mean there isn't someone there.'

When she looked in her face Petronella could see she wasn't joking. 'Is there really someone? Who is it? Please, please tell me.'

'Well, my heart, if you must know I'll tell you my secret, but first you must promise me never to tell anyone.'

'I promise.'

'Because if you do, people will think I'm dotty and I don't want that.' She tapped her forehead with a finger. 'They might lock me away.'

'I won't, Granny, I really won't.'

'Well, it's your grandfather, my Gianni. He promised to come back and haunt me after he died. I ask his advice sometimes. And we have a little laugh now and then, too.'

'What? You mean he really, really haunts you?'

'Yes, I'm never lonely for long and I can discuss with him whether I need to call the plumber or when just to ask your dear father to fix something for me.' She smiled conspiratorially.

Petronella asked, 'Isn't it horrible to be haunted by someone?'

'No, not in the least. It's lovely, my heart,' she said, clapping her hands.

'What else does he say to you, Granny?' She moved closer to watch her eyes.

'Oh, he hums tunes from our favourite films. Sometimes when he speaks to me he puts on a Clark Gable voice saying, 'Frankly, my dear, I don't give a damn!' He also does a very good Judy Garland voice: 'There's no place like home. There's no place like home.' He makes me laugh out loud when I'm sitting here alone or even in the bath. If I feel sad he says to me, 'Rosa, get a grip!'

'Does he always tell the truth?'

Rose emphatically said that he did. After that, Petronella often felt someone was sitting there in the corner of their conversation—maybe silently joining in, although however hard she strained she could never hear him herself.

One time after seeing her grandmother talk with her lips, but not her voice, she felt an urge to tell someone. So she wrote Grandfather Gianni's name on a stone and let the river carry the secret away. She threw the stone into a pool above the mill wheel and his name, like a message, flowed out into the water. When she heard the mill wheel churning round and round she fancied it murmuring, 'Giannigiannigiannigiannigiannigianni...'

5

When there was fruit to spare my mother made jam, and she also preserved olives and tiny onions in oil as if she were compressing and bottling our happiness. All the time that Pappa was absent she sewed our lives together. I didn't notice, day-by-day, how much this cost her. It wasn't long before the seams came apart.

In those first days without Pappa I couldn't bring myself to eat. He wasn't here where he should be, chatting to us, sipping his coffee with that sucking noise he made with his lips and spilling the crumbs over the table. He'd said, as he left the house that night, that he would be back in the morning, but he wasn't. I knew my mother knew this because of the violent way she washed the dishes. I thought she might break them. After he'd gone, I missed him so much it was as if there was a Pappa-shaped hole in my mind dislodging everything. To fill the gap I wanted to talk about him all the time.

My mother said I had to go to school as usual every day even though I was tired because I dreamed about him. It was hard to concentrate on lessons when my mind was in such disarray, so I was often told off.

I thought the sky was watching him and that the moon knew where he slept at night.

I went round the house looking at the things he used. There was the silver cigarette case inscribed with my parents' names and the date of their wedding, *Gianni Petrini e Rosa Roberts Agosto 16 1923*. I knew he would be missing me, and it was worse for him because he didn't have any of my things to look at. I slipped my hand inside a pocket and found a bill, a key and some fluff. The inside of his jacket smelt of him—I put it on. I saw all his papers lying on his desk and I looked at his handwriting as if it could tell me where he'd gone. I wiggled my toes in his leather slippers that were moulded to the shape of his feet.

There was a photo of him in a silver frame beside my bed. As I closed my eyes I heard him say good night to me. From the photo, he watched over me as I slept, greeted me when I woke. He spoke in the same absent-minded way as when he was listening to the radio that my brother, Cristiano, had assembled in the sitting room. I could see from the expression on his face in the photo that he was thinking about something far away, as if he were looking into the future. I had his colour hair, but I looked more like my mother and my brother, who looked like my father, had my mother's fair hair. Our parents had crossed over each other in us, so that we reflected each of them, perfectly. We Four. *Noi Quattro*.

Sometimes, I reached up high to get one of the albums down from the shelf in the drawing room. I imagined my father sitting beside me at the table and telling me some of the stories of the people who were photographed. I wanted to squeeze inside each frame as if it were a miniature doorway to walk through into the past so that I could hear birds singing and people talking to each other, at the very time it was taken. Like the ones when he was young, with my grandmother and grandfather, standing to attention as if they were having to wait a long time for the camera to work. From under the black cloth, the photographer was saying something like, 'It won't be long now. Hey, keep looking. Just another minute. Now, watch the birdie!' Someone had written the place and the year underneath each photo. I wondered who had taken the trouble to do that.

In one picture, my grandparents were standing outside the front door of their house. As there was no road to the village where they lived, we had to walk a long way from a town called Trondo so we only went there for holidays. At the top of the steps were my father, my Uncle Luciano, whom I knew, and my Aunt Maddalena whom I'd never met because she had died in hospital when she was young. I was named after her, but nobody could ever tell me anything about her because their faces screwed up when she was mentioned. In the photo they were all talking to each other and I wanted to know what they were saying because, oddly, no one was taking any notice of the person holding the camera. As if there wasn't anyone there. They seemed pleased about some good news. Underneath it was written *Meraldo 1914*. I remembered enough history to know that the Great War had started then, but I couldn't think that they'd be pleased about that. I wanted to join in and get excited about whatever they were excited about, to call out something like, 'Hey, one day you'll have two lovely grandchildren called Maddalena and Cristiano.'

As I was looking at this page, my mother came in the room and leaned over to see what I was doing. 'So you've got that old thing down, I see. Found anything interesting?' she asked. We flicked through some of the pages in the album and she pointed out some of the people. 'Look, there's Aunt Marjorie when she was young. Pretty, wasn't she?'

'Why didn't she get married, Mamma? I thought everyone had to get married.'

'Well, she just never found the right person. It happens sometimes, you know. She just never loved anyone enough to want to marry them.'

'Oh! I see. Here's Pappa again!'

'That was when he and Luciano bought one of the very first motorcycles. It looks so funny now.'

'And here he is again!'

'Yes, didn't he look handsome? His hair was jet black then.' She studied the pictures as if they were fortune-telling cards that could tell her what to do next.

'And there's a picture of you, Mamma, when you married Pappa.'

My favourite pictures were these ones of my parents' wedding. My father was standing to attention in a suit with a rose or a carnation in the buttonhole. Underneath his smart moustache he was smiling his enormous smile as if his face was going to crack with it. In the sepia photo I couldn't be sure of the colour of my mother's dress. I thought it was mauve or even grey? 'No, it's more of a violet colour. Violet crêpe de chine it was.' she said. The material looked as if it had been dipped in silver. I spotted Uncle Luciano wearing a boater hat, tipped rakishly on the back of his head. In another wedding photo, my grandfather had his arm round my mother's shoulder. His fingers touched her bare neck. She was looking at him as if she relied on him to protect her from something that frightened her.

When we'd finished the photos, I closed the album and it made a sound as though there was a little catch in its throat.

'I've still got that dress, you know. Do you want to see it? It's in a box upstairs.'

From the wardrobe she took down a thin cardboard box from the hat shelf at the top. When she'd unfolded the layers of tissue paper, she shook the dress out so that it swished and then she held it up against herself. I fingered the mauve-blue material, which was cool and silky. It was trimmed with a few ruffled bits around the bodice and the sleeves came to just above her elbows. Whenever she moved, the lining whispered as if it was full of secrets. 'Do you like it?' I nodded and smiled. It was so beautiful I couldn't speak.

6

Petronella worked at translating the account until streaks of light appeared at the window. A bird chirruped. She needed to sleep. Although she was getting used to Maddalena's handwriting the language was slow in coming back to her. If only she'd kept up her Italian over the years. There had been a time when she'd understood a lot, even if she couldn't speak so fluently. She'd once accompanied her mother to that place where she'd been born and, by the time they came home, Petronella had thought she was able to pick up much of what was said.

She made herself some tea, went back upstairs to sleep in the spare room. Although she was tired she couldn't resist the urge to open the door of her old bedroom as she went past. The leaf-patterned curtains seemed to twitch. On the floor by the bed lay a scatter of dead bees. She gasped, hesitated, her fingers gripping the door handle. A chill flooded through her. 'You came back when I wasn't here for you', she said, flopping down on hands and knees on the worn carpet to look at them closely. They seemed to have dropped to the ground in a crescent shape while in mid-flight—their wings frayed at the edges, their bodies hollow. It felt like a supernatural visitation. She scooped them up onto the fly-leaf of a book and, opening the window, sprinkled them on the sill where the wind would blow away their husks.

Whenever Petronella returned to this house and reached the corner on the stairs she would visualise bees, forgetting they were not still inside her room; for years of her childhood she used to fall asleep to the tiny sounds of the bees' activities, which seemed to her like the breathing and shuffling of another's body close by. She did not mention their presence—their striped topaz and copper-coloured bodies filling a cavity behind her bedroom wall.

Occasionally, she saw her father standing on the garden path looking up at the slit in the stonework they used as an entrance. She never said that the wall behind her pillow smelt of honey and vibrated like an engine, day and night.

As she climbed into bed Petronella stroked the almost-warm wall with her fingers pressed flat against the wallpaper to feel the hum. Tapping on the wall seemed to make them cross. She didn't want to disturb them because they might buzz angrily or even fall silent, think she was eavesdropping. She had read that bees do not hear, they only sense vibration—but she thought they must be aware of her, picking up her movements with their radar.

Petronella liked the thinness of the wall between the bees and herself. There was just this small partition between her life and theirs. She read that a bee space is exactly the width of a bee; any bigger and they seal it with hexagonal comb, any smaller and they block it with waxy stuff, called propolis. The exactness of it was marvellous.

She could be herself here, in this room. Everywhere else she was on the alert to what others said and did. She told the bees her secrets and they sent answers in dreams that she forgot on waking.

That was why what would happen to them later hurt her so much. Especially when she thought maybe it had all been her fault.

Years later, bees came back into her life and created happier times. It was 1976, the year of the drought. It was her first proper job, teaching English in the local comprehensive, and she shared a house with others in a mini-commune of sorts on the edge of the town. They were all devotees of John and Sally Seymour's book, *Self Sufficiency,* and grew their own vegetables and made compost. They had a house cow for milk and a pig to fatten on the leftovers. They would have felt themselves in tune with *The Good Life* if they'd had a television to watch it. One of Petronella's duties was to care for the two hives of bees.

On an appointed afternoon during the school holidays she waited at home for the government Bee Inspector to arrive. His job was to inspect all the hives in the area every couple of years to check for foul-brood. If bees were found to have this disease they would be destroyed. It was a routine visit but she couldn't help feeling nervous as she was painfully aware of her own ignorance. She admitted that she kept bees in a slap-dash and unmethodical way even though she went to bee classes and knew how the order of the experts' hives did not correspond with the chaos inside her own.

The man who arrived was new to the job. He explained that the old chap she'd met once before had retired. Before he stepped into his bee-keeper's suit, she noticed with amusement that this new inspector wore a jumper with a honeycomb pattern.

When he lifted the top of the hive the bees seethed. Opening the lid always seemed to her as intrusive as if something sacred was being exposed. With gloved hands he winkled out the combs, lifted each one towards the light, and ran his gloved fingertips over the mass of bees as if he were stroking them. The hive's engine noise increased. Some of the guard bees were checking what he was doing. They danced round his head as if they were connected to him by elastic strings. Ignoring them, he puffed smoke into the hive from time to time and continued riffling through each of the combs, scrutinising the cells. He didn't say anything. She imagined that he was communing with her bees and felt envious of his confident handling.

After a while, he gently replaced the lid and started on the other one. By the time he'd finished looking through the two hives the air was full of guard bees. As he walked away, they followed him as if escorting him off their territory.

'Did you say something about putting the kettle on?' he asked. He unzipped his bee veil and it tipped onto his back. His eyes were the colour of the bees.

'So, are they okay?' she asked.

'Yes, they're all fine. No sign of foul brood.'

'That's good then.'

'But if you'll pardon my saying so...' He was stepping out of the protective suit. 'You could do with tidying up those hives or you'll end up with virgin queens hatching and you'll lose a swarm or two, especially if this warm weather continues.'

'Oh, did you spot queen cells?'

'Yes, I saw lots of occupied queen cells. It needs sorting soon or there'll be trouble.'

'I can't bear killing the queen cells. I do know I'm meant to do it, but I didn't start keeping bees to have to kill any of them.'

'But you'll have to or you'll seriously weaken your hives, you won't get any honey and the bees won't survive next winter.'

'Couldn't you have done it for me?'

'It's not my job as inspector. I'm only paid to inspect for notifiable disease.'

'I see. But still... You wouldn't, would you?'

'Well… not during my working day. It's a long job going through each and every comb. Let's have that cup of tea and I'll think about when. Have you any biscuits?'

He was called Todd and had curly hair the colour of a polished conker. She liked the look of him the minute she saw him. His features were still until he smiled. She liked the way he'd stepped unselfconsciously out of the bee suit.

She was really grateful to Todd when he came back one evening after work and went through the two hives to check for new queens and did the job of smudging out the new larvae. When he arrived she'd just washed her long hair and it was wrapped in a turban.

'That may or may not work. You'll have to see,' he said when he'd finished the job. 'It might help you if you talked to your bees. Do you?'

'Not exactly, but I try to listen to them.'

'You need to tell them about important events. If you don't, they fly off. Depart forever. Swarm!' He was tying up his shoelaces.

'What do you mean exactly?' She was laughing, but he looked absolutely serious.

'It's part of the folklore of bees. When there's a death in the family or anything important happens, you must tell your bees. I suppose it means you're out there working with your bees rather than neglecting them. There are a lot of stories about bees. The Greeks believed they were the guardians of the natural order and their comings and goings were always looked on as an omen, sometimes for good or sometimes for bad.'

He came back after work a second and third time that month. She thought it must be an omen because the third time was the first night he stayed. She assumed it couldn't work between them because he slept sprawled in her bed as if he owned it and she noticed that his skin was clammy, that he smelt slightly of damp leaves.

His hands on her skin made her forget where her body ended and where his began. He made her laugh. Her thighs ached from so much sex. When he wasn't there she couldn't believe he would come back, but his smell lingered on her body. She discovered that missing him filled her to the ends of her toes. One time, when he left his honeycomb jumper behind, she carried it round her shoulders as if it was hugging her. She felt desire rise in her when she looked at the purl and plain stitches of his hand-knitted woolly. Love affected her like alcohol.

They had much in common—enjoyed the same books, went for long walks he'd planned out using the local map. He liked to walk to places that suggested something to him, to a place with a mysterious name; to a bridge, with no marked path to it, over a river running through a wood; to a knoll that might have been a fort; to a clump of trees in a bare expanse. He made every outing an adventure—she thought she was dangerously in love.

On these walks he told her what he had read about the destruction of the rain forests, the pollution of the seas, acid rain. He talked about there being a hole in the ozone layer. She saw that he was caring and selfless, that her own efforts at self-sufficiency—the bee-keeping and vegetable growing—connected her to a global movement.

Often he led her down paths that were not marked on the map. It involved battling their way through undergrowth or ending up looking dishevelled in someone's farmyard. Sometimes they arrived at a river where they swam naked in the cool water in the searing heat.

She remembered once he'd said something like, 'I want to know where your bones and your tears and your laughter really come from, Petronella. Will you take me there, please, one day?'

She replied she had no idea where she came from. 'You have to take me as you find me!'

7

'How did you know it was Pappa when you first saw him?' I asked. It was a story I knew, but I never tired of hearing it because new information always came out. I could improve my picture of him. 'Well…' She draped the dress across the pillows as if someone were lying there, checking up on the truth of what she was about to say. She sat down beside me.

'…I was staying at the Grand Hotel. You know the one I mean, down by the promenade?'

'You'd come to Porto Romolo from England?'

'Yes, with your Aunt Marge. She came for the company, but really she was keeping an eye on me. She was what used to be called in the olden days a chaperone. Young women weren't meant to travel and socialise on their own. It wasn't done. But, because I was asthmatic, the doctor said I might become seriously ill if I spent another winter in England. My parents sent me over here because the Riviera has warm winters and it was thought the air would be good for my lungs. Coming to Italy might have saved my life.'

'Which is when you met Pappa?'

'Yes. He was working for the local paper and was writing a feature on the town's hotels—so he happened to come to the Grand Hotel to interview foreigners like us who were staying there to find out what they liked about the resort. But, unfortunately for him, none of us were grand lords or ladies, as he'd hoped—only a few minor ones—and other people like Marge and me with no fashionable clothes at all in our wardrobes. But the hotel did look very elegant, with tables made of glass, and chandeliers everywhere.'

My mother and aunt arrived in Porto Romolo in the autumn of 1922. The train had chugged its way along the coast from Marseilles, passing graceful villas in pink and yellow, tall pine trees, magenta and scarlet roses. The carriage wheels clacked in and out of tunnels, the rails curving along the shoreline of the blue Mediterranean where waves seemed to break into white-toothed smiles along the rocky coast. Rose stopped exclaiming to Marjorie and fell silent because she could see her more serious older sister had grown tired of her enthusiasms. When the train jerked to a stop at their station the hissing of steam and the screeching of brakes drowned out what Marjorie was saying. Rose could see Marjorie making shapes with her teeth and tongue and her eyes looked cross, focussing on something slightly above Rose's head. She didn't want to hear whatever it was her sister was trying to say. It was certain to be some sort of complaint. Or perhaps she was trying to tell Rose the news that Mussolini's Fascists had marched on Rome and, in front of ecstatic crowds, he had just been declared Prime Minister by the king. But she never did find out what Marge was telling her because she was too excited to concentrate.

Stepping down from the train into the sunlight, the glare drained all colour away. Rose always said that the most striking thing of all, for *stranieri*, was how the air was fragrant with the smell of mandarins. It was like arriving in paradise.

The platform was in pandemonium with people arriving and departing, steam from the train billowing out over the platform, doors banging, and a babble of voices. Rose giggled and said that Marjorie's face looked quite lugubrious. Perhaps it was just the heat and the whooshing noises.

Marjorie signalled to a porter who ambled over to assist them and when she waved an arm in the direction of the luggage he touched his cap, smiled at them both and said, '*Ben venute, signorine inglese*,' but Marge was already taking Rose's arm and frog-marching her away.

A motor taxi whisked them through wide streets lined with palm trees to a hotel that looked like a whipped meringue. When Rose opened the shutters of the window in her room there was a little balcony with a view of the wide sweep of the glittering bay. It seemed to her as if sunshine was revealing a new way of looking at things. And she could breathe without a wheeze in her chest.

The two sisters were swept up into the life of the hotel: lunching together in the shade, dinner every night with the band playing, jolly outings with other English guests to places along the coast, tennis in the morning and a siesta in the afternoon. These people behaved as they did at home, taking tea in the afternoons, the men drinking their port after dinner while the women had to withdraw to a lounge.

Sometimes, while Marjorie rested in the afternoons, Rose slipped away from the hotel to explore by herself. Round the corner was a Russian Orthodox Church. Its dome looked as if it might take off, for the coloured tiles with their upturned ends seemed to flutter like feathers. The fragrant pine trees made her feel clear of the prying eyes that watched her every move in the hotel. Inside the church, the Russian icons, painted with gold leaf, shone out of the cool dimness. She liked the dark shadows and heady smell of incense, which lingered in the corners.

Lady Firth and Mrs Thetford were perfectly dreadful, in Rose's opinion, so she avoided sitting with them: they smoked cigarette after cigarette with their scarlet nails tapping on the long, thin holders held between fingers weighed down with jewels. The smoke circled round their made-up faces and rose to the ceiling. If she sat too close to them, she'd start to cough.

One evening, Mrs Thetford coiled her long body next to my mother on the settee and hissed in her ear, 'Feeling a bit low this evening?'

'No, I'm fine, thank you very much. I was only thinking.'

'Might one enquire as to what you're thinking about? Or rather of whom?' She stretched closer.

'Oh, I wasn't thinking about anything in particular really.'

'Are you missing someone then?' and when Rose shook her head Lady Firth, who had come to sit beside her on the other side, asked, 'Are you not engaged yet?'

'No, not yet.' Rose wondered if the men spoke to each other like this when they drank their port, lit up their cigars.

'Perhaps she has a lover here?' The two women caught each other's eyes across her. She laughed and said that she didn't, as a matter of fact. But they noticed a blush. 'Ah, but there must be someone here you rather fancy?'

'We'll worm it out of you eventually, if you don't tell us.' Lady Firth spoke in a low voice so that Marge would not hear what she said. Carroll Gibbons and the Savoy Orpheans were playing *A Nightingale Sang in Berkeley Square* on the gramophone.

'We'll be thoroughly disagreeable until you spill the beans.'

'I bet he's married!' Mrs Thetford blew smoke rings, like kisses.

'We'll keep our eyes peeled. We'll be implacable.' Rose assured them there was no one she had a crush on and Lady Firth leaned towards her so that my mother could smell tobacco on her breath and said, 'We'll rectify that soon, dear girl. You're much too pretty not to be having fun, you know.'

'You must get away from that sister of yours and come out with us to the casino one night.'

'We'll teach you to play Black Jack or *Chemin de Fer*. It's easy and frightfully exciting!'

'There are some very eligible young men there. Not like these fuddy-duddies in the hotel.' Mrs Firth added this in an undertone and Rose felt her breath against her cheek.

'Don't worry, darling, we'll take you clothes shopping with us first.'

Then, from across the room, Marjorie called her to start a game of whist and though she didn't want to play that evening she was relieved to get away from their embarrassing conversation.

At the card table, Marjorie was mimicking the head waiter. 'I only asked for a knife to cut up my spaghetti. Impossible to eat without cutting it. I can't think why the tables are not laid with knives. Do you know what he said? 'Signorina, permeet me to show you 'ow to eat ze spaghettee.' And then the scoundrel took my fork and plunged it into the spaghetti and twiddled it round and round and then laid the fork down expecting me to open my mouth that wide. I ask you! Disgusting, I call it.' Rose looked around the room, thankful to note that none of the hotel staff were present.

The truth was that by then my mother had met the man who would be my father. He was giving her classes in Italian once a week and she didn't feel any desire to meet any other smart young men at the casino.

While he taught Rose Italian, Marge insisted on sitting with them. 'It would be a pretty kettle of fish if tongues started wagging,' she said. When a waiter poured milk into his tea and Marjorie offered him the sugar bowl my mother could see he was unaccustomed to the milk and nonplussed by how much sugar to take. His dark hair was curly but he had made no attempt to quell its springiness with hair cream. His moustache was glossy black. She thought she could see from the expression in his eyes what he was thinking, like light on water. She wanted to protect him from Marjorie who would make sneery remarks later about his wayward hair and his tie that was not perfectly straight.

Rose liked his smile and the way he laughed at what was funny and not just to please. She stumbled over the accent and the new words. After the half hour, he always punctually stood up to leave and warmly shook both the English women's hands. Rose liked the feel of his palm in hers, firm without being too soft. Perhaps he held it just a shade longer than was necessary.

One day he offered to take them for a drive around the town in a motor. On the street corners she noticed there were posters with a portrait of a politician with a prominent forehead and black hair, his face angled sideways. The signature, *Mussolini*, was printed in one of the corners; the *M* was large and bold.

They drove to the old port where men sold gargantuan fish and brightly coloured fishing boats were among the yachts. In the flower market he bought the sisters multicoloured bunches of roses. In a café on the promenade they drank tiny cups of sweetened coffee with almond cakes. She saw groups of men walking about wearing Blackshirts and knee boots, some carrying coshes that they twirled. When Marjorie asked who they were Gianni frowned, leaned across the table and said, 'Those are Fascist squads. Try not to look at them: they are already too full of their own importance.'

Rose decided that Gianni's eyes were the same colour as the sea. And like the Mediterranean they seemed to change colour with the weather, or his mood. She wondered if things appeared bluer to him, as if he were seeing through water. She didn't spot any other Italians with sharp blue eyes like his.

8

Petronella could remember a time when grandmothers were only young in sepia photographs, looking innocent and hopeful at their weddings, before colour was invented and showed everything up.

Petronella once asked, 'Granny, can you tell me something? Are you really called Rose or Rosa?'

'It's quite simple really. Italian women's names usually end in a. And, as you know, we used to live in Italy.' Her throat sounded dusty.

'Oh, please tell me the story.'

'I don't know if I've got a story.'

'You must have. Everybody has.' But something about the set of Rose's mouth made her stop wheedling and she never was told the story of how Rose became Rosa and then changed back again.

And there was another thing; although both Maddalena and Rose often spoke Italian to each other Granny Rose rarely spoke any to Petronella, except to teach her some rhymes.

Dante Alighieri
Spacca bicchieri
Sulle teste dei carabinieri.

She chuckled like a girl when Petronella repeated it. She said it meant 'Dante Alighieri broke glasses on the heads of Italian policemen.' It was a silly rhyme, but it seemed to mean a lot to Rosa. 'We used to sing that in the playground.' Petronella noticed that Granny Rose's eyes looked blurry as they searched her own face. What was she looking for? She always seemed to be on the brink of overflowing.

When Maddalena went into hospital to have another baby Petronella went to stay with Granny Rose for a few nights. But the stay went on for ages. Silence spread over everything. It collected in corners. Time seemed to slow. The baby was called Johnnie.

But he died. Petronella never saw him.

No one came to take her home. Staying so long with her grandmother made Petronella begin to hate her just a little. Granny Rose's hands were all knots and knobbles, as if she was collapsing inside her body. Her varicose veins flared red if she sat for long, close to the coal fire. Her blood seemed to be gradually draining out of her body somewhere as the skin sunk lower.

But her hair stayed beautiful—shades of grey folded and pinned up on the back of her head. She let down Petronella's hems because she was growing and the small neat stitches were pulled a little too tight by her bony fingers so that the material puckered slightly all the way round. Like the lines round her lips.

Her grandmother had irritating theories about many things—that you should not wear bright red until you were a certain age; that silver tongs should be used to pick up sugar lumps; that biscuits should never be dunked. Petronella noticed that Rose started to lose things—her needles, the door key, her purse.

One afternoon Petronella stirred eggs into flour mixture to make their favourite Cheery Buns while Granny Rose cut glacé cherries in half. Petronella was thinking so hard her stirring wasn't strong enough.

'Is the mixture too thick, dear?' Rose asked.

'I was wondering, Granny. Do babies turn into ghosts as well?'

'I expect so, dear. Why? Perhaps you need a bit more milk in the mix. It must be too dry if it's stiff.'

'Do you think that Mummy is like you and can see ghosts? Maybe she's being haunted by the baby ghost.'

'Perhaps she is, my heart. I wouldn't know, I'm afraid.' She put the knife down. 'Oh dear, there aren't enough cherries for the mix.'

'Mummy didn't say anything about a ghost though. Perhaps baby ghosts aren't able to talk.' Granny Rose turned away and went over to the window. Her hands tightened, as if she was about to yank the curtain material.

'Just because people can't talk doesn't mean they're not thinking thoughts.' She slowly pulled the curtains shut. 'Now, dear heart, if you divide the mixture in half we could put currants in one half and cherries in the other.'

'Granny, do you think ghosts will talk to me?'

Rose didn't answer. She collected the dishes off the table and washed them up noisily. Her cheeks looked damp and she brushed her rubber-glove fingers across her eyes. Petronella thought she was crying but it was difficult to tell because the hot tap was so steamy. When Rose tipped the water out of the bowl she seemed to be trying to force something down the plughole.

9

I can visualise flower buds opening in the hotel garden that spring, and the sea turning from grey to navy blue. Marjorie was making arrangements for the long train journey home. 'Oh, I'm having such a lot of fun, Marge. Let's stay a while longer,' Rose said to her, 'it'll only be raining in England and I did so want to see the agapanthus and the agave in flower. It's going to be simply lovely here in the summer. Please say we can stay for a little bit more.'

Marjorie was adamant. 'I find the heat at midday absolutely hateful and it is only April. I think it's high time we returned.'

'Well, you go on without me. I'm not quite ready to leave and if it is cold and wet in England I may find all the good work on my health is spoiled. I shall stay for another three or four weeks and you can tell everyone what a difference a dry, mild winter has made to my health.'

As Rose waved her sister off on the train she did have a guilty feeling about making her travel all that way on her own. Did Rose really have no suspicion about what was coming next? Marjorie obviously hadn't guessed, or she would never have left her behind.

Lady Firth and Mrs Thetford kissed Rose goodbye as well. 'You simply must come and stay with me when you come up to London for the season, dear girl, and we'll find you someone really entertaining, not these old fogeys we've had to live with all winter.'

Drifts of small red roses shimmied in the warmth, scattering their scent like a spell. Rose and Gianni were practising Italian in the hotel garden. He spotted a tortoise in a flower bed. They bent down to look at the beady eyes and Gianni lifted it up, its legs waving in the air as he turned it over to show her how to count its age by the spots underneath. *'Una tartarugha,'* he told her. She couldn't pronounce the long word without watching his lips as he repeated it for her. Perhaps that was a little too familiar. She touched the tortoise's head with a forefinger and it withdrew, then popped out again and winked at her. She laughed and Gianni put it back on the ground.

'How come there's a tortoise here?'

'They live here. They go to sleep in winter.'

'Well, I never knew that. He's just woken up then? A wild tortoise. I can't believe such a thing.'

'Yes, wild. They came out of the forest – oh, long ago, you see. They live in peoples' gardens now.' They walked on, peering under the bushes to see if there might be other tortoises. Gianni touched Rose's elbow, 'It's nice to be in love.' She didn't think she'd properly understood what he said. For a long moment, she felt confused. Tortoises one minute, love the next.

She thought he was about to tell her about another woman he had fallen for. She felt a bit disappointed, but thought he might need a woman friend to unburden himself to—or was it simply conversation? It's nice to be in the warm sunshine, something like that. When he didn't follow this up she opened her mouth to ask him the time. He looked straight at her, with his eyebrows raised. A shiver crept across her body so that she felt it flush across her face.

'Yes,' she said, 'It is, isn't it?' Doubt prickled her mind until he stepped in front of her and kissed her lightly on the mouth. The feel of his lips on hers was like the touch of a butterfly and she couldn't say anything more. When he kissed her again she knew that she had loved him all her life and that this was where she had wanted to be.

They arranged to get married in the early autumn, telegraphing Rose's family in England. From the photographs I can see that neither my grandparents nor Marjorie attended the wedding. Gianni arranged everything so that her family would feel comfortable about the ceremony. Perhaps it was a snub when they made no arrangements to come. Rose received letters wishing the couple happiness, but making excuses about the long journey. They would have considered her marrying an Italian unsuitable; even worse with no title or property to make it a topic of dinner party conversation. She knew she was no longer a credit to her parents.

The honeymoon was spent at Gianni's parents' house in their tiny mountain village called Meraldo, perched on the edge of a precipice. It was a perfect autumn for fungi, which they collected in baskets and dried on sheets in the sun. Rose had never seen so many colours and varieties. Gianni's mother taught her what was safe to eat; it was often difficult to tell. In the mountains, she felt her blood quicken and her skin lost its fashionable pallor. Her nose freckled like the inside of a foxglove petal. She tied her hair in a ponytail and felt it bounce against her neck. She felt a new person. And she was, because the marriage certificate said she was called Rosa and, because of that, everything would be happy ever after.

I wriggled towards her on the bed because I could see she was crying. My mother cried easily and now that Pappa had gone tears always hovered near the surface of her eyes. As I shuffled the bedclothes the dress rustled as if it wanted to comfort her too and she jumped up and started folding it away, wiping her eyes on her pinny so as not to mark the material with her tears.

'Mamma?'

'Yes?'

'He will come back, won't he?'

'Of course he will, my darling. You could start crossing the days off till the end of the year. Time will fly.'

10

That summer with Todd was early and hot, an unusually dry year. By late May, the fields turned blond, then ginger. One morning the air started seething. The second Petronella heard it she recognised the sound. She involuntarily looked up, eyes scanning the trees to watch if the nimbus of bees would settle in the vicinity. The clouds were moving in the bowl of the sky as if they were being stirred together. She spied a few stray bees circling the tops of the trees on the edge of the woods, just beyond the garden gate, so she rushed through it to watch them. These scouts were looking for a suitable new home for their colony while the main swarm was closely protecting their queen in the centre. The scouts rotated in the air as if they were spinning on an invisible leash. They were dancing the language of bees. Soon, the swarm gathered like a single creature made of many particles, dangling from a low branch of an ash tree.

She phoned Todd about the arrival of the swarm. She needed help in collecting them. He asked where they were and said he'd be over shortly with a box, but to let him know if they flew off. He thought it likely they'd stay there for a while. When he arrived, about an hour later, the bees were still hanging in a huge cluster from the branch. He stepped into his bee-suit and zipped himself up. When he saw the location of the swarm he said, 'I might need your help.' Then he went out into the garden and lit his smoker, picked up his cardboard box and took them over to the tree. He came back to her and asked if she had a pair of sharp secateurs. 'I thought we'd be able to shake the swarm into the box, but the whole branch needs snipping as they're hanging on to the twigs. It's a bit tangly.' She fetched some heavy-duty secateurs and stepped into her bee-keeper's outfit.

'Do you want to cut the branch or hold the box up underneath?' Petronella chose to cut the branch. She knew it must be severed in one snip and not be allowed to shake. She'd need to be sure of cutting right through it. There was a satisfying chopping sound as the branch fell and then the swarm plonked into the box as if they were one creature. They sizzled deeply and some of the bees welled over the sides and then ran back inside again. Todd shook the few remaining bees off the branch. Then he turned the box upside down and laid it on the ground, propping up the front with a stout twig so that the bees were free to fly in and out.

'It's always a wonder,' he said when he had taken off his bee-suit. 'I'll put them in a hive for you later on.'

That evening he spread a sheet on the ground, like a cloak, in front of the hive that stood at the bottom of the small garden. 'Come with me, if you like,' he called.

'I'm ready to run.' She hesitated behind him.

'That won't be necessary.' They fetched the box from the edge of the wood. Petronella carried it while Todd kept his hands on the base to stop the weight of the bee colony dropping out. The cardboard was fizzing in her hand. It felt like a live bomb. He took hold of the box and shook it decisively. Out plopped the seething contents onto the sheet. The knot of bees unravelled and scurried about in all directions. After a few minutes of frantic running around there must have been a signal—some tails lifting into the air beaming a pheromone flare across the colony—because they made a decision and marched as one over the white sheet and up into the dark door of the hive.

'That's your home now. Don't go off again. And you, Petronella love, must remember to always tell them what's important to you and what's happening in your life.'

She didn't say what was in her mind, that in the future she would tell the person she loved that she loved him. She wouldn't let someone drift away because he thought she didn't love him enough to tell him so. But she couldn't say this aloud.

They skipped some of the usual steps of courtship. When they were married the next year she wore a short plain purple dress she'd bought in Biba with a floppy hat and knee-high boots. She refused to be given away.

'I'm not a chattel to be handed over by my father. I give myself away freely.'

Had Alex minded? She wondered now. The thoughtlessness of youth! So many things she had never asked him.

11

Every moment that we lived hung on the moment that had just gone, like words in a sentence relying on each other to make sense. One thing must have led to another, but I saw no pattern. There were plenty of warning signs before they actually took him away, but Cristiano and I never spotted them. Fascist life was all we'd ever known. Besides, even if my father had suspected what was coming he would have carried on the same. He saw the gradual fascistization of institutions, the danger to civil liberties, and was determined to resist whatever the cost to himself.

And I'm sure my mother knew well enough that Gianni was dragging us all along with him. She had no power to steer, only to hold tight to what she believed in and hope we'd all get through intact.

At first my father complained about restrictions placed on his newspaper reports by obstreperous local officials. I heard him grumbling to my mother that they were bureaucrats justifying their existence by inventing problems. The Fascist government was run by the diminutive, pugnacious Mussolini, who specialised in rousing speeches. There were photos of his bald head and thick neck everywhere – in the streets, in my classroom, in the school hall where, every morning, we had to chant, *Hail to Il Duce, Founder of the Empire*. On the corner of the main piazza in the town centre was a picture of Mussolini riding a horse and brandishing a sword. He was often on the front of newspapers too.

My father began attending anti-Fascist meetings. There were rumours about what happened to people who challenged the state and my mother questioned his involvement. Opponents were sometimes forced to drink a litre of castor oil or were beaten up by the Blackshirts. Rumour soon turned into anecdotes and then into news about someone's brother or a friend's brother-in-law, arrested or exiled down South. We knew a boy called Gino in my brother's class at school whose father—an outspoken opponent of the Fascist state—was found mysteriously shot dead in the street. Gino refused to sing the Fascist anthem at school and was expelled.

The only person who felt able to talk to us was Uncle Luciano. But when he came round to see my father he would repeat his warnings, telling us about the new phenomenon of informers, a species of people who would tell the police about any suspicious expression of dissent. My father seemed to think he would always get away with it. My mother's concern was that he might lose his job; he'd never be able to find another. Unemployed people were begging on the streets. Having some money was far better than having none at all. Even as a child I dimly sensed a threat like the rumble of summer thunder. When it appeared to fade away I hoped it had gone forever, but it always came back, growling in the night.

Soon the English newspapers became unobtainable. The man at the newspaper stand on the street corner shrugged his shoulders, 'I'll try and order them for next week,' he said. But they never reappeared. My mother had often bought *The Times* or the *Daily Telegraph*, whatever was available, to give my brother and myself practice in contemporary English. When the newspapers stopped she was completely cut off from her country.

My father said, 'They've been banned for good, I expect. They're quite happy to let you read about the coronation of King George and Queen Elizabeth, but they don't want you to be able to read the truth about Italian troops slaughtering Abyssinians trying to defend their own country. They also don't want you to know about their allies the Germans who have been bombing Guernica to pieces. Fascism is nothing short of terrorism.'

My mother said he was exaggerating and that the papers would be available the next week. They weren't.

One evening I heard my father speaking quietly to Cristiano after a supper of my mother's minestrone. She had been taught how to cook it by my grandmother and she took special care with the broth, tasting it as it simmered, adding a dash of salt or oregano.

'Don't tell your mother where I'm going, if you can help it. It will only worry her. Let her think I've gone to see your uncle.' Cristiano remonstrated that he wanted to go out with him, but Pappa wouldn't allow it. My mother must have overheard because she did not look at Cristiano again that evening. She did not want to force him to lie. And she didn't ask Pappa what he was up to either.

She didn't need to ask because she already knew. He had helped to establish a newsletter called *The People's Voice*. It contained the news he couldn't write about at work and publicised illegal anti-Fascist meetings. The current issue contained a cartoon depicting a diminutive Mussolini standing on a hidden stool to address a crowd of people who were all dressed-up security guards, made to look like ordinary townsfolk.

Could she have stopped him? It was becoming more discomforting, like feeling the approach of a mistral; and now it was about to arrive inside the house.

Cristiano turned to his homemade radio in order to discover things for himself. He said that Italian radio was full of Fascist propaganda. 'If I hear the *Inno Fascista All'Armi* again, I'll go mad!' And he mocked,

> *To arms! To arms! We are the Fascists,*
> *Terror of the communists...*

He strung wires in the tree outside and built the set out of bits and pieces. It took up a corner of the sitting room. He was happiest when wearing the ear-phones, twiddling the knob until his face lit up when he found a station. He'd yell and bang the table, losing the connection, and I'd shout at him to be quiet. Then he'd settle back down again and look for another frequency. Cristiano's radio started off as a bit of fun, but his growing proficiency soon made it more dangerous.

Even though it was not permitted Pappa encouraged Cristiano to tune to the BBC's *Radio Londra* to hear the real news because Italy was not broadcasting the truth about the political situation. With the start of a civil war in Spain, he was desperate to know what was happening.

One night he and Cristiano tuned the radio carefully and we sat down to listen. My father had found a way of amplifying the sound so that earphones were no longer necessary. That evening when we were all gathered in the sitting room, he exhorted us to be absolutely silent. From Radio Barcelona there came an Italian voice; it was a man called Carlo Rosselli speaking to Italians in Italy: 'Brothers, Italian comrades, listen...' he said.

My mother interjected. 'Can you not turn it down lower? They could punish us for listening to a foreign radio station, you know.'

The voice on the radio spoke about sabotage and supporting Spanish workers in the trenches. My mother jumped up and tried to coax me to leave the room, too. I didn't take any notice as I was enjoying being cuddled, sitting on my father's lap, dovetailed neatly under his chin. My mother went to the kitchen to knead her dough, to stretch and fold it, to lighten the politics that kept creeping closer.

12

Petronella and her father sometimes sat at a table playing Liar Dice when her mother was busy in the kitchen. She learned how to cheat. Her father said to watch people's faces to see what they were hiding. Secrets get reflected in their eyes. She thought at first he meant the actual figures on the dice. She learnt to control her wayward eyes so that she could disguise her thoughts, but an involuntary movement of his might distract her. Through observation, she found that mouths revealed more because it isn't easy to hide the truth with your lips. You only need to offer little truths to make people think you are honest. Did her father know truths he'd never reveal? His mouth seemed to have no lips, as if he had clamped them shut or drawn them back to guard his tongue.

He was given to funny turns. One evening he was alone in the sitting room—the door was closed and the hall was full of cooking smells. Television voices leaked out from the room and Petronella went in to tell him his tea was on the table. As she entered he looked across at her as though he didn't have a clue who she was, which made her stomach twinge. When his eyes flicked back to the television her cheeks flushed hot as though she had been slapped across her face. Then he rose from the settee as if nothing had happened. In the kitchen Big Ben struck the time for the radio news. Petronella glanced back at him and saw him run both hands over his face and through his hair, but he didn't smile.

She always thought her father saw something wrong in her, something shameful. She wanted him to forget whatever it was and never tell anyone about the thing that was inside her. It made her feel as though she was living in a disguise and that her real self had no substance.

When she discovered that a school friend had been adopted it occurred to her that she might be too. It worried her at night. The bees were becoming dormant; she heard nothing more than a faint wheeze from them, as if an old man turned over in his sleep. She didn't like to ask her mother because Maddalena wasn't the sort of person you questioned much. But the doubt niggled at her; she had to know the truth.

She was helping her mother sort through the washing for the new twin tub: all the sheets in one pile, whites in another and coloured things to wait for last. The air grew steamy as the water in the washing machine heated up. The clothes smelt of the person who had worn them. They were all jumbled, empty arms and legs wrapped round each other. The sound of her voice broke through the machine's swishing and swashing,

'Do you think I might have been adopted?'

'*Carissima*, whatever made you think that?'

'Oh, I just...' She couldn't remember how the thought had arisen.

'You have such curious ideas sometimes.' Maddalena was checking the buttons on one of Alex's shirts.

'I can't help it.' She wished her mother would answer the question. The suspense felt like a hornet buzzing round her head.

'But what made you think that? It must have come from somewhere.' Maddalena stroked Petronella's hair into a curl behind her ears. 'What a strange idea to enter your head. What makes you ask?'

'Oh, I don't know. '

'Is it Daddy? Has he said something that's upset you?' She was frowning. She bent down to lift a pile of towels. 'Because you mustn't mind him. It's what happened to him in the war. Sometimes he doesn't sleep. He loves us, you know, he loves us very much but he sometimes has to switch off and he seems... distant, doesn't he? I know he does. He can't help it; it's just what comes back to him now and then. You see, your father... unfortunately he...' She walked away with the towels, came back towards Petronella. 'One day, your father...' she began and stopped. She pushed wisps of hair from her face and looked away. 'No! No, it's me. What I mean is... I just don't make him very happy some of the time.'

Maddalena untangled a sheet and a pillow-case. The conversation was left like that and Petronella didn't ask any more. She didn't understand what her mother meant. Unfortunately what? How could that become Mummy's fault? There was something mysterious about the world of adults she didn't think she'd ever understand. Or was marriage an impossible and unworkable invention? Perhaps her mother was not the marrying kind and had made a mistake. Maddalena offered her one of Granny Rose's peppermint creams, crunchy on the outside and gooey in the middle, but the feeling of being adopted didn't altogether fade.

Years later, it was Alex's decision that Petronella should be sent away to boarding school. He didn't ask her if she wanted to go. She ended up spending seven years imprisoned at that school. She learned to hate sewing because the needlework teacher always made her undo whatever she had just sewn. Sometimes the food made her gag, but she wasn't allowed to leave any and, if she made a fuss, the school matron spooned on to her plate an extra helping of what she hated the most. The same dictator checked she was wearing regulation grey knickers when uniforms were inspected before going to Sunday morning church. At night, she read *Lady Chatterley's Lover* by torchlight under the bedclothes. This was interspersed with school holidays spent in front of the television at Dale View with her unfortunate father or blissful times cooking with Granny Rose.

13

Pappa had been hoping that I would win the year's Dante prize in my class. He coached me, as he always did, listened to my recitation endlessly and made me practise over and over. Every year a pupil in each year group was given the award for the best rendition of a chosen canto of Dante. I knew mine by heart and lungs, as did he. He knew screeds of *The Divine Comedy* and he expected the same from both Cristiano and me. But without his presence at the event, it hardly mattered. I wanted to shout, 'Why aren't you here, you stupid fool of a man?' I felt guilty raging at him, but I wanted him to know what it was like at school with a family like mine; how I was teased for being half-English and how, every day, I had to try and evade the Fascist bullies. They would push me around outside the school gates because my brother and I weren't like them.

On the day before the final announcements were due, as I walked across the school playground to line up for the bell, my friend Angiolina accosted me.

'I've a bone to pick with your brother.'

'Why?'

'He's so big-headed his cap's too small for his head.'

'What are you talking about?' I always defended him from other people.

'He thinks he's so good-looking that every girl will fall at his feet,' she said, keeping a little distance from me as we walked past the dusty tennis court.

'Well, he has that effect. Can't be helped. Do you fancy him or something?'

'Fancy him! No, I do not! As a matter of fact, I don't go for boys of mixed race. Thinks he's too grand for the Young Fascist Scouts!' As she said that I cancelled her name from my list of friends. I didn't mind what my brother had done to upset Angiolina; the lines I'd had to learn for the Dante competition were still dancing in my head and were connected with the grief I felt in my heart for the loss of my father.

'You are both just so stuck up,' she continued ranting. 'Just wait until we're at war with the English! That'll pull you down a peg or two. Just you wait!' She hissed right into my ear and I couldn't wipe her spit from my earlobe until I could get to a basin and wash it out. Even then my ear felt invaded by her inexplicable venom, which felt like a stain right inside my eardrum—a private place, so close to the brain. I couldn't erase the noise of her words.

At home that evening, I tried my best to practise the Garbo expression in the mirror, to fend off the likes of Angiolina. Later, I decided that the Harpo Marx strategy of being dumb might suit the situation better.

The next day it was announced that I was the winner of the Dante prize. My mother made my favourite meal: stuffed zucchini flowers followed by peach torta. The day after, the Italian teacher made me stand up in front of the whole class. I thought she was going to congratulate me about the prize. At the same time, something about her tone of voice alerted me—as if she was about to tell me off. But as I stood up I felt a smirk twitch the corners of my mouth. She flabbergasted me, 'Maddalena Petrini, I regret to have to tell you that we have to strip you of the prize you have been awarded. It has come to my notice that you are not a committed member of the Fascist Girls' Association. For this reason you are not eligible to receive the prize. If you want to get on in life you must learn to toe the line.

'Instead we are going to give it to the runner-up who came very close behind you, Angiolina Bernini. Angiolina, stand up! You are going to be the recipient of this year's Dante prize. You need not feel you were second best because you were almost neck and neck with Maddalena. Unlike her, you show respect to *Il Duce* and the eternal values of the Italian race by attending Fascist Girls' activities. I would like everyone to applaud you. Now, stand up boys and girls! Long live *Il Duce!* Everyone in the class echoed her. Angiolina had spat in my ear only the day before she won the Dante prize over me. From that moment, I started to feel angry deep inside.

If Pappa were here I would have had someone to ask what to do. But he wasn't.

The incident made us all aware that whatever we did was going to be noticed by someone. Mamma said my brother and I had no choice and must regularly attend the Fascist Youth Movement. We had to wear uniforms and I remember the blue kerchief, pinned with a badge showing *Il Duce* in profile looking like a Roman emperor, because it was scratchy round my neck. As Cristiano and I walked to the compulsory drill practice on Saturday mornings I'd nag him, 'Do a Mussolini!' and he'd stick out his chin and his lips and bulge his eyes so that we arrived at the Casa del Balilla aching with laughter.

Mamma was cooking some cherry buns one evening. She used morello cherries and the juice bled into the dough. As she pulled the tray out of the oven she dropped it, burning her fingers. She kneeled on the floor picking up the broken buns and tears sizzled on the hot baking tray. I asked what the matter was. 'Is it Pappa? Have you heard something?' Cristiano came into the room. The water was on to boil for the evening's pasta and the kitchen was filling with steam.

'No, it's not your father,' she said as she got to her feet and wiped her face with a tea-towel. 'It's what's going on at my school. The head master said it's been decided that Italians no longer need to learn English. I must teach German if I am to keep my job.'

'Do you know any German, Mamma?' I was being practical. She had taught English part-time for years at the private elementary school in town. She had signed the oath of allegiance to *Il Duce* and wore a uniform.

'I'll manage somehow. I'll have to. I'll keep one step ahead of the children and mug it up as I go along. After a year or so I suppose I'll know what I'm doing.' She drained the pasta and gestured to us to take our places at the kitchen table. There was pesto and ricotta cheese, to be followed by apple *crostata*.

'But why German? Everybody learns English. I don't see the point.' I had sat down in my usual place by the window. My father's seat was empty beside me, but I had laid him a place at the table as I always did.

'I'll tell you what this is about,' said Cristiano. 'It's what father feared the most. If there is going to be a war, which seems likely, then Italy, now so pally with Germany, will join forces with Hitler. And when they win the war against the English then obviously speaking German would be far more useful. It's the future of a Fascist Europe as perceived by our glorious *Il Duce*.'

'This is all morbid speculation. There's nothing we can do about it anyway so I think we will stop talking like this any more. It's just upsetting. Now, who'd like to have a piece of *crostata*?'

'Apparently, the alliance between Italy and Germany is going to stabilise the whole of Europe before a crisis. It helps, of course, that the Italian people carry the mysterious power of eternal youth. It says so in my Fascist textbook so it must be true, mustn't it?'

'I wish Pappa would come back. I wish he'd never gone away,' I burst out, tears clogging my eyes. My throat felt full of bits of glass. Whatever we did was wrong. There were dangers hiding round every corner, even in our home. I ran out of the room and flung myself on my bed, weeping into the pillow. My mother followed and sat beside me on the bed. She stroked my head so I knew I was not alone. I tasted salt in the corners of my mouth. My nose ran.

'I expect we'll hear from Pappa soon,' she said. I sat up and flung my arms round her neck and we wept together.

She pulled herself away, took out a handkerchief from her pocket and wiped her eyes and then my own. 'If only we could visit him sometimes, hey? It's the never knowing when we'll see him again, isn't it?' Evening sunlight filled the room. Everything outside looked so calm, so normal. Birds singing in the garden. A tree swaying in a breeze and shadows on the wall.

'I don't know what war is like, Mamma. What will become of us?'

'Let's hope it won't come to that.' She wiped her nose.

'But, why do you suppose wars happen? And what will Pappa do?'

'I don't know any more than you, my love.' Her voice was shaky.

She never told me about the rat-infested trenches of the Somme, which her own father had managed to survive, or the thousands of men who went missing in the mud. I discovered all this much later. She didn't describe shell-shock or the effects of a gas attack, or a massacre, or what happens to ordinary people like us.

14

Petronella dreaded finding out what would happen next. She wanted to take them back in time, urge them not to take risks. Her family had walked into disaster.

Her head felt as though she had drunk too much red wine. During the long school day one class after another trooped into her room and slumped down at their desks to discuss what Piggy said and did in the next chapter of *Lord of the Flies* or to yawn through *Hamlet* and her thoughts returned again and again to Maddalena's account. Maybe she would find the truth that would explain the mess she'd made of her life.

She was meant to be at a staff meeting after school; she forgot and drove almost all the way home before remembering. She couldn't get involved with the discussion about various miscreants or the subsequent debate about what to do with children who consistently refused to wear the school tie. 'Are you feeling all right, Pet?' one of her colleagues asked her afterwards. 'You don't seem quite your efficient self.' She hated being called *Pet.*

'Does uniform really matter so much we have to discuss it for so long? Oh, sorry… take no notice of me—I had a late night. It's my age, isn't it? Nothing that a good sleep won't cure.'

The following Friday evening she cancelled an outing to a film she had arranged to see with a friend, explaining that over the half-term break she had to go back to her father's old home and get on with clearing it up. 'It's a pity you haven't got someone to help you,' her friend said. Petronella wondered if Matt might find a weekend to come with her. He always used to enjoy coming to the house.

But she wanted to be at Dale View on her own, for just a little while. It was half term and she had the whole week ahead. Things that had happened in her childhood seemed to be making sense and she wanted to be there to think about it in case she lost the one thread back to the past.

On the drive back to Wikeley it struck her that everything in Dale View was so out of date she doubted a charity shop would want it. The furniture was old fashioned and she had no use for it. Yet how could she get rid of it? The kitchen table had been a constant companion throughout her childhood and every scratch and dent told a story. It would be a terrible wrench to get rid of it all, but her house was already full of clutter.

She automatically chose to sleep in the guest room, as she always used to do when Matt and she came for their customary week in the summer holidays. Matt used to sleep in Petronella's old room with the single bed. After Todd left, she knew it would have been more sensible for Matt to have the double bed in the spare room as he was tall like his father, and she had remained small despite having been force-fed vitamin drops as a child. But she hadn't suggested they swap. There were ghosts in her old room and she still wouldn't sleep there.

That night she dreamed again about the man in the photo that she'd found in the trunk. Her mother walked into this dream. He was standing in a queue at the fish counter in the local supermarket. He looked beyond Petronella and gestured to her mother who was coming up behind. Together they walked straight out of the store, without paying, and clambered into a huge car, like a film star's Chevrolet with the sun-roof folded back, and they drove away. It wasn't much, no blinding revelations or anything like that, but the dream inexplicably agitated her.

In the morning she phoned Matt to tell him she was going to stay at the house for a bit longer than just the weekend. She knew he wouldn't be up yet so she spoke to the answerphone.

She rang Todd and left him a message, too. 'Todd, it's me. Look, I'm at Dale View and I'd like to be able to stay a few days. There's a lot to sort through. Can you keep a bit of an eye on Matt? If you can, will you please make sure he doesn't stay out all night every night? And can you possibly try and talk to him again? He's got some serious studying to do or else he'll fail everything. You've got this number to ring me back if there's a problem at all. Ring me any time. Okay? '

While she concentrated on the translation she kept Maddalena's photograph beside her on the desk. She found that glancing at the portrait from time to time helped her to extract her mother's tone of voice from the foreign words. The deepest shock was the feeling that she was hearing her real voice speak for the first time. It was like meeting her mother again now that she had become an adult. Perhaps this was what had been on the tip of Maddalena's tongue as she mouthed her own language to Petronella when she was a child, anticipating where she might stumble over the foreign words. She had been this close to telling. A bee-space close.

15

The year went by. Pappa might come home any day. We'd calculated when to expect his return and I'd been crossing each day off on the calendar. But then he didn't come and he still didn't come. A new Pope was elected who was Italian. What more could Italy as a nation hope for? As time went by and Pappa didn't appear our fresh sense of expectation turned sour with desperation. In the end, none of us was quite prepared for the evening when he did turn up. He walked in and called out, 'Hello, anyone at home? It's me!' I remembered the sound of his voice as if he had just come back late from work, and my mother's excited shriek.

He sat on a kitchen chair and we couldn't stop hugging him. Mamma turned her back while she made him some coffee and then slipped the cup across the table. 'Let him drink his coffee, Maddalena, please!' she said as she sat next to him, holding his other hand. Cristiano sat opposite with his elbows on the table, cupping his head in his hands, and just grinned across the table at him. I hugged him round the neck and rubbed my cheek against his, all prickly because he hadn't shaved. There was a horrible musty smell coming off his threadbare clothes. His coal-black hair was greying at the edges and his face was so thin his cheeks were crinkly. He reminded me of the unemployed men I'd seen hanging round every street corner in the city centre.

My mother was crying without making any sound and leaned on his shoulder. I said, 'Mamma, you are funny, crying now Pappa is back!' Everything for the next two or three days looked as if it was brand new—the sky was clearer, the trees and the flowers in the park were more beautiful and the waves made the pebbles on the beach glisten like gems.

For a while life went on as it had done before, although he was very tired and napped when he came home from his work as a machine grinder. Every time he left the house I was afraid he might disappear again. I felt more confident after he continued coming home in the evenings for two or three weeks. He often listened to foreign language stations on Cristiano's radio as if they might tell him something important, like the meaning of life or how to avoid the future we faced. He hung a heavy curtain behind the front door so that no one would overhear him listening to the banned BBC.

I overheard my parents talking to each other at night as I fell asleep. His rumbly voice was soothing. Once I caught bits of conversation, 'Let's just hope it won't...' and, 'You're living in cloud-cuckoo land, you know, if you're thinking...'

When I woke a bit later they were still talking in their bedroom, next to mine. I heard him say, 'It's inevitable... Italy's honour...' I was drifting off as he almost shouted out, 'He's bloody well sold us down the river.' But to me nothing seemed to be threatening now that Pappa was home. He could sort out whatever we needed.

16

'If you dream you've died, do you think that means you're dead?' Mother and daughter were folding sheets in the kitchen. Outside, a chill April wind flowing from the moorside above the town billowed the week's starched washing dry.

'Well, how would I know the answer to that, *mia cara*?' Maddalena replied. They each held one end of the starched sheet which lay stretched between them, difficult for a child's small arms.

'But, have you ever dreamed you've died?'

'My dreams die when I wake. So I might have done, but I couldn't say.' They walked toward each other, their fingers joined at the top crease of the linen. 'Now, just hold tight for a second, will you?' Petronella's hands became fists. Maddalena looked at her daughter as she took hold of the edge hanging down and then walked backwards. Shaking out a crease in the fabric almost pulled it out of Petronella's grasp. Maddalena walked towards her again to finish the dance of the sheet and laid it down folded and flat on the ironing board.

Petronella decided to keep an eye on her mother. She did it so that Maddalena wouldn't guess. She would look at a book and pretend. Sometimes she even turned the page, although she hadn't read more than a few words. Or she'd be colouring a picture, but would only half concentrate. Since Petronella had come home after the death of baby Johnnie she noticed that there was something new about her mother. Ordinary-seeming questions sometimes ignited a flame within her. Petronella knew her mother was changed, but wouldn't say anything about it. She was not so much different as somehow more herself—edgier, wired, as if something inside had been exposed.

She would have liked to help in some way, but couldn't think how. She wanted to understand the territory of grown-ups before she had to become one. And learn how to be one.

Whatever the circumstances, her mother contrived to look glamorous. When Maddalena came to Parents' Evenings at that time Petronella wished she didn't look quite so smart. She embarrassed Petronella more and more the older she grew. 'Don't be so English, *mia cara*,' she heard her mother's voice.

Maddalena wore expensive perfume that wafted in the air around her. She used scarlet lipstick and painted her nails bright red when other people's mothers looked as if their nails were damaged from scrubbing the kitchen floor all morning. She smoked, using an ivory cigarette holder, which was considered fast. She wrapped her hair in a scarf, wore dark glasses like a gangster's moll because she said the whiteness of the clouds in this bloody country dazzled her eyes.

Petronella observed her friends' parents watching her. Their eyes snapped on to her as she entered a room, when she arrived at the end of a birthday party or on Sports Day. Did they know that there was a white gap at the top of her seamed stockings that were kept up by a rubber button on her suspenders? Did they guess that things were not what they seemed?

Maddalena was capable of anything—wearing a pink suit or having her hair done in the latest style before anyone else realised it was fashionable. Her hair was naturally wavy and its blackness shone like coal, or as if it was oiled. She preferred to wear full skirts with belts that nipped in her waist. 'Zip me up' she'd command and her spine wriggled her tight-bodied evening dress into position in front of the mirror. She never wore stilettos, not even when she went out for the evening. 'Bad for your legs and feet,' she said.

Her dressing table was like an altar, the lipsticks standing in a row, with names like Petal Blush, Starry Kisses, Cherry Velvet next to bottles of matching nail varnish. She painted her toenails in winter, when no one would see her feet.

Petronella was fascinated by a curious little wooden hat with a feather, carved from one piece of wood. Because it was a little incongruous amongst the cosmetics Petronella picked it up to hold it in her hand. Maddalena slipped it from her and placed it back in front of her mirror.

'Not that, *mia cara*. Please.' There was some indecipherable writing scratched into the base.

'What does it say?' Petronella asked.

'Oh, I can't read it. It must be the name of the person who made it. Now choose me some perfume, *carissima*.'

There was a silver hairbrush with a matching hand-mirror inscribed with her initials. Petronella picked it up to study her reflection as if she could see the future in it. Maddalena sat her on the stool in front of the dressing-table mirror and brushed her hair a hundred times, or until her neck was tired from holding up her head. The hair flew upwards with the electricity and Maddalena said she looked like an angel.

17

But it wasn't long before everyone talked about this thing called War—in the streets, in the shops, everywhere. Everyone reacted differently. As if it was in the air, animating us. I remember walking past the newspaper stand on my way back from school and the billboards caught my attention: 'Fascism will Conquer' or 'Our Relentless Advance'. It felt as if an unstoppable herd of horses was on the rampage. We were never sure what the next day would bring. Everyone was buying food as if there would be none left in the shops to buy tomorrow. Pappa was still in poor shape after his period of exile, but he said it was inevitable he would have to join the army soon, too, because they would need complete mobilisation.

'They'll need every man they can get,' he was talking to Mamma.

'What? You and Cristiano, too?'

'Yes, certainly me. Cristiano isn't old enough yet. It depends how long it goes on for, of course. Let's hope it'll be over soon.'

Then my father received a letter announcing that he'd been selected for deportation to a German labour camp. He had been right: Hitler had ordered Mussolini to provide him with men to replace all the German workers who'd been required to become soldiers. My father was to be one of these. We calculated that he'd be safer in Germany. He'd be so useful they'd have to look after him well and we were thrilled he had been spared having to fight against the British. He'd be back before long; *Il Duce* assured everyone it would be a lightning war.

He was instructed to arrive at the station on a certain day and to bring a few clothes. Suitable work clothes and accommodation would be provided. He'd receive a wage in German currency and this could be sent back to the family.

Outgoing and incoming mail would be subject to censor. My mother packed up his bag as before and added chocolate, coffee and olive oil. 'I'm sure they do not have olive oil in Germany,' she said. We all went to the station to wave him goodbye, but he was bundled into a carriage so quickly we didn't see where he was sitting before the train bound for Verona pulled out of the station. There were hands fluttering from all the windows, but we didn't know which one was his.

I'd seen the headlines at the newspaper stand on the corner: Germany was about to invade Britain, and London was being systematically bombed. The Axis would soon be declaring the speedy victory *Il Duce* had promised. This didn't seem to happen as we had all hoped and the months of the war dragged by as we eked out our existence day by day. We had little money because Mamma didn't teach at the school any more. Cristiano worked hard all that year and finished his final school exams.

Just when Cristiano would have been about to go to university, he received his call-up letter and he went away for two months' military training. He came home on a weekend's leave before being posted somewhere, not that he knew where. He had to take his own leather boots because the army only provided a thin beige uniform and a helmet. We waved him off at the station where he jumped into the packed train to be with his old school-friends, Pierino and Enrico. My mother held on to him tightly. He took her hand and kissed the palm of her hand and closed her fingers round it. 'We'll be back soon,' he shouted as he jerked the window down. 'We know what we're doing!' Then the whistle blew, steam hissed and the wheels shrieked as they started to turn.

My mother's face remained impassive until the train reached the bend past the station. Then, she cried so much I thought she would be unable to walk home. Outside on the crowded street, the police were trying to round up the people into organised groups, one pavement for those going east and the other side of the road for those heading west. If you found yourself being carried in the wrong stream you couldn't cross to the other.

Later, when almost home, we passed a newspaper stand and the headline said, 'Italian Heroes in Greece.' We bought the paper and I read the piece out to my mother as we walked. It said that we were the superior force in the Axis because the Italian army was well-equipped and imbued with the spirit of order and discipline, unlike the Greeks who were being liquidated. When I had finished, my mother took a while to say anything at all. 'Don't you remember, dear, Pappa always said not to believe everything we read in the papers?' I wasn't sure which bit I wasn't to believe, but whatever she meant her words spoiled my relief that he wasn't directly in conflict with Englishmen.

18

Matt was already older than Cristiano had been when he received that call-up letter. Had it seemed like an adventure to him, going to another country with his friends? Petronella felt an inkling of what it must have been like for Rosa and pictured her own son's five-year-old body in the bath, squealing when the bubbles she squeezed from the flannel landed on his skin, the tip of his penis floating upwards to the surface as if to take a breath. She kissed the pudgy flesh of his arms. She remembered him filling the basin over and over again to watch how water spiralled down the plug hole. Always in the same direction.

Todd had been the sort of father to push his son in the pushchair. He even carried him in a pack on his back when they went on a long weekend to walk Hadrian's Wall. But the midges bit the baby and he became irritable. Todd developed a headache. Petronella couldn't carry Matt for long so they bought lotion for the bites and gave up on the walk.

In those days babies were put in a pram outside to sleep in the garden under a tree. Granny Rose said fresh air was good for him, but she didn't hold with leaving infants to cry, not for a minute. And Matt hadn't been the kind of baby to be content watching leaves. He never liked being alone. Todd grew fractious.

She wondered how much Matt had been damaged by her and Todd splitting. Once she really had been in love with Todd, but it hadn't worked because they argued over everything. He had a temper and she couldn't understand the way he would flare up. It wasn't much and he didn't mean the things he said, but his occasional outbursts hurt. She couldn't get used to his way of pouring out every frustration. As his concerns for the world became bleaker she struggled not to become depressed herself. She wanted holidays, but he wouldn't go with her. He told her it wasn't anything to get fussed about; he simply wasn't going. She wanted to move, but he didn't. Sometimes silences lasted for days—one of them had said something hurtful, but neither was clear who had said what; it was always the other one.

There was often plenty for him to complain about: the phone bill, Matt's fussy eating, or his forgetting to turn out lights or leaving the television on stand-by, which wasted electricity and created emissions from power plants. Petronella tried to steer a middle course for all of them, but the marriage was coming adrift. She had to admit the day-to-day realities of living with worsening global crises and Todd's consequent moods were not easy. Especially when so few other people sympathised with his grim predictions.

Into her mind rushed the memory of the night he told her he wasn't able to continue living with her and Matt. She remembered exactly when it was because he announced it just after the news describing the Serbian siege of Sarajevo. As the pictures flashed across the screen he said he needed to talk. Always ominous that phrase. She found it difficult to concentrate on what he was saying. He explained that he needed time to himself because he wasn't sure if he was cut out for a lifetime of marriage. 'I can't sit around here while the world is heading for annihilation,' he said, ' it's either going to be a nuclear bomb or ecological collapse.' He said he had to make a stand, do something to save the world. He didn't believe in anything except the imminence of global collapse. 'I'm a miserable bastard,' he said, 'and I'm not cut out to be just a husband.'

'Please be straight with me, Todd, is there somebody else?' she asked. It wasn't that, he said, he just didn't have the gifts to share a happy life with any one and because he was so fond of Petronella he felt she'd be better off without him: 'Happiness is ephemeral. It's in my genes to be gloomy; you know that because you saw it in my parents.

It catches up with me and ruins what I've tried to create. I have this predisposition to be pessimistic. It's like an illness. Better if I move sideways, before I infect you.'

She'd weakly argued with him that it would have a really bad effect on Matt, a sensitive teenager. What she failed to tell him was that it would also hurt her. She never thought to say that. The right occasion to tell him that she loved him hadn't arisen. She blamed him for not knowing what was in her heart. It was too late to tell him now.

It felt as if he was saying he didn't even like her. As she looked back over the last year or so she began to think he had more or less hated her for quite a while. In the morning he always complained that she yanked the duvet off him, as if she did it deliberately to prevent him sleeping. He was too depressed to feel any sexual urges. When she came home from work later than usual he expected her to wash up and to make him a cup of tea. She knew that plenty of men were like that, many could be much worse and that those marriages survived, but it was an expression in his face, she thought, something about the way he looked at her or didn't look at her, that made her feel she might hold her wrist over a candle-flame till the skin singed. Even that would fail to make him notice her for more than a minute.

Once he left he didn't return. She knew that there wasn't much likelihood; claiming he needed time to himself was just the sort of thing people say. Three years had gone by and he was living with his latest girlfriend, Tree, who ran a stall in the market, selling natural cosmetics and candles made from beeswax. She wore flowery trousers, sandals and a jumper she'd knitted herself from wool dyed with berries and roots. She was twelve years older than Matt.

Petronella was head of department by then: timetables, meetings about the curriculum, about staff, about budgets. Once, she'd thought it was possible to just shrug off unhappiness. If the timing was inconvenient you could put it off till later or, maybe, if you ignored it long enough, it would go away of its own accord.

But when Todd left she couldn't get away from herself and she kept falling asleep so much that she had to take time off work. She'd get up and make herself a cup of coffee or a sandwich and watch day-time television, but then she'd wake up to find that she'd been asleep again. Her friends rang up and she told them she was fine, just exhausted, she'd see them next week.

19

In July 1943 the newspapers announced that the king had imprisoned Mussolini. The new Italy would soon be on the side of the British and the Americans. Everyone could see the end of war on the horizon. In the park the town band played music I'd never heard before and people were dancing on the grass. Men climbed up buildings and lampposts, tearing down the portraits of Mussolini, setting fire to them in the street. They entered the Fascist headquarters and threw the bronze and plaster busts of *Il Duce* out of the window, flinging them on to burning pyres. Overnight Mussolini became reviled as if they had secretly hated him all the time. We had survived the war, and Pappa would soon be coming home. When both he and Cristiano returned at last, we would carry on from where we'd left off and everything would improve.

Next thing, Mussolini escaped from prison and was flown back to Rome by the Germans in a small aeroplane. The extremist Fascist militia proclaimed him their leader and in just a few days the Nazis occupied all of Northern Italy. New portraits of Mussolini appeared, but in these he was thinner-faced and ghostly. His bald head looked like an iron helmet. So, a different war was detonated. But, from where we were, we couldn't see what was going on. Nobody could have done, except perhaps for Pappa.

It was around this time that Mamma sent me out one day to see what food was available in the shops, because we needed flour and salt. I knew from experience that having a ration card didn't necessarily mean that I would find any. The sight of Nazi soldiers on the streets nearly made me turn back home. Armoured cars were parked down side streets. A motorcycle with a machine gun sticking out of the sidecar whizzed down the road and made me feel sick. I steeled myself to walk on. The soldiers looked like walking bullets with their helmets so low that they didn't seem to have faces and didn't notice how I glared. Knots of people gathered to talk about their arrival in our town centre. When Gino approached from across the street it was not apparent that he had been waiting for me, but later I realised that he must have planned the meeting. It was wonderful to see him again. He couldn't have known then that he seemed to me like my only friend.

We walked behind the gathering crowds of people along the pavement, swearing under our breath at the soldiers. Then he asked me to drop off a letter at an address in the town. It seemed a strange thing to ask; I wondered why he couldn't do it himself as it wasn't exactly on my way. I didn't mind the extra walk for the air was bright and there was a sharp smell of salt and seaweed blowing off the sea. Every now and then, between buildings I caught a glimpse of turquoise sea with white horses breaking, like rows of teeth snarling at each other.

The address Gino had given me was in a quiet alleyway off a main road. German trucks were grinding down the road and I had to wait for them all to pass in order to cross. Crowds of people were watching them. No one was singing or cheering any longer. The rumbling of the heavy tanks made the pavements tremble. One vehicle followed another, like an unbreakable chain.

I nipped through the scrum of people and into a narrow cobbled street, where many of the doors stood open so I could hear a baby crying and an old woman shouting. A dog barked half-heartedly at me as I passed. Washing was strung across the narrow street and smells of cooking were in the air. I knocked on the closed door of a tall house. I waited a short while and then the door opened a crack. A woman's head appeared in the gloom. When she saw me the door opened wider.

'Yes?'

'Gino asked me to give this to Yolanda,' I showed her the letter.

'I am Yolanda.' She snatched the envelope, looked up and down the alley, showed her teeth in a half-smile and closed the door. I thought she was a bit brusque, especially as I had walked out of my way just for this.

The little money I had didn't buy us very much as the prices had risen dramatically. The lira was just toy money. My eye caught the headlines as I passed a newspaper booth: *Victory in Greece Imminent.* Good, I thought, Cristiano will be home soon.

It was difficult to know whom you could trust in the streets. Mamma told me it would be better never to express any opinion to a stranger and even to be circumspect with people I considered a friend, but I knew Gino and on several occasions all through that winter he asked me to get messages to Yolanda and then, later, to other people in the city. A girl on a bicycle was far less likely to arouse suspicion. I thought Pappa would be proud of me.

20

Maddalena's description of glimpsing the sea between the tall buildings and her mention of narrow cobbled streets made Petronella's throat tighten. It was exactly what she remembered of Porto Romolo on that trip when she was eight years old.

There had been a long train journey to get there. She'd sat by the window in the train with Maddalena next to her. She recalled how the landscapes drifted past; flat plain, as far she could see, gave way to ranges of hills covered with trees, shimmering like the backdrop to a film. To Petronella the significance of every detail was intensified because as they drew near to their destination she noticed how her mother appeared happier.

If her mother was happy then so was she. Being in Porto Romolo signified ice-cream and shopping and roses and the whine of mopeds. She visualised the market stalls selling huge bunches of multicoloured flowers, as well as shiny bags, rainbows of scarves and lacy bed-linen embroidered with birds and butterflies in coloured silks—things she hadn't even dreamed of.

In her mind she saw her mother's friend, Renata, with the wayward hair she kept forcing into a chignon. Yellow shoes, she'd worn sun-yellow shoes. She was always teasing, a little alarming to an eight-year-old English girl. Maddalena and Renata spoke very fast in Italian and she didn't understand it at first. She'd forgotten what it was they talked about. Perhaps she hadn't listened.

Reading about her mother walking in those streets reminded her of the narrow medieval alleyways, and a small, sunny piazza with an old house that had ornate patterns on the ceilings and a decorated cornice. A bright purple bougainvillea grew against the wall. There was the stink of drains, children played in the streets and washing dangled above their heads. A canary was singing from a cage in a window, a woman was ranting from deep inside a house and a man was painting a door. Maddalena and Renata were arguing about something. Their voices rose and then her mother started crying in the street, weeping so that Petronella thought her mother wouldn't be able to stop. And nobody was taking any notice.

It came to her that she ought to return there, in the next school holidays maybe. She'd be able to brush up her Italian and being in the same environment might help her understand the unfolding story. The thought of it made her jump up. She wished she wasn't on her own.

She felt that what had happened between her and Todd was her fault, a flaw in her personality. He would never guess what she had done to spite him. On an impulse she had gathered sticks to make a fire in the grate. Flames chewed through the laminated cover and caught the corner, exposing curling pages before the whole book was satisfyingly consumed. My friend the fire: she bent down and fed it more wood. All those names and phone numbers going up in smoke. When he asked her if she'd seen his address book she answered, 'It must be around somewhere.' But his connection to his past was nothing more than a little heap of ash. And the worst thing was that it still made her want to laugh. She was far more deceitful than she let on and would never admit that one of his cuff-links might eventually be found somewhere in Lyme Bay. She'd dropped it off the end of the Cobb in Lyme Regis, refusing to be the French Lieutenant's woman watching out for his returning ship. The remaining cuff-link useless without the other. Because he rarely used them he might take years to discover one was missing. Rather pleasing, she almost giggled out loud. Like winning at Liar Dice.

She'd have to think about this trip to Italy for a bit longer before making any decisions.

21

It was a Tuesday evening in March and Yolanda sent me with an envelope to an address I knew. I had been there once before. An unshaven man wearing overalls asked me to take a package in my basket to an address in a quarter of town I seldom visited. I was searching for the street when two Blackshirts in long boots and gun belts appeared round a corner. I felt as if something had electrocuted me when we almost collided. I quickly said, 'Good evening.' I tried to say it in a cheery voice, but something caused a blockage in my throat and it came out as a squeak. They stopped and demanded my name.

'Maddalena Petrini,' I said without thinking.

'What are you doing here?' the younger one asked. I explained that I was going to visit an aunt but when they asked me where she lived I was unable to furnish them with an address in this quarter. The hesitation gave me away. They started peering into my basket and soon found the package. I didn't know what was in it, but panic welled up in my belly so I turned and bolted like a frightened horse. I ran and ran, away from everywhere I knew. I was lost in the maze of narrow streets.

They didn't catch up with me, but I knew for certain that I couldn't return home to my mother. As I had given them my name, I'd placed us both in danger. How could I go home to her now? If they looked up my father's name they'd soon put two and two together. I wandered the streets for the rest of the night, listening for footsteps behind me. I kept hearing the sound of my own shoes on the cobbles and couldn't distinguish mine from someone else's. I started running again in case I was being chased. In the distance, I could hear the sound of shelling, lighting the sky orange and white somewhere out to sea. It was Allied ships attacking German positions along the coast. Tonight, our town was spared. After curfew, the streets were empty and I felt trapped in a loop of terror and indecision, which made me keep walking on further and further away from the places I knew.

I must have sat down on a doorstep and fallen asleep. When I woke at first light I found myself near Yolanda's street. I'd been going in circles. I knocked on her door; I could think of nothing else. I feared being captured and shot and thought she might tell me what to do. I was hungry and exhausted. An old man answered and led me upstairs to an apartment where he sat me down and gave me coffee and a piece of bread and jam. He said he was Yolanda's father and that he could take me somewhere safer, to a house he knew in Caraggio, where we'd find Yolanda. He told me to hide under some sacks in the back of a three-wheeled pickup truck. The drive was bumpy and I thought my bones might be broken. I had to find a way to protect my head from smashing against the floor so I cradled it in my arms.

When we arrived I was relieved to step safely onto the ground and to see Yolanda there. Another girl was with her. She was called Renata. About my age, she had dark skin, an aquiline nose and wavy hair scraped back with a ribbon. She showed me where I could wash the grime of tears and sleeplessness from my face. After I'd cleaned up, she put a plate of pasta on the table in front of me, saying that she was pleased I had come because now she and I could escape together. I didn't grasp her meaning; because I was so tired everything was surreal.

I felt ashamed of myself—I had failed everyone by running. But Yolanda told me that I was lucky to have escaped because the package I'd been carrying contained cartridges. Without a doubt, they would have put me in the city gaol and then shot me. Renata said that she herself had only managed to escape arrest, in a similar situation, when one of the young men took a fancy to her and she promised to meet him that evening if he would let her go. He had turned away for a moment, giving her the chance to disappear down a side street.

After the meal, Yolanda gave us some lipstick and rouge and she told me to tidy up and use plenty of the lipstick. I hadn't used make-up before so Renata showed me how to apply it. She said to stiffen my lips and I felt the cold smear of the lipstick, 'It's a bit smudged now, silly. Can't you keep still?' Then she said to rub my lips together and took me to a mirror. I didn't think the colour suited me. We were given some warm clothes to fold up in a bag. Yolanda explained, 'You'll have to stay with a partisan band up in the mountains for your own safety. You can be of use to the Resistance fighters, cooking for them, cleaning, things like that.' She handed each of us a letter to keep in our knickers, along with an identification card and the name of the local Partisan Association.

'With these, if you are caught you might be lucky and be treated as an enemy combatant, but it may also be your death warrant. You cannot tell which way it will go. Anyway, you'll need to prove your identity to the fighting bands, who must be sure you are one of us.

'If you are stopped by the Germans you must smile and be friendly. Do not, under any circumstances, show any fear. You can be as flirtatious as you like. No one need suspect you are anything but silly bimbos. Now, you must spend five minutes learning the directions to where you are headed. When you arrive you must show this letter to the commandant. He will tell you where to go next. A map is too dangerous in case the Nazis get hold of it. You must not tell anyone where you are going. No one at all, do you understand? You can say that you have been to see a grandparent in Caraggio if anyone asks why you are on the road. You each have a letter in case either one of you is captured. This is not a game; your lives depend on each other.'

I rushed after Yolanda as she went out of the door. She snapped, telling me to obey her orders and learn the directions quickly as there was little time left.

'Please can you listen, just for a second?' I was almost choking. 'My mother will be very worried about me. Please could you get a message to her that I am safe and will return as soon as I can?'

Her eyes relented a little and she said that she would get someone to deliver a message. 'You must now stop thinking of your families and get on with your first task. Your lives are at stake. Renata and the others will be relying on you, I can't emphasise this enough.' The words both thrilled and frightened me.

22

After Todd left the sleeping problems grew worse. Petronella was so tired during the day she could not work. She went to the doctor for a certificate and he gave her sleeping pills, but her body clock was the wrong way round and the pills made her sleep more heavily when she ought to have been awake.

Meanwhile, Matt, who was seventeen, was getting himself to and from school just as he had done when she was working. She didn't take much notice of his comings and goings, left him to his own devices. One evening she fell asleep on the sofa in front of the television and woke when he stumbled through the front door.

'What time is it, love?' she called. She heard a retching sound.

'What's the matter? You okay?' A tap was running. 'For heaven's sake, why are you out so late? Haven't you got school in the morning?'

She didn't recognise the tone of her own voice. It sounded like someone else, a teacher or someone. Her heart lay in pieces and she was shouting at Matt. She got up to apologise to him and looked at him as if seeing him for the first time. There was a boil on his lip and he had red marks round his mouth and nose. His lip was split open. His eyes were filled with something, not tears, the pupils like dots. He was looking past her. It gave her a shock in the pit of her stomach.

'What's happened to your face, Matt?'

'Someone had a bit of a swing at me. It's nothing.'

'Oh, Matt. You poor thing. Doesn't it hurt a lot? Let me clean it for you, put something on it. Come over here; let me look at it properly. Does it perhaps need stitching? Were the police called?'

'Leave it, Mum.' He backed away waving his arms at her, nearly stumbled. 'I'm okay.' It came out slurred.

'Have you been taking something?'

'Been to see *Silence of the Lambs* with Dan and Mike. We went to the pub afterwards.'

'You have been taking something, Matt. I can see it in your face.'

'Oh yeah, so I've got a sore lip... Have you got that stuff I can put on it?'

'You've got more than a sore lip. I think it does need stitching, Matt.'

'So would you, if you saw that film! Oh, you always imagine things, Mum.'

'No, I do not, Matt. I'm not blind. What have you been up to?'

'Oh leave it, will you? Get off my back!'

'No, Matt. I'll get your father to talk to you about it and he'll want to know what you've been taking. It's dangerous, you know.'

'Yeah, whatever.' He was half way up the stairs.

'It matters a lot to me. What is it?'

'Oh just a bit of this and that. Nothing very much. Nothing 'dangerous', Mum. Keep your hair on.'

'Mixing things, I suppose. That's the worst possible thing you can do.'

'It was nothing, Mum, nothing you haven't taken in your time. Leave off, will you?' He looked down at her from the top of the stairs.

'But I only smoked the odd spliff, Matt. I didn't take pills ever—or concoctions. And nowadays they put chemicals or other substances in the weed.' She added, 'Just look at the state of you.'

'Look at the state of yourself, mum. Look, I'm off to bed, g'night.' And he stumbled across the landing, slamming his bedroom door. She ran after him, knocked on the door. 'Look, you might need a glass of water, Matt.

Please get me up if you need me in the night, Matt. Don't worry about disturbing me. I'm here for you.'

She sat in the dark listening for sounds of Matt. His words came back to her, 'Look at the state of yourself...' She wondered how others would see her now. All her confidence turned to flab and this sleepiness making her lazy and unfocussed. She had to get out of this mess. Had she needed the arguing to keep herself upright?

She felt she'd been indulging herself and neglecting her son. But how long had this been going on without her noticing? What substances was he taking? She'd have to get Todd to help; she'd talk to him tomorrow. This was already more than a little cannabis smoking. She knew what might happen if he started taking harder drugs, but how far down the road was he and would he talk to her, or to Todd?

She thought how Matt's young beauty was already spoiled by living—blotched skin, reddened eyes, unwashed hair. She thought how she and Todd had failed him because they hadn't loved each other enough. That had never been part of the plan—to let him grow up like this, secretive and disappointed by the age of seventeen. She'd only wanted to give him a secure home with two loving parents. And yet she'd felt that with Todd she had to compromise on everything to keep the household peace. It was too much, it couldn't have worked.

She wouldn't have admitted as much to Todd, but she'd have believed him if he had come in the door at some point and put his arms round her and said, 'Let's get Matt sorted. He'll be fine if we're together again.' She would have wound the clock back if she could. She considered going to Todd's and begging him to return, even though she knew they would only argue again. She'd ask him to forgive her, anything was better than this; not that it was she who needed forgiving. But she would forgive him if he asked and then everything would be all right and they could try again. She wouldn't tell anyone. She was good at keeping things secret

But when it was clear to her Todd wasn't ever coming back, she and Matt moved to a smaller house. The rooms were pokey, but she liked living in her own burrow. She painted the walls different colours—flowerpot pink, cinnamon, allspice. People live in rooms like foxes live in dens, she thought. It was new and it was hers and Matt's. Todd had had nothing to do with it, but would be welcome to visit—so long as he phoned first.

She remained friendly with Todd, so sensible of them. He'd always been a good talker—perhaps not a good communicator, but in the early days of their marriage he had talked about bees, politics and clouds. She had listened. Matt often went to see him and she never thought that Matt felt like he had lost his father. But she couldn't ever know what he felt he had lost.

At Dale View, Petronella started taking down the china and cutlery from Alex's cupboard and putting it all into cardboard boxes. No room for them in her spice coloured kitchen. The patterns on the plates were hieroglyphs—memories of ravioli and spaghetti that her mother had cooked. Later, Miss Brown's lumpy rice pudding and gristly steak and kidney pie made her gag and that voice of hers droning on, 'There are children starving in Africa who'd be glad of that food you're leaving. Spoilt little madam, you are!'

By teatime she was weeping in the garden under the monkey puzzle tree.

23

I had the sensation of being swept away by a strong current that I couldn't swim against. The only thing to do was hope that eventually it might carry us to safety. I missed my home so much, I was frightened that I might cry over nothing. I didn't know who to trust so I did what I was told; there was no alternative.

Yolanda said to choose two bicycles from the pile parked at the bottom of the stairs. Around mid-morning we set off out of the town. Our journey took us up the winding road beside the river, past small farms and olive groves. Our first night was to be spent in a house in a village, but we were not to arrive before dusk and if we ended up being much later than that we might have to fend for ourselves.

As we cycled, the road got more winding and steeper, following the twisty river. I knew this road from visiting my grandparents in the village of Meraldo. The last time our family had come we travelled by bus to a village up in the mountains and then walked the rest of the way. Before that, we used to hire a horse and cart. But it was all new to Renata. As we climbed higher the spring air blew viciously cold on our faces and legs.

On the approach to Lucco, roadside walls were daubed with *Il Duce* and Fascist insignia. Pictures of Mussolini greeted us as if to proclaim the town's loyalty. When we discovered that the bridge over the river had been destroyed we were directed higher up the valley to a steep hump-backed Roman bridge. This was our first encounter with German guards. We were both tired and numb with cold and I admit that I faltered, wanting to give up right away. Renata murmured, 'Watch this,' and, to my horror, called across the bridge to the two German soldiers on guard on the other side.

'Help,' she called, 'We can't push our bikes up this steep slope.' Despite the sound of the rushing water below they must have heard her shrill tones. They both came across the bridge towards us and Renata smiled broadly at them, 'Could you possibly give us a hand?' She pushed her bike slightly towards them. 'Our bikes are heavy and this is so steep. Do you think you could push them over for us?'

The two men seemed to understand. I could not look them in their faces. I shook with nervousness and felt self-conscious about the lipstick. Both smiled and talked in German, seized the handlebars out of our hands and wheeled them to the other side. Renata touched one of them on the arm, hitched up her skirt a little as she stepped through the bike and waved as she pedalled away. I managed a smile and a wave as I sped off as fast as the hill would allow me. Around the next bend we both convulsed in nervous giggles.

The rest of the journey that day took us a long time, as we had to get off and push the bikes up the unrelenting hill. We saw no one except a few old men tending their plots. The wind rattled the eucalyptus leaves like gaolers' keys.

The turning up to the village of Gorli was welcome and the track ran up between the sheltering trees. Daylight was fading as we approached the first few buildings. From the path through the village we could see the last of the milky sun gleaming on our beloved Mediterranean in the distance and we realised just how far from our homes we had come. I lingered a moment, felt the jagged edges of a groan rising up in my throat. Renata bustled me along, said that we should make tracks as we had better not be seen outside after nightfall and we didn't know how far we had to go. We had to find a path through the village to where we would see a pink church in the woods at the same height. The house we were looking for was in a bend just before we reached the church.

Bats were flittering in the sky as we tapped on the door. An old woman peered at us in the dim light and we showed her our letters and identification card. She didn't speak, but beckoned to us to follow. She led us up behind the house to a goat byre and said we could sleep in the hay mangers. She'd bring us some food and a blanket. We were out of the wind, but the thought of sleeping in a goat byre with those animals for company filled us with disgust. We were town girls, had barely touched a goat in our lives and here we were, expected to sleep with the smelly animals, share their air. My grandparents kept goats and on holidays I helped feed them. Their horizontal glassy eyes used to alarm me as a child because I thought they could see something that I couldn't.

After a sparse meal of salty cheese and bread, I wept myself to sleep, exhausted and still hungry. My tears were as salty as seawater. I often jolted awake in the night only to hear the goats chomp at their hay and the young bleat to their mothers. The morning light was a small relief, but I was stiff with discomfort. We were just rousing ourselves when someone opened the door of the byre.

'Hope you girls are decent,' he called as he walked straight in. His short, dark hair was smoothed and shiny. He must have seen the looks on our faces because he said, 'I'll tell you something for free, this place is going to seem like a luxury hotel to you in a few days' time. You'll be longing for it.'

'I doubt it! Not for the smell of those goats,' Renata grunted.

The man shrugged, 'They've been doing you the favour of keeping you warm.'

'Thanks,' I said. 'It was kind of you to let us sleep here.'

'Right.' He lit a cigarette. 'I've come to tell you where to go next and to give you a package to deliver to a man named Fuoco whom you'll find there.'

'Fuoco?' Renata gulped. 'What kind of a name is that?'

'A code name. It's generally considered a good idea not to use your own name if you're useful. That way no one can really identify you if you are captured and tortured.'

'What's your name then?'

'My name is Volpe.'

'Will we get funny names, too?'

'Oh, shouldn't think so. You're only girls, so no need to bother. Now listen to me and I'll tell you where to go next. You go back to the big road and head right up the mountain till you get to the next proper town with an undamaged bridge across the river. With bikes you'll probably prefer to stick to the road up to the village on the hill, though there is a safer but steeper zig-zag path up the hill if there are German patrols about.' He went to the door to stub out his cigarette and came back to us.

'After Trondo there is no road. You will just have to take the footpath to Taretta. When you reach the church find the third house down the hill on the left. That is where you are spending the night. If there are German patrols about you can hide yourselves in the woods below the houses until they have passed.' Everything he said made the situation feel worse. I was so grateful to have Renata with me. I knew I couldn't have faced this without her.

'Be careful of the package for Fuoco and swear to me you will give it to no one but him. You will find him where you end up.'

Renata took the package and put it in a cloth bag in the basket on the front of her bicycle.

'Mother says you're to come to the house now and get something to eat before you set off.' He peered out of the door, then loped off down the hill.

'Did you ever have a sinking feeling before now?' said Renata. 'I'm so relieved I'm here with you and not on my own!'

We followed Volpe down the terraced hillside that we had walked up the night before. It was a fine day and a blue haze had settled in the valley as if we were so high we were already in the sky.

Inside the tiny house the woman we'd met the night before placed milk and bread on the table. She waved her hand at us to eat and, as there was nowhere to sit, we ate standing. As we were supposed to be looking like girls on an outing, not girls who had spent the night with goats, Renata asked if we might wash somewhere. The old woman gestured at a pump outside the door. We had to make the best of it.

As we were about to leave, Volpe's mother gripped both of us by the hand. 'I pray that you will return to your poor mothers by Christmas.' She would not let go and tears were welling in the creases of her eyes. 'You are brave young women. May God protect you.' She leaned towards us and kissed us both. Then she pushed us gently towards the door, turned back to her chores. Volpe pointed back along the path we had come the night before. 'Go quietly through the village. You don't know who is watching or who is spying on whom these days.'

That day, as we cycled higher up the valley, the slopes on either side became steeper and closer. Immensity crowded in around us. The road was busier with German traffic. In the town with the bridge over the river a lorry-load of Germans halted in front of us. Two soldiers approached, stretching their hands for our papers. We drew our identification papers from our coat pockets and handed them over with a smile. Renata said, 'Good morning to you, gentlemen. What a fine day it is. You seem to like stopping young women on the road.'

The soldiers stood together, their eyes scanning the documents. Then they looked at our faces, frowning. I felt my cheeks burn. One jabbed his finger at something on the paper and they talked to each other in German.

I scowled at Renata while they weren't looking at us and she said, 'They don't know a word of Italian. Don't worry so much.' The wait seemed a long time. Renata took a powder compact out of her bag and flicked it open to look at her face. One of the soldiers motioned at the baskets on our bicycles as though asking what was in there. Renata laughed and shook her head, miming that it was too dangerous to look, 'Bombs!' she shrieked and crouched down, covering her head with her arms. The two soldiers smiled half-heartedly and both turned away. They were going back to the lorry when Renata followed them, 'Hey, can you give us a lift? This hill is horribly steep and you've got room in your lorry for us.'

She stood behind the tailgate of the truck, gesturing and smiling. The older of the two took hold of the seat and handlebars of her bike as she fished out her cloth bag with Volpe's package in it, and they swung the bike over the tailgate. The men moved up to give us room. She stepped on to the bumper and willing hands hauled her up. My bike was tossed into the back of the truck as well and someone pulled me by the arm into the truck as if I weighed nothing.

We found ourselves sitting on a narrow wooden bench with a group of young German soldiers. Renata kept her bag on her knees. As the engine started up Renata chatted to them in Porto Romolese dialect so that they wouldn't follow her even if any of them happened to speak some Italian.

'Kind of you to give us damsels in distress a lift.' Her voice rose a little, 'Anybody speak any Italian? No? No one at all? Oh, come on. You've been sent to take us over and you haven't yet learnt the language? Shame on you. Well, I don't know any German either.' She smiled and smoothed down the skirt of her dress.

'So, then, where do you all come from? How do you like our lovely country?'

Because the men were wearing helmets it was not easy to calculate how young they all were. But apart from the two who were in the cab who had looked at our identity cards, I guessed that they weren't much older than us.

I managed to shout across to her, 'I can't believe what you've done. How could you?'

Renata winked at me. 'I'll do anything for a free lift. Aren't you incredibly grateful?' I smiled, unconvinced, but the jolting of the lorry was preferable to the ache in my legs and the pain of the cold.

'What about a song then?' she asked and she started humming a tune. One of the boys joined in with the words in German and then another, *'Es ist ein Ros entsprungen…'* The others smiled and tapped their feet a little. I thought that she was stringing them along, like lapdogs.

'How do you know that?'

'I was in the school choir and we learnt some German songs then.'

Because the noise of the engine was so loud nobody spoke after that and everyone fell into a sort of reverie.

The engine clattered over every bump and the gears scraped. We were all swung together round the sharp corners and I couldn't stop myself being thrown against each of the two youths sandwiching me. At first, I tried to hold myself away, but the force of the cornering meant I had no option. I could smell their cigarette-smoke breath and feel the warmth from their bodies. I could see the lad next to me had red hair because he hadn't shaved his chin very neatly and little stubbly bits flashed gold when any light came in the back of the truck. His skin was pink and slightly greasy. Somebody's brother, I thought. Instead of hating them as my enemies, I noticed all these young soldiers seemed harmless and I felt almost sorry for them. They must miss their mothers as much as I did. I smiled at my other neighbour, saw he was covered in acne. He leaned slightly forward to put his hand in his pocket and drew out some chocolate. I took two pieces and handed one to Renata. Suddenly several hands were stretched towards us offering us chocolate and cigarettes. I declined the cigarettes, but Renata told me to take them. 'You never know when you might need them. They might come in useful.'

We'd climbed a particularly long, steep hill when the lorry braked to a standstill. The flap was let down and one of the men in front stood there, gesticulating at us to get down. The bikes were lifted out and we waved to the men.

'Danke schön,' I said and the soldier nodded at me. As the lorry lurched away from us we looked down on a deep gash between two mountain ranges, the river coiling like a snake far below us. My ears popped like corks being pulled and the sound of river filled my eardrums.

Round the bend in the road ahead of us we found two small houses and, even further up, we could see the village of Trondo. Above us was a steep battlemented wall surrounded by trees looking like a fortress. 'I expect they couldn't be seen driving through the town with us on board,' I said.

'Well, that saved us a lot of work at any rate.' Renata was leaning over her bike, checking the tyres. 'Lucky they didn't know what they didn't know.'

24

The last time Petronella saw Maddalena was in the hospital. Someone had brought in a big bowl of strawberries. They lay together like small pouches with their green leaves and shreds of white petals still attached. Petronella ate lots, hulling them as she picked out the gleaming red fruits. Maddalena said she didn't want any. She seemed quite well, smiling and talking. After that, whenever Petronella saw strawberries in a bowl with their leaves still on, she always thought of that unremarkable day and something caught in her throat. Petronella assumed her mother would be home soon and they'd have lots of days together, maybe like Porto Romolo once more. But Maddalena stayed away for a long time and, after a certain point, no one suggested taking Petronella to see her. So she was never able to tell her mother she missed her.

After that visit her mother drifted from being ill in hospital to not being there at all. There was never a point at which Petronella realised that she had died. She didn't get better and come home. She didn't remember ever crying for her mother. Later, she was afraid that if she started, it would be too difficult to stop. Better never to start. In those days children were not considered capable of understanding. There was a theory that being very upset was bad for you or even harmful.

Petronella began to wake in the night when everything was dark. She didn't like the way air, which was normally see-through, went black at night. Even the bees were quiet. In winter they always fell silent, dozing through hibernation dreams. She found it difficult to breathe the black air because it was heavy and thick. She could never push it away. It seemed to enter her nose and mouth at night and made her nearly choke. She wanted to have a light on for when she woke up, because she forgot where she was. But the light only deepened the blackness in the corners and she was more afraid of what could not be seen. Ideas that came to her out of that blackness made her whole body go rigid. When it's dark, she thought, my mother won't be able to find me.

She listened to the small night-time noises of the house on the stairs and along the landing. The house came awake at night; its secrets moved around between the rooms. If she slept they could come closer so she decided that sleeping was risky. Secrets on the loose at night knew about things she didn't know, shouldn't know. She thought she heard them nudge at the door, as if a hand were groping across the paintwork, trying to find the handle. Heartbeats bumped inside her ears so loud that she could not hear what it was they whispered. She couldn't quieten her mind enough to hear properly. She wanted to call out for her mother because then she would make them go away. But no one would be listening.

Her mother's absence filled the house. It was the silence in the hall when she walked in the door. It was the way pipes creaked at night and the way owls hooted in the tree outside.

And whenever she woke she was always afraid, just for a second. There was a threat but she could not quite remember what it was. Sometimes she felt the huff of its breath on her neck or smelt the faint scent of decaying rubbish that trailed behind. While sleeping she seemed to know what it was, but as soon as she woke it faded in the daylight. The thing to fear was always forgotten. When she lay very still it came to her that whatever it was had already happened. But she still waited for it; in her muscles and sinews she was alert.

Then spring arrived at the head of the bed, sporadically at first, as the bees started their labours, with the morning sun fingering the outside of the house. When their treacly, viola noise started up again they made Petronella feel her mother had been re-incarnated as a bee; she heard a trace of her voice in their humming. They repeated whatever they were saying as though they were trying to tell her something. And on sunny days they were always flying out to the blossom on the trees and the flowers in the gardens, with names like wallflower, sweet william, lady's mantle.

While her mother was in hospital a housekeeper came to look after Petronella. She was called Miss Brown. She had dandruff and her hands felt cold and limp. For tea she made fish paste or jam sandwiches. But on Tuesdays and Thursdays, which were Miss Brown's afternoons off, Petronella would go to Granny Rose's house for tea after school.

Rose played Glenn Miller band music sometimes and one winter she was singing 'Let it Snow'. After tea she would tell folk stories, drawing out a spell of words as delicious as the aroma of chocolate brownies. There were magic horses that could talk because they were really princesses under a spell. There were kings and queens who lived in palaces next door to one another, and princes who were transformed into dragons. As Petronella grew older, she thought there were stories hiding everywhere. It was Granny Rose who let her see there were so many ways of telling stories and that beginnings and endings were infinite.

The old woman gave Petronella *Adexoline* vitamin drops and glasses of milk. She said Petronella was on the small side for her age because her mother had not had enough nourishment during the war. 'This will make your bones grow stronger,' she used to say, as she offered another spoon of revolting cod-liver oil. But Petronella didn't seem to grow any faster.

Whenever Rose went out in winter or summer, she always dressed herself up in a hat stabbed with a special pin and gloves, even on a warm summer's day. She kept an assortment of such hats with matching gloves and sometimes she would let Petronella choose the colour she would wear that day. Every so often she manicured Petronella's fingernails and rubbed the skin growing over her cuticles. Petronella sucked her thumb and bit her nails but Rose never told her off. She used Glymiel Jelly on her own hands and smeared it liberally onto Petronella's, telling her to rub it well in. For a minute afterwards her hands felt sticky. Petronella could taste the jelly in the buns Granny Rose made for tea.

25

We pushed our bicycles up the hill until we spotted a secluded chapel, perched on the edge of a steep drop. The unfamiliar chocolate had made my mouth dry. Outside the chapel was a fountain from which we drank. In the covered portico we found a spot to rest out of the wind and gratefully dropped our bikes on a grassy bank. Exhausted by fear, cold and the jolting of the lorry we fell asleep.

In my dream, a man's voice was speaking urgently to me, but I couldn't catch the words. Then I heard, 'You will catch your death of cold, signorina. Come with me. This place is not hidden. Questions will be asked.' Renata must have heard him too, because by the time my eyes had opened she was already up. 'Come, my dears. This is too exposed. Anyone can see you from above. You are not from round here so people will wonder who you are. It's not safe here.' An old man in a dark blue hat was standing near us. He pointed upwards and we could see that the houses of the town stretched up the hillside above us, full of narrow streets and tall buildings with windows glinting like watchful eyes. He beckoned us to follow him to a house at the back of the chapel. He sat us down in his only room and threw a log into the stove. The air was warm and we were stiff with cold. I began to shiver. He set down two cracked cups filled with milk. 'I have milk, but nothing else to give you,' he sighed. He watched us as we gulped it down. I remembered the cigarettes and pulled them out of my pocket. His eyes brightened and he nodded at me gratefully, putting them carefully into a drawer in the table. 'I won't ask how two pretty girls came by good German cigarettes. But I will ask, if I may, where you are heading.'

Renata spoke. 'We're going to see our grandmother at Taretta; I expect you could tell us how far it is from here.'

'The quickest way is to follow this path through the woods. It is less steep and you don't have to go through the town. Not everyone knows this path. I will show you.'

He pointed along a footpath leading across open fields before disappearing into the woods. 'It will be an hour, perhaps longer pushing bicycles. You can ride at first. You'll see a sign on a rock to Taretta.' He paused for a moment to look at our faces. 'There are no German patrols on this path, but you must be vigilant all the same, listen out all the time and don't relax or start chattering. You want to hear them before they hear you. Just in case.' He stood over us as we picked up our cycles and set off downhill.

The forest was dense and gloomy, with mist rising from the river and catching in the trees. We met no one on the path, but as we climbed the hill to the village of Taretta we saw two wiry old men working on the terraces. They stopped and waved at us. In the village, outside one of the houses, stood two old women. When they saw us they fell silent. I thought they looked like old witches, hooked noses, deep creases around bright eyes, gnarled, bent fingers. We said 'Buona sera' to them both and went on up the hill. Before I turned the next corner I turned round to look; they were still watching us. I waved and they waved back. There were bright flowers in old containers outside front doors and on balconies, the birds were singing, a cat kept an eye us from a step; everything was perfectly ordinary.

We spent that night in an old shed. The mangers were too rickety to hold our weight so we had to settle down on the soiled straw the animals had used. They weren't in residence, but their smell permeated everything.

'Tell me about your parents,' I said. I was afraid of the complete darkness in the windowless shed, wanted to hear the sound of my new friend talking, so that panic wouldn't overpower me. Renata said that her parents grew flowers in a greenhouse on a hillside above Porto Romolo and Fontalena. Her mother sold them in the market or to hotels. Her father was from a flower-growing family and knew a lot about orchids. Her parents were of Jewish descent. She had become 'radicalised' (the word she used) when *Il Duce* had instigated the Racial Laws, which prevented her from getting a job or even being a member of the Tennis Club. 'It's mad. I love tennis and was going to play in the team at school. But they wouldn't let me because of being Jewish. We're not practising Jews and we don't go to synagogue. And what if we do go? Loads of people are Jewish. I don't see the point of it. Anyway, that's why I'm here really. If I wasn't Jewish, I don't expect I'd know what the hell was going on.' I could hear the pattering of rain on the roof and realised she was drumming her fingers on the wall. 'You know, you mustn't tell anyone I'm Jewish. It's dangerous to hide Jews. And if they know I'm a Jew they might not want me around.'

'I don't see why not, Renata.' I heard my own voice in the darkness. 'But I'll never tell anyone, don't worry.'

'So, then…what about you?'

I told her about my family. I felt free to tell Renata about my English mother because of what she had said about her parents. I sensed that others might not consider me fully Italian. After all, the English had been at war with the Italians. At home, it had all felt clear. The government was wrong and the war was wrong. Away from home, I wasn't sure what to think. We fell silent. Sleep overcame us and the straw kept us from the cold.

The next morning, we were woken when the door opened. A woman with a green scarf tied under her chin came in. She gasped when she saw us. We apologised, but she was adamant that we must leave quickly.

'Has something happened? Are there German patrols on the road?' asked Renata. 'Would we not be better off hiding here?'

'We could say we found it empty, that you hadn't given us permission.'

'It doesn't take much for them to react. They may come searching houses and outbuildings. It is very dangerous for my parents for you to stay here. Haven't you seen this?'

She showed us a leaflet that had been handed out to villagers by German soldiers:

> Whoever knows the place where a band of rebels is hiding and does not immediately inform the German Authorities will be shot. Whoever gives food or shelter to a band or to individual rebels will be shot. Every house in which rebels are found, or in which a rebel has stayed, will be blown up. So will every house from which anyone has fired on the German forces. In all such cases, all stores of food, wheat and straw will be burned, the cattle will be taken away and the inhabitants will be shot.

Until that moment we had not understood the danger we were in, or those who helped us. The terror was too much. I said to the woman, 'Does this apply to us? I had no idea. We'll go, of course we'll go… straightaway.'

'You see they could be shot if you are found on their property even if they only suspect you. You're strangers in this area and will automatically be under suspicion.'

'But where do you think we should go?' I asked.

'The path from here takes you beside the river and then you'll have to follow your nose into the mountains. You pass one village and then another and after that the path divides at the top and you go right. You must be especially careful that you are not shot by mistake. If a partisan sees you, he may shoot before asking questions. That is the way. If I were you, I would sing out if you see anyone and drop to the ground. Now be off with you.' She turned and walked away down the slope.

Outside, in morning light, the mountains rose up like a crowd of giants staring down at us. I thought they could read our minds, knew where we were going and what was going to happen to us. It felt as if we were entering the maw of the mountains and would be slowly masticated by the chunks of rock that lay everywhere, like stone teeth.

The woman had not told us that other paths peeled off from the main one; it was not so easy to follow our noses. Often we stood at a fork and wondered which way to go. Sometimes we set off and found ourselves going down to the river, which felt wrong. When we could see the two villages we felt more confident about which route to follow. Pushing the bikes along these narrow, stony paths was tough going. It was only higher up between the two villages that we could actually ride them.

Looking down on the second village we could see activity. Washing had been innocently hung outside the houses, but there were some German soldiers running up and down the alleys and banging on doors. A woman shrieked. A baby was howling as if it had been abandoned. It made our hearts turn over.

We realised we could not go any closer so we turned back to where another smaller path had peeled off across the mountain-side. We ran down a zig-zag path through trees and crossed a hump-back bridge. On the next bend, we nearly bumped into a man who, as soon as he saw us, signalled to follow him. We did so without question, as we could still hear alarming noises from the village. He led us up the path to where it joined another one and got wider. Then a tall house appeared as if it was coming to the rescue. The man took our bikes and hid them behind the house before leading us through a narrow doorway and up some steps into a warm kitchen where a woman stood slicing apples at the table.

'We have visitors, Tina.'

She looked at us for half a moment and then put her arm round each of us. 'Welcome to you both. Poor girls, you look all done in. It is dangerous out there today. You had better stay here for now because the Germans won't bother coming all the way over here.'

'I don't think you'll want us to stay for long. It's dangerous for you to hide rebels even for a short time.'

'Well, you don't look like rebels to me. What do you think, Tina?'

'No, you look like two hungry, tired women. Not at all like rebels.'

'So, take a seat, make yourselves at home. You have nothing at all to fear with us.' The man put out two chairs beside the fire where a log blazed, filling the room with the aroma of burning wood. The heat penetrated my bones. I took off my shoes, which rubbed; the hearth slates were warm on my bare feet. He said, 'I'm sorry that we have very little to give you, but we will share what we can spare.'

The woman went to the window and called out, 'Francesco!' A boy walked in the door as she set out five bowls on the table; she served out some thin soup, which we gulped down. Our stomachs felt full.

'My name is Bruno and this is our son, Francesco. Our other sons are grown up and are away fighting in Russia. We have not heard from them. We do not know when they will return and, at the moment, Francesco is all we have.' His words were flecked with dialect so I could not easily grasp what he said and whenever I glanced at Tina she was always smiling at us quizzically. 'Now, if you can, tell us what you are doing up here in the mountains. It is unusual to see two young women on their own.'

Renata explained what had happened to us. She didn't say anything about being Jewish. I told them about how she had managed to get the two Germans to help us over the bridge and had wangled us a lift in a German lorry. The two of them exchanged glances.

The twinkle in Tina's eyes drained away. 'Your mothers must be so worried about you girls, alone out here in this dangerous place. I don't know how you have done what you have. You are both very foolhardy and very courageous.' She handed us some cooked apple sweetened with honey.

'You can stay with us for the night. No one will know that you are here.'

We spent that night in beds with sheets; it was a luxury even though the mattresses were stuffed with straw, which made the bed lumpy. Wind tapped on the windowpane all night. I woke from a dream about my brother playing music to me on his radio, in our sitting room at home, and the tapping seemed like Cristiano's foot on the floor. At the moment I woke, I thought he was knocking at the window to rouse me. My heart hammered inside my chest—I felt sure it was my brother rapping on the window and yet I couldn't understand how he would know where I was. I got up and fumbled my way to the window. It was not until I looked out on the moonlit night that I realised he couldn't be there. We were on the first floor. Something inside me curled into a tight knot. I fell back into a deeper sleep, almost comatose until morning. When Tina suggested we stay for longer, Renata said that we should push on to our journey's end, because of the package. Tina made us promise that we would look on her as an honorary aunt and, if we ever needed her, we could just turn up.

Bruno told us that the village had fallen quiet that morning. Even with his binoculars he could see no sign of Germans. He said, 'Remember you always have friends in us.'

26

When her father was away from home for more than one night Petronella stayed with Granny Rose at Middleton Villas. He often went away on business. He bought Granny Rose a new television with wooden doors and they watched programmes together. *Dixon of Dock Green* and the *I Love Lucy Show* were the favourites.

Even though the linen sheets in the spare bed were licy, Petronella preferred them to staying at home with Miss Brown, who had a habit of saying, with her lips curved in a sneer, 'Just wait until you find out what life's got in store for you, young lady.'

And she liked to read Granny's old books. Some had thin, gold-edged pages and opened to reveal the marbled flesh inside their covers. On the flyleaves of each Rose had written her name and the date. She particularly liked *The Children's Life of the Bee*. She learnt about drones, queens, worker bees, swarming and how they communicate with each other about the good sources of pollen and flowers by dancing in spirals and circles.

She had just finished this book when Granny Rose put her head round the door and said, 'Can you make yourself ready, dear, at the front door at two o'clock please? We're going on an outing as it's stopped raining and I've ordered a taxi. You'll need your hat and coat.'

The taxi driver held open the door for them to get into the car. He smiled and said, 'Lovely day for a drive.'

'Granny, where are we going?'

But Rose looked away. It wasn't like her to be quiet.

Petronella watched how the trees on the road bent over as they drove past. She couldn't think of anything to say to the back of the taxi driver's head. When the car stopped outside a church on the edge of the fields the man came round the front of the car and opened the door for them.

Rose headed off round the back of the church to the cemetery where there was so much bright green grass it billowed. The wind that came blowing from off the moor was so cold it stung Petronella's eyes. There were wobbly iron railings and rooks cawed in the huge trees, their wing feathers tattered and raggedy. Nests swayed in the tops of the branches. As they walked beneath the trees the rooks jumped into the air, creaking noisily like witches cackling.

Rose had brought flowers; yellow chrysanthemums and dahlias with pink and white petals. The two of them walked along the paths to a grave inscribed with Maddalena's name. Petronella caught sight of baby Johnnie's name and something jumped in her stomach. He had been born, but had not lived and his name was never mentioned.

Rose removed some old flowers from the vase and they walked to the far end of the cemetery to fetch clean water for the new flowers. She threw the old ones on a rubbish dump in the corner of the cemetery. The rank smell of rot and damp filled Petronella with nausea; she hated the decaying stalks stuck together on the heap with the flowers all faded and flopped. It made her feel sick. On the other side she could see the river flowing between the trees. It looked like freedom, flowing without a care past this dismal place.

She read the inscriptions on the stones, bewildered because the people in this cemetery all seemed to be asleep. 'Only Sleeping' she read on one gravestone. 'She Fell Asleep…' on another. 'Asleep' was also written in wiggly letters beneath someone's name. She could see no connection between sleep and death. She supposed that 'Dead' was one of those words you weren't supposed to say. Similar to being told off for saying 'toilet' instead of 'lavatory'.

There were small mausoleums with columns and architraves and carved stone angels and cherubs, praying or singing. Some of the angels were so old their fingers had fallen off. The writing on these graves was worn away and was covered in lozenges of lichen and fingers of moss. Birds sang from a laurel hedge. It was oddly comforting here. 'Why are these graves less haunty than the other ones?' she asked her grandmother.

'Perhaps because they are much, much older and nobody comes here any more to look after the graves.'

'But, poor things! It's awful if nobody thinks about them any longer.'

'Now, come along. We'd better go now or we'll be keeping the taxi driver waiting.' Rose headed down the path. Her shoes made a tapping noise on the paving stones.

'And everyone seems to have forgotten our baby.' Petronella ran to catch up.

The taxi driver started up his engine as they approached. On the way back Petronella looked out of the window, but didn't see anything because she was thinking so hard. Rose was also staring out of the window and Petronella thought she must be thinking, too. So as not to interrupt, she snuggled up to her grandmother and held the hand that lay in her lap. Even though it was a warm spring day, her hand was cold as if she had turned to ice. Her fingers squeezed her granddaughter's.

Petronella was surprised that they didn't go straight back to the house, for the taxi stopped before they reached Middleton Villas. They went into a little café with net curtains and teapots on the window-sills and Rose said, 'Let's have a treat, something to cheer us up.' They sat at a table next to a window and Petronella looked at the teapots; one was in the shape of a kitten dressed up in clothes. The lid was a hat and the handle was its tail while an outstretched paw was the spout. Another one was in the shape of an elephant and his trunk was the spout. A woman with a white, frilly apron and a little hat brought a plate of iced buns with crystallised flowers on top and coconut fancies. She brought Petronella a glass of fizzy orange; the bubbles went up her nose and she sneezed. A bee was buzzing at the windowpane, trapped behind the net curtain. Petronella stretched up to help it find the opening at the top of the window and escape.

When her mouth was gummed up with the icing off a mud-coloured bun she had a really horrible thought. Perhaps her father had never shown her the grave because he did not know where Maddalena was buried. He never mentioned it, after all. And, as if to prove the point, all her things were still locked in her wardrobe. When she could open her mouth she gasped, 'Why does Daddy never talk about Mummy?'

'He doesn't want to upset you, I expect.' Rose's voice was like milk. 'Now stop talking with your mouth full. Eat up and have another bun, if you like.' Something in Rose's voice made Petronella understand that she would never be able to tell him about the grave in the churchyard with the rooks in the trees or ask him to come with her to see it.

During that long summer holiday she often played in the shrubbery after tea while Rose snipped at stray twigs or dead roses. Sometimes her grandmother fell asleep on a deck chair. To keep an eye on her, Petronella made a design of petals and pebbles on a stone slab beside her. She wanted to know if a person could go from being asleep to being dead. Rose's breath squeaked in her throat. Her mouth fell open. When she woke, Petronella ran back to the shrubbery and Rose pretended she hadn't been asleep.

Petronella was uncertain whether she thought and felt like other people. Perhaps she was like one of those children who were rescued and suckled by wolves. She always felt there was something missing in her, some important thing that she had never understood and that would make her more human—or perhaps more grown-up. If only her mother could come back. She felt that she had such a lot of things to ask. But she wouldn't know what the questions were. If she could see her, the questions would not matter any more. Things would just fit neatly into place.

After a time she began to feel that her mother must have forgotten her. The thought of this seemed to become true over time because more and more often she found that she had forgotten her mother. Only then did she know Maddalena had left forever, that 'falling asleep' is what people say because the finality of dying is so painful nobody, not even grown-ups, can bring themselves to say the word 'dead'. Such a flat and final word. When someone dies people just have to live with it, as best they can, day after day after day.

Sitting in the garden at Dale View, Petronella recollected Granny Rose dying in 1982 when Matt was six years old. Rose was still living at Middleton Villas and even in her eighties she used to make Cheery Buns with Matt. She ended up having a heart attack in the bathroom. The morning home-help had found her there in her nightie. Petronella wished she hadn't had to die there on her own. Rose had left detailed instructions for the service and the wake. It was her final message to the world. She had written her own eulogy, which included a brief mention of both Gianni and Cristiano. At the crematorium the organist was to play her favourite *Tara's Theme* from *Gone with the Wind*. Every time it came on during Sunday's film matinee Rose had watched it, mouthing every word of the script.

During tea and sandwiches at Alex's house after the service Petronella put on another of their favourites, *Somewhere Over the Rainbow,* on the old record player. She proposed a toast to Rose and Gianni with prosecco. She made a large plate of Cheery Buns and handed them round without apology for producing children's food at a funeral. She was glad for Rose, thought of her reunited with Gianni. Rose had found her own way to make peace with grief.

27

Francesco ran ahead of us on the path for a while until we arrived at the edge of the village, after crossing another bridge and following a path through the chestnut forest. He pointed up the hill. 'That is where you are headed, up there over that hill; the path is twisty but it will get you there in the end. Then just follow it between the rocks.'

When we had panted our way up the tortuous mule-path, we eventually came to the fork at the top of the mountain from where, remembering what we had been warned, we moved forward slowly and nervously. The slightest movement made us jump as if we were wild creatures—being townsfolk, we couldn't tell the difference between the sound of twigs rubbing together and a gun being cocked.

A figure moved among the trees. We dropped to the ground. A rough-looking man emerged from the gloom, came up to us and stood above us for a moment. I thought he was going to shoot us. He asked us what we were doing and we explained that we had been sent there by the Women's Defence Group and that we carried a parcel for someone. He was holding a rifle, but he pointed it away, 'I've been watching you.'

He gestured to follow behind him before disappearing between some tall rocks, so we jumped up and ran after him. No alternative, not knowing what else we could do. The narrow path opened into a glade in which there were dilapidated buildings. Smoke was rising languidly from a chimney. He told us to wait at the edge and he hurried into one of the buildings. A group of men were standing around outside. They stared at us until a tall man emerged. I could tell he was angry from the way he walked.

Towering over us, he made me feel small. Though his faded uniform had almost become a suit of rags I knew that our future depended on him. His eyes were blood-shot and his hair was filthy. His beard was going grey. He was a stereotype of a brigand.

We showed him our papers and Yolanda's letter. We gave a garbled explanation of our journey.

'I can't understand how you've got here from Porto Romolo. Two girls won't fit in here.' He started shouting. 'Really, this is no good. Our radio has been damaged and we can't use it. I have had no prior warning of your arrival. You turn up here, out of the blue, and expect to be fed. I don't have any spare food and anyway, I don't think having women in camp is a good idea. Bad luck, in my opinion.'

'We have nowhere else to go. The Fascists will kill us if we are captured. I'm sure we can be of service.'

He was gruff, 'This letter tells me you have been sent to me by the Women's Defence Group, but why do they think I want women in my brigade? What use are you to me?'

'We have followed the instructions given to us and we have brought a package with us. We must give it to the man named Fuoco.' Renata tried her charm but he didn't notice.

'We are Resistance members and believe in freedom for our country just as you do,' I said to him. 'We can do as much as any man. You need not think of us as women.'

'Oh yes? You know how to handle a rifle, do you? Go on, show me what you can do.'

'No, I can't use a rifle. But I can work a wireless set,' I said rashly, wondering if I really could.

He relented and said, 'Well, I doubt that you can, but you'd better stay a few days while I consider what to do with you. Hey, Fuoco,' he shouted across the space to the men who were watching the proceedings, 'get yourself over here. These girls have something to give you, apparently.'

A man broke away from the group. 'You are Fuoco, are you?' Renata asked him.

'Yes, Capitano,' he answered, without smiling.

'I am under orders to give you a package but, first, I must have verification that you are who you say you are.'

The brigade capitano stood over us. 'Of course he's Fuoco. I'll vouch for that.'

Renata wouldn't give in. 'I really need to see your registration card first.'

The younger man pulled a small wallet out of a pocket and showed her his card. She looked at it quickly, passed it to me and I gave it back to him. She pulled the cloth bag off the package and handed it over to him. 'Mind, it's heavier than it looks.'

As he took it from her, he made a play of nearly dropping it. He put it down on the ground, squatting next to it. He turned his head and winked at me. Carefully, he undid the brown paper, revealing that, for the last few days, all the way up the mountain valley Renata had been carrying grenades. We gasped. The leader motioned to one of the other men to show us where we could sleep. I felt we'd proved ourselves.

The accommodation was rudimentary inside the ruined house. There were several sacks filled with straw in the larger of the two rooms. 'We'll be sleeping with the men, I take it,' I groaned, 'Suddenly the goat shed does feel like a palace.'

'I hope to God you can use that wireless. Do you think you really can? Whatever made you say that?'

'My brother taught me a few things. He built his own out of bits and pieces. I don't know all that much really. Let's hope it'll be enough. Got to stand up for ourselves among this lot.'

'Oh, the Capitano will come round, I expect.'

'I hadn't realised how heavy those grenades were.' We were sitting on the straw sack that had been allotted to us. 'I'm sorry I didn't help you carry it.'

'As Volpe gave it to me I had to be the one responsible for it.'

'God,' I groaned, 'think of the joke you played. Think of the risks you took. Where do you get your courage from, Renata? I am not as brave as that and, if it wasn't for you, we wouldn't be here now. We might have been arrested just because I can't stop myself looking scared all the time.'

'You'll learn,' she said. 'Looks like you'll have to, doesn't it?'

That night I cried myself to sleep. The straw sacks must have been full of lice because I was soon itching. It was the smell of sweaty men that frightened me as much as the sound of their breathing, their restive discomfort. We were lying so close together I was anxious lest one of them kick me in the face as he turned over. It was cold. I don't think I could have got through without the slight warmth from Renata but, all the same, I could feel fits of shivering from time to time. I couldn't work out if it was me or her. We held each other's fingers all night.

28

At the back of Dale View was Alex's workshop, where he used to keep his tools and his collection of old wireless sets. As Petronella opened the door she felt uneasy, as if intruding on his territory. On the work surface there were two mugs, encrusted with dried mould. A pair of his spectacles had been left next to a grimy ashtray. His tools were where he had left them. A notebook lay open with some calculations written down in pencil. Piles of old newspapers and catalogues were stacked high on top of the shelves, which she recalled as being orderly—now covered in cobwebs as though he had just popped out and forgotten to come back.

Petronella thought that the house was always like one of her father's radios; the three occupants were tuning in and out of one another's frequencies. The landing was the place where interference was picked up, voices, imagined or real, leaking out of bedroom doors. Had she heard or imagined her parents' voices like scraps of sense among the white noise between stations?

'Why didn't you?'

'I can't undo…'

'If you'd moved… only locked up, not tortured, not killed.'

'You torment yourself. Stop this… before…'

'And… you can't face the truth… they wouldn't have murdered you—like a beast.'

'If only this had happened and if only that… Leave it now, can't you? Drop it!'

Afterwards, Alex had fallen silent for days. Whatever wasn't audible seeped into the curtains and carpets through the house; the fabric looked exhausted.

This space at the top of the stairs was the transistor—like a cistern enclosed by banisters, where people pass through on their way to sleep or on their way down to daily life, where nothing actually happens, and yet everything happens. And baby Johnnie, who had barely breathed, became an unvoiced whimper on the stairs, muffled by faulty circuitry.

What was it about her childhood? She often felt she was growing up wrong, as if a limb was being forced into the wrong position, her neck permanently bent or a foot clubbed. But it wasn't something visible; it was too difficult to describe. Maybe nothing had happened and that was the point—something should have happened and it hadn't.

Her father had only become real to her on Saturdays and Sundays when he watched television in the sitting room. He liked to see the news, which was about the past, and the weather forecast, which was about the future. She learned about the world from keeping her ears open because sometimes he muttered under his breath, like Granny Rose, only louder. When somewhere called Bikini Island was obliterated by an atom bomb, she heard him say, 'It should never have been invented.' When Britain invaded Egypt over the ownership of a canal called Suez, he said there was probably going to be another really big war.

He was always watching TV programmes about The War. Sitting in his armchair as if it were a throne, he stared at the screen and Petronella saw the flash of pictures reflected in his glasses, as if the lenses were small televisions. His favourite seemed to be *All Our Yesterdays,* on Sunday afternoons. She sat beside him on the sofa and when there was a dead person she shut her eyes. She watched the pictures on the screen that looked like carnage and people walking around amongst ruined buildings and rubble. It looked unimaginably frightening.

Supposing they were to send my father away to a new war, she thought. 'Away to war' sounded terrible, but perhaps it was meant to sound heroic, manly, patriotic.

Such a big thing to be described by such a nondescript little word—'war'.

He told her once how he had walked out of a prisoner of war camp and then took to the hills to fight the Germans with Italian partisans. She didn't understand who they were. She knew her father had been born and brought up in Rome because her other grandmother, Granny Mary, had told her about it. She had said something like, 'The Fascists finished your grandfather.' To prove it, she and Grandpa Bill had both died when Petronella was young.

Petronella and Todd had once taken Matt to Rome on a holiday to see the city where his grandfather had lived as a child. They had strolled past the marble lions mouthing water in the Piazza del Popolo and the marble bees drinking from the pool in a hidden corner of Piazza Berberini. Alex would also have touched the cool stone flesh of the many statues, might have wished that his physique would one day match the magnificent Tritons in their fountain.

Looking back now, she could see that was how he had spoken Italian well enough to be useful to the Allies liaising with the Italian Resistance. That was where he met her mother because she, Maddalena, had been there, too. He made it sound like an adventure story. The word 'partisan' had a ring to it. She savoured the new words she learned in this way. The partisans hid in old houses and caves and were sometimes supplied with provisions by the villagers. Resistance fighters laid explosives along roads or bridges used by German convoys with ammo supplied by the Brits. Sometimes they ambushed the Jerries and shot at them from behind trees and then they legged it to the hills to hide. But, in Alex's version, nobody ever got killed or even wounded.

The stories used to make her restless. There was an electrical charge in her body as he spoke and she waited for him to carry on. The undercurrent of what was not being said made her concentration slip, as if he was making it all up. She thought he must be fantasising; war looked horrible on the television screen but, after it was over, people remembered it all with a strange nostalgia and sang songs about it, saying it was 'fun'. What was the truth of the matter? Had her father really done any of that? He seemed so ordinary in his tweed jacket and lace-up shoes that she could barely believe it.

Between his favourite programmes, he sometimes played Liar Dice with her. By that time Petronella could often outwit him; after Maddalena died he was only half-there. Petronella was afraid of being close to him—once, while they were watching a television programme, he grabbed her to him, trembling, pressing his face in her hair so tightly she felt his jaw against her scalp. When she squirmed away he let her go and she saw that same distant look in his eyes.

What did he want from her?

Matt was always in her mind. Before she left he said, 'It's okay, Mum. I'm not going to smoke or take E again. Well, I might smoke a bit of weed now and then, but I've learnt my lesson. I won't mix weed and E and alcohol again. I had such a bad trip I thought I was being hunted down. I locked my bedroom door and barricaded it one night. I imagined that if I fell asleep they'd come to get me. The next day I had the most terrible pain in my side. I thought I should go to hospital, but knew they might refuse to treat me when I told them what I'd done. It had never been like that before. Never. The first couple of times were the best, but it wasn't like that again.'

She knew he meant what he said—he wasn't a liar—but could he stick to it?

29

...fasciati quince e quindi d'alta grotta.
Poco parer potea lì del di fori;
ma, per quel poco, vedea io le stelle
di lor solere e più chiare e maggiori.
Sì ruminando e sì mirando in quelle
mi prese il sonno; il sonno che sovente.

(Purgatorio Canto XXVII)

(...all of us hemmed in by high rocks on either side.
Little could be seen there of the world outside;
but, through that little space, I saw the stars
both brighter and larger than they are accustomed to
be.

As I was thus ruminating and looking at them,
I was overcome by sleep, that sleep which frequently
knows what is to come before the reality arrives.)

It was as if we'd broken into a prison camp and all the
inmates came openly to inspect us—some friendly, others
hostile. We were a spectacle. Renata and I were smart town
girls, not built for roughing it. We had had no preparation,
hadn't lived a peasant's life. We understood little about what
was required. Capitano Umberto didn't need the
responsibility of extra mouths to feed, especially people
who were not fully contributing to the resistance effort. He
distrusted us, thought we were only there to deliberately
distract the men. He must have thought we were loose
women.

Yolanda had instructed us to make ourselves useful.
Without help, however, we would have failed. There was an
old stove that was a pig to light. It was capricious and if the
wind was in the wrong direction the wood wouldn't catch.
Luckily, Fuoco was there when we needed him. He helped

us by fetching wood, chopping it and lighting the damned stove. He showed us what to do with the staple food of the camp, chestnuts, which we often had to eat to put something in our bellies. They needed boiling up to be shelled and then roasted. In the cold, our fingers lost all feeling, and peeling those chestnuts took the skin off our manicured fingers. Occasionally we were given something different, potatoes or a few carrots. Sometimes some supplies arrived by mule. And sometimes someone shot a squirrel or two, a rabbit, even a small deer. We also ate hedgehogs, small birds, frogs, snails, fresh-water shrimps. These needed preparing too and we didn't have a clue where to start. Gutting a fish from Porto Romolo market was not the same.

Renata was surprisingly squeamish and couldn't pull a skin off a rabbit to save her life. I listened to what Fuoco taught us and when I'd got the hang of it I could get on by myself. After a time I certainly didn't want him hanging around as if he was checking up on us. There was what I would call an atmosphere sometimes. So that he might get the message, once I muttered the words, '...getting under our feet'.

One of the men, called Stefano, suggested that we boil up all the clothes to see if that would kill the lice. We rinsed everything in kerosene and had to wash that out too. I asked Capitano Umberto to requisition some louse powder. Small hope. So Renata and I asked permission to go to Bruno and Tina's house to fetch an iron so that we could iron the men's shirts...more like pressing the rags together, so that the lice in the seams of the fabric might be killed by the heat. Renata scrounged needles and thread to patch the clothes. After a time we really were making ourselves useful and we felt determined that our presence among them would raise the tone of the place, put a stop to the men behaving like louts. By then, I think if Capitano Umberto had proposed sending us away he would probably have had a mutiny on his hands.

To start with, he would have had to deal with Stefano, who was always first in line to have his clothes washed and repaired. He said that if we had come this far there must be good reasons why they should look after us. He was always chivalrous. He came from a village close to Porto Romolo. His parents worked the land and his father grew carnations and owned a greenhouse. He had been studying medicine before war broke out and he was here to fight for his country's freedom. He understood the sort of people Renata and I were. From the start, I guessed he was a bit sweet on Renata and this led to a lot of banter, much disapproved of by the Capitano—as well as myself, come to that.

Stefano was an example to everyone because he was fastidious, washed himself every morning. I overheard him once tell off some others for not bothering. 'The trouble with you is that you have no dignity. Washing means you care about yourself.' Fuoco, who was listening, peered theatrically at the small amount of cold water in which Stefano was washing himself, checked behind his ear lobes, looked at the state of his clothes, and said 'Yes, I see exactly what you mean.' But I think he must have learnt something about self-respect because it was noticeable that he looked less unkempt from then on.

From Umberto's perspective I can see how difficult it must have been. Although he had travelled away from his native countryside and had fought in the Spanish Civil War, originally he'd come from a remote village where women were submissive. He was used to women who belonged to their fathers, and, when married, belonged to their husbands. Even if they argued, and they would always argue about certain things vociferously—you would hear excitable women's voices like yowling cats raised in any street in any village—they still fell in line behind the menfolk. But I didn't feel this philosophical at the times when Capitano Umberto was being abrasive.

He saw our hands were not those of peasant women who worked the land. Our skin was untouched by wind or weather. We addressed the men as equals. Italian was another language to him, learnt at school, so it did not come naturally—he had his own Abruzzese dialect. We were better educated and spoke Italian naturally. It was no wonder he was edgy around us.

Fuoco was more objective, the more pragmatic of the two. He showed us how to use a pistol, how to aim accurately and how to look after it. He said we would need to be able to handle guns for our own safety. If we didn't know, we would be a danger to the others, as well as ourselves. Umberto expressed his annoyance about the squandering of valuable bullets, saying it wasn't something women would need to know. Renata and I kept our mouths shut, letting the argument rumble on until it fizzled out. To show us the small parts of the revolver and look over our shoulders while we took aim, Fuoco had to stand close up to us. As I grew more confident in my marksmanship I stopped noticing his stale-sweat pong. Once, when he brushed the back of my hand, it held the feel of his touch for a while.

Occasionally messengers from other brigades arrived at the camp, bringing news about paramilitary operations. One of the most regular contacts was Captain Alex Latimer, the chief liaison officer between the local Resistance groups and the British. It was tactically important for partisan brigades to communicate regularly with the Allies to hammer out coordinated strategies. He was useful to the partisans as he was a trained wireless operator and, because he spoke Italian well enough, he could decode ciphers and translate what came over the airwaves. When he came he usually brought a few necessities as well. The first time we met him he brought a new wireless set to replace the old broken one. He was perplexed to find us women in the camp. Renata said she overheard him say so to Capitano Umberto.

'If you wish to make a complaint there are official procedures.' She mimicked Umberto perfectly. She thought he was almost begging the English captain to complain.

'I wouldn't go that far.' The English captain had no authority over Umberto.

'*Certo,* if you think that the presence of women compromises us as a fighting force then it is your duty to say so.'

I thought I'd better explain our situation to the Englishman, let him understand my background. I went up to the captain as he was speaking to Fuoco and addressed him in English, knowing the others wouldn't understand what I said. 'Good afternoon. I wonder if I can be of assistance to you, sir?'

He spun round to see who was speaking. 'Oh! Good afternoon. How do you do? By Jove, you speak English, do you?'

'Yes, I speak English. And I hear you speaking Italian, sir.'

'Well, I get by.' He squinted at me, looked at my forehead, not in my eyes. He continued abruptly, 'Excuse me for asking, but how come you speak English so extremely well?'

'We are taught English at school, you know.'

'But you speak like a native.'

I could see he realised he might have—how do you say it—put his foot in it. I relented, explaining that my mother came from Yorkshire originally, that it was she who had taught me the language. He said he was pleased to meet me and we shook hands. I noticed his white teeth, how his pale lips fitted together like pastry. 'What a coincidence this is. My parents live not far from York, too. I wonder if I know your mother's family.' I told him my mother's maiden name, said I'd never been to England, but would like to go there one day.

'Can I ask how you ladies come to be here? Do you think it safe? It's a dangerous place you know. Some of these men are uncouth, uneducated people, riff-raff. Between you and me, I wouldn't trust many of them.'

'We're here to be of service to the war effort just like the men. We're all in this together.' The pupils of his eyes registered surprise. I added, 'If I can be of any help please let me know. But you'll have to excuse me as I have the washing and the catering to see to, now.'

During the evening meal (Captain Alex had brought us some horse-meat) Fuoco asked me, 'What were you and the Englishman talking about?'

'He said you are all very generous to look after us and that we're very lucky to be here.'

'How did you learn to understand the language so well?' I explained again about my mother. It made me think of her alone and worrying about me, waiting for us all to get back home. I had been so preoccupied with my own situation in the last few days I hadn't thought of her as much as I had at first. I wondered how she was coping—an Englishwoman living in a country at war with her own. I hoped they weren't going to imprison her as an enemy spy.

'But your father? He is Italian?'

'Yes he is, his family came from the mountains originally. Now he's a newspaper reporter, or was, until he lost his job when they exiled him to Calabria for a year.' I told him about the anti-Fascist newsletters my father distributed round Porto Romolo. I shrugged my shoulders, 'That's probably part of the reason why I find myself here with you lot.'

It occurred to me that he could have been offended by the way I had said 'you lot.' It must have seemed dismissive considering how the band was giving us food and shelter.

He continued, 'But what about you? How do you come to be here?'

'Oh, the Blackshirts caught me delivering cartridges to a house in Porto Romolo. I managed to escape them and then got sent here by the Women's Defence Group.' I smiled and asked, 'So what brought you here?'

'Ah, now you're asking. That's because I want ordinary people to take control of their own destiny, run the country, put an end to hunger amongst the poor, ease the tax they have to pay towards *Il Duce's* wars, provide decent jobs for everyone. I want that for Italy. I am determined that after the fighting is over we will have a people's government. And right now, I want the German occupiers to leave us to live in peace.'

'I didn't realise so much was at stake,' I replied. 'But I think that's what my father wants, too.' My cheeks flushed. I felt tearful again, controlled my urge to cry by looking away. And because he, too, came from a poor mountain village I had assumed he was as uncouth as the rest, except perhaps for Stefano.

'Well, that's how it is for me.'

'I think you'd better get on with the delicious chestnuts. And you can have some more after that, if you like.' The thought of my father had upset me more than I could say.

'I'll have you know, young lady, that's no way to speak to Fuoco, the Brigade Lieutenant who also holds a place on the local Committee of National Liberation,' said Stefano sitting next to him, 'and did you perhaps mention second helpings? I'd like some of that delicious lasagne with parmesan and basil that I smelt cooking earlier.' He looked around mock-hopefully. 'Oh, no, has it all gone? Poor me!'

30

Half-forgotten pictures of her father kept breaking into her mind: the leather elbow pads on his tweed jacket; the fountain pen he kept in his breast pocket; his other pockets full of small change so that he jangled when he stood up. He watched BBC, but never ITV. If there was kissing on the telly he tutted. The whisky in the decanter was kept filled to the brim so that the level never went down and yet his tumbler was rarely empty. He mended punctures in Petronella's bicycle tyres and never made her try herself. He had never been the kind of father to drop pennies in your pocket to buy Sherbert Fountains. He disapproved of gob-stoppers and liquorice sticks—all that licking and sucking. He didn't hold with the imagination because he didn't see the point of making things up.

On Saturday afternoons he was usually busy in his workshop. Because of the tools lying about, he would never let her in. 'Dangerous,' he said. Having nothing to do she sat by herself on the warm step outside the door. He didn't like her to talk to him when he was repairing things —he couldn't concentrate. Sometimes, when he was working on one of his old-fashioned radio sets, voices or music would jump out of the workshop. Petronella was intrigued by this, thinking that because the radios were old, the sounds materialised out of the past.

Bees were sliding in and out of apricot and scarlet snap-dragons, humming in roses with centres like egg yolk, their stamens filled with pollen. They sucked up nectar and carried bags of pollen on their legs, making a heavy burden for their wings—and yet they continued to fly in and out of the hole in the wall of her bedroom.

Tiny red spiders were running round on the step. They were replicas of big black spiders, but perfect and minute —so engrossed in their own world they didn't notice a giant face peering at them. She laid a finger flat on the slab amongst them to see if one might run onto her hand. They avoided her finger, swerving away as they approached. They were running as if there were some hidden purpose to their endless motion. Alex appeared beside her, squatted down to watch what she was doing. 'Those are money spiders,' he said. 'It's good luck to have one on your hand.' He was slurping whisky, swirling all golden in the glass. He had a cigarette in his other hand.

Then bingo, a spider was running up the length of her finger and across the back of her hand. She was afraid it would go up her sleeve.

He stood up and said, 'If you wait a while it may leave you moneybags'. She observed the speck of a spider for what seemed like ages. She grew bored of waiting, but wanted the money. After a time, tiny black dots appeared on her wrist. He looked down at her, smiled and nodded, announcing, 'That's it. Those are moneybags. You are very lucky. One day you are going to be wealthy'.

When he said that, she'd felt as if she was swimming by herself in the clear, blue-green water at the Lido on the edge of town. And just for once all the older girls and boys weren't sitting on the concrete fountain, laughing and shouting, so she was able to swim right up to the middle of the pool and, even though she was small for her age, haul herself out and sit on the jet of water as it spurted out and all the bubbles gurgled down her legs like silver ribbons. How she had hated being so small. She wondered if there was something wrong. But not in her imagination on that day—so she asked him if they could go and see Peter Pan at the theatre in York and he said, 'Yes, of course' and went back inside his workshop and didn't say anything more all afternoon. But they never did go. That was the way things were at Dale View.

31

Shirts and vests were blowing in the wind, sleeves catching hold of each other, snarling on twigs and brambles. The clothes looked like ghosts coming out of the woods. Wind swelled them as if they were filled by bodies suspended from the trees. We two had scrubbed and rinsed all the garments that were handed to us, then tied the clothes to branches to dry. It took a lot of wood to boil so much water to clean so many clothes and we were lucky Fuoco had asked Renzo and Stefano to chop wood and keep the fire going.

But, in my book, cooking wasn't a job for a man. Is that where Fuoco (meaning 'fire') got his code name from? If the other men weren't out on a raid or an ambush they sat around playing Liar Dice, but he was always helping us prepare food. Whenever he was around I felt irritation creeping over me, as if he was implying we couldn't manage on our own. Hadn't he anything better to do? He said he liked cooking, that he used to help his mother by organising the meal for the family some evenings. She would come home from working on the land and find a meal on the table. After he'd explained that, I said that I was sorry that we had perhaps usurped his position as cook, but he said not to worry about it as he had plenty of other things to do, like eliminating Fascists.

We couldn't have managed without him. He would bring wild plants and edible fungi he found in the woods. And somehow I knew when he was near. We did ordinary things; fetched water, peeled chestnuts, sliced potatoes, skinned some wild creature, scrubbed clean the cook pot. In the daylight, as we prepared a midday meal, everything was calm, but in my muscle and bone I felt watchful, alert. I turned my head away when he approached. I didn't want him to see my face, catch my eye.

Around this time I woke one morning with cramps in my belly, traces of blood in my knickers, that familiar ache in my groin as I got to my feet. I didn't know what to do with myself, having no towels with me, nothing to soak up the blood. When I told Renata, she shrugged her shoulders and rolled her eyes. 'Oh, who'd be a woman?' By noon, it was seeping on to my thighs and I was uncomfortable as well as embarrassed that it would soon show. I whispered to Renata, 'What am I going to do? I can't wash out here.'

'You'll just have to use rags from something, if you can find any. Go into the woods when no one is looking and see if you can sort yourself out. Then, we'll have to do some thinking about what we're going to do. I'll be in the same boat soon.' I dashed into our sleeping quarters, found an old shirt, tore off a sleeve and ripped it into strips, which I rolled and tied uncomfortably into position. It would have to be washed out in the stream, dried and re-used.

When I next met Captain Alex I was relieved to be feeling respectable again. We must have looked like frights anyway. Renata said she'd die for a hot bath, clean underwear and an ironed blouse and I think I might have committed murder for that, too right then.

'What exactly does he do here?' Renata asked Stefano who was feeling the clothes to see if any of them were dry. 'Oh, the English Captain comes to organise things with Capitano Umberto from time to time. They discuss military tactics and he coordinates parachute drops of supplies from the British—ammunition, boots, maybe cigarettes, if we're lucky.'

I was intrigued. From our point of view, it was astonishing to see a man of his position in a god-forsaken hole like this. The English captain was tall and slightly stooped, his smooth face almost expressionless or perhaps inscrutable. He smiled a lot, but the smile could disappear as if he'd swallowed it. He wore a smart uniform and spoke

Italian passably well, but made no attempt to disguise his English accent. I peeked at his suitcase radio, which was one of the very latest Type B Mark 2 versions. I know that because I asked him about it, being interested in radios; Cristiano would have been impressed by how neatly it fitted inside the case.

We felt altogether safer with the English captain around, as if he proved we had a purpose in being here and had proper links with the English. They recognised the part we played in the war. We partisans would not be abandoned.

Because someone had magicked in some bottles of wine that night there was singing round the campfire instead of the usual Liar Dice game. I hoped the wine wasn't looted but I suspected it might have been. When the captain left the next day he shook my hand and Renata's. He was really quite affable by then. I noticed that he had green eyes and I wondered what his hair was like beneath his peaked cap. I thought he looked so incongruous here; it was almost amusing.

It was Fuoco's job to lead Captain Alex to various local partisan encampments. They were on good terms, I thought, but Fuoco knew well enough that his paymaster was British Intelligence. He wasn't one of us, however friendly we became.

One of his duties was to inform us about what was happening on various fronts of the war. Once the Allies landed in Sicily it was assumed a quick victory would secure the country's liberation. But the war was dragging on. Every inch of the country was fought over and countless people lost their lives, both partisans and civilians. News was patchy even from the English captain. The picture was all highly confused—chaotic, with some Italians fighting others in a civil war between the fanatic Fascists, loyal to Mussolini, and the Anti-Fascists who were either Royalists or Republicans, united only by their determination to free themselves from German occupation.

On a later visit, he brought good news. He said that Rome had been liberated and was under Allied control. The American CO had praised the local partisans for their resourcefulness and co-operation. There were loud murmurs of approval, a cheer and some back-slapping. From out of the darkness a voice growled, 'Both of our enemies are fighting it out in the Eternal City. Pah!' A gob of spit landed in the dirt.

The captain hadn't understood what was said in the local dialect because he asked me about it. I told him they were grateful for the enormous efforts of the Allies, that they appreciated the advances being made towards the liberation of their country.

I asked him, 'Can you tell me anything about the war in Greece? Have we at least kept that for the Italian Empire?'

He replied, 'Your *Duce*'s Greek expedition turned into tragedy, I'm afraid to say. We received reports that, owing to the procrastination of Italian command, their soldiers stationed on the islands were massacred by the Germans.'

'Which islands?'

'Cos and Cephallonia, as I understand it.'

'Did any manage to escape, sir?'

'Maybe, maybe not—but those that did get away are likely to be trapped in the mountains.'

My brother, Cristiano, might have been sent to one of those Greek islands. I wasn't sure which. My heart pounding, I got up and walked away, nursing my small hope that Cristiano might be surviving in the mountains.

I'd never told my brother that I loved him. And I hadn't known, till the day when my mother and I were waving him off at the station that what I felt for him was called love. That night, when the Englishman told me about the news from Greece, I thought that perhaps they would have to go on killing each other till everyone discovered they had lost the ones they loved.

I had this picture of my brother Cristiano. When I was young, he'd been my hero, one of those bronzed, epic figures with eyes as blue as the summer sky, just like Pappa. He went mountain climbing with his friend, Pierino. He had strong leather boots and wore shorts. They climbed without ropes, using their fingers to probe ledges and handholds, which then became their toeholds as they ascended. I can remember him going off on his bike early in the mornings during school holidays, leaving a sense of drama in his wake. He'd come back with his knees scored from the rocks he'd climbed. All my friends were a little in love with him. But it was only I who knew how he farted in the bath to watch the bubbles rise, and how his socks smelt.

And I thought of Gino, how his father's murder only hardened his resolve. I reasoned that Cristiano would have escaped and that I had no reason to assume he was dead. Out here, I couldn't be certain of anything. I wasn't going to let myself feel beaten. And I would be sure to tell him how much I loved him, the next time I saw him.

32

Petronella wasn't confident about the order of events. Scenes from the past played out in her mind as if two time scales were operating together. In one she was a watchful, rather fearful child; in another, she was her adult self—still watchful, still fearful. She opened the lid of the upright piano and tinkled some of the keys. It was out of tune so she gave up the idea of warming her fingers with the old Beatles tunes she used to play and headed out for a walk, passing an estate that was built in the 80s between their home and the river.

Above the rows of brick houses she could make out the Mare and Foal Rock, its top encircled by clouds. The path along the river bank was now securely fenced and gated, reminding her how the river had the potential to turn wild and uncontainable when rain saturated the moors—and only flowed down its channel because it chose to do so for the time being. There was a smell of wet stone, mud and peaty water. Where it was deepest the water flowed black. White bubbles circled slowly on the surface and on a huge bend there was said to be a whirlpool. As children they used to chuck twigs and leaves to see if they were swallowed up into the vortex. They'd whirl round and round in the water shining like a blank mirror.

There was the mill where they used to play, but it had fallen derelict; only the outer walls of the building were still standing—fenced off with barbed wire, punctuated with crooked 'Trespassers will be Prosecuted' signs at intervals. The old sluice gate was stuck open. A child had been swept away in the current near that place, now a forbidden area.

After lunch she went through the books in the downstairs sitting room. The leather-bound covers and their titles brought back memories, half-forgotten, but familiar like the taste of salt dissolved in a broth. Her eye was drawn past the Winston Churchill diaries, past the Rider Haggard and the Gwen Raverat, to a blue book called *The Children's Life of the Bee* by Maurice Maeterlinck. This was the one Granny Rose had given her; she'd read it from cover to cover. The book fell open next to an illustration of the mysterious Sphinx moth, a piece of paper between the pages. Unfolding it, she found it covered in a child's script. All the stories she'd ever written were lost —so she was intrigued to find this one, on forty-year-old paper. She sat on the wide arm of the sofa to read it.

The Story of the Bees

Once upon a time there was a huge family of bees. The mother was called Queen Mellifera and she lived in an acorn-shaped cell that was called the Throne Cell. It so happened that her husband had died. He had never been called King because he had died just after they were married, up there in the blue sky far above the apiary. There was a curse on all male bees and they had to die at an early age. Maybe that was because they were just drones and sat around all day with their feet up, drinking whisky and smoking, leaving all the work to the Queen's many daughters. But still the Queen was sad.

The hive was later invaded by a man dressed in a veil-helmet and bearing a smoking bomb. He stole all the honey and then banged the lid tight shut, which made all the bees shudder. After the bees had worked their socks off bringing in more honey to replenish their stocks the workers had to send out a warning because a moth called Atropos, with the sign of the death's head on its back, had entered the hive and was gobbling up precious honey while it squeaked, pretending to be the Queen. The bees could not tell which was the true queen. The whole population was in an uproar while the creature crept back to the entrance and flew off, its body full of the honey it had stolen. The guards were powerless against the honey stealer and everyday the moth returned to gobble up more of their liquid gold.

The next morning it happened that Queen Mellifera went for a little walk by herself before she started her important work of laying baby bees and she stood at the entrance to the hive to watch the sun rise. She liked being by herself because the retinue of bees that looked after her always walked backwards and this made her feel cross.

She sniffed the air and on the breeze that floated past she smelled a voice. Bees don't have ears. Some bee was calling to her from far away. She recognised the voice of her recently dead husband. He was beseeching her to fly to him because he had found a new home where there would be no beekeepers plundering the hive for their precious honey. 'Fly to me', he called, 'and bring all the worker bees because there's room for everyone.'

So Queen Mellifera sat in her throne, and commanded all the bees to pack their sacs on their legs with honey and royal jelly. Tomorrow they were going to leave for pastures new but only if the sun was shining.

The next day dawned bright and the bees were all ready and waiting at the door of the hive. Queen Mellifera gave the secret signal and all the bees flew together in a tumbling golden ball. There was a tremendous buzzing sound and a whirring of all their tiny wings and they flew high into the radiant sky. They were intoxicated by the breeze and their eyes shone.

The voice of her husband grew louder as the swarm of bees drew further away from the hive. When they looked back their old home was just a speck and then it disappeared from sight.

Soon a house with a beautiful garden full of flowers appeared. There was buddleia and lavender and roses of every colour around the house in every direction. It was bee paradise. The guard bees formed a defensive ring around their Queen and she directed them to go in a little hole in the wall of the house. Inside it was a large space which was just lovely for a bee home though they had to work very hard to build new combs. These were hung like stalactites from the ceiling. Queen Mellifera laid lots of eggs that turned into larvae and there was plenty of room for everyone however large the family became. They never saw the beekeeper, who always spoiled everything, or the greedy Atropos again so they lived happily ever after.

The End

She didn't remember writing it. How old could she have been? Ten or twelve? Is it true that a Hawk Moth could get inside a hive? Does it really squeak? How had she known that Atropos is the name of one of the three Fates, the one that snips the thread between life and death?

And it was no wonder that she'd behaved as she did a little while later, when she discovered the fate of her bees.

33

It was an evening towards the end of the summer of 1944 and the partisans were huddled, talking amongst themselves. A tension hung in the air. Everyone was waiting for some signal. I asked one of them, a younger man called Renzo, what was going on.

'There's going to be an attack, a coordinated push, you'll see,' he answered, 'any day soon, before autumn sets in. That's what the English want. We'll see some big action.' Some men had already gone on a reconnaissance trip and in the next two days we heard that all the men would be leaving to link up with the other partisan bands in the region.

Everyone was on high alert, waiting for the go-ahead. The atmosphere was like a taut balancing wire—weapons primed, cartridge belts filled. Stefano and his explosives team were busy stuffing mines in pipes to lay along roads used by German soldiers. They waited for Fuoco and the others to return with information about where everyone was to meet.

As Renata and I crept onto our lice-ridden straw sleeping sacks I wondered what was to become of us. No one was willing to tell us anything. Before they lay down, the men formed into small groups and gathered guns and ammunition. At intervals they rose, did up their boots, buckled on cartridge belts and left. Lined up and marching. Through the night, all of them disappeared.

At the last minute Umberto came back and shook us both by the shoulder, as if we could still be asleep after all the noise. 'We are going into battle with our comrades to finally oust the Germans from the mountains. Your job is to guard the camp and to be ready for when anyone returns. They will need food and there will be some wounded. Be prepared. If we don't return, we have failed in the attempt. Here is a pistol for you in case any enemy soldiers appear with any ideas of torching our camp. You are under orders to shoot.'

'Oh, can't we come with you?' I started to argue, 'I want to fight too.'

'Don't be so ridiculous', said Umberto. 'You're girls. You've not had formal training; you can't be brave like men. Your orders are to defend the camp and keep the fires burning for when we return.'

After he'd gone, Renata said she couldn't stand the sight of blood, hoped she wouldn't faint if anyone was wounded. 'So,' I was thinking, 'this is what it's really going to be like all the time: we're just dogs-bodies.' I said as much to Renata, but she replied, 'Imagine it, though. Suppose they did make you go and fight. Could you actually go ahead and shoot someone dead? Could you do it? I couldn't. I just could not do it. Could you?'

Left by ourselves, the place was desolate. Every little noise was a potential threat. When something creaked like a rusty door hinge I flicked round, but it was only branches rubbing against each other. Old leaves rustled as they were lifted by gusts of wind between the trees. The expanse of mountainside was desolate.

Renata hummed to herself. She hugged me once, squeezed my hand. 'We'll be all right. They'll be back soon.' She was scraping away at a blackened cooking pot. 'If we could get rid of the burnt stuff on the bottom the heat might cook the food more quickly,' she said. The noise of her scrubbing got on my nerves. How far would the sound travel? Jays squawked at each other somewhere down the valley. The river was shushing.

'Do you want to give me a hand or something?' her voice was parched.

'I was wondering about airing the bedding, see if that'll get rid of the bugs.'

We didn't talk much. It was better to say nothing. The mountain peaks appeared to wait too. All day nobody came and nothing happened. As night fell we agreed that one of us should stay awake while the other slept.

Because of the unaccustomed silence I couldn't sleep when it was my turn. No snoring, no muttering or coughing, no restive turning over. I'd got used to the sounds of men at night, their closeness, the smell of them. I must have dropped off, however, because Renata woke me when it was her turn to have a sleep. She lay like a stone, as if she had fallen asleep immediately.

The next day we heard the sound of shells exploding in the distance. So we climbed the hill and scrambled on to a rocky outcrop, hidden behind some scrubby bushes. Thick smoke rose beyond the horizon. Occasionally we heard machine-gunfire. No indication which side was winning. We waited and watched for hours.

If our men lost, the Germans would swarm all over the mountains and come looking for the various encampments, to check for munitions and clear any partisans in hiding. They would capture us; maybe shoot us after interrogation. Was this the end of all safety? We had heard about the reprisals: ten Italians would be shot for every single dead German. We both knew the possibilities if things went wrong. What remained unspoken became like some malevolent creature watching and waiting for us from between the trees. We slid into living entirely through our senses, quivering in every pore like vixens.

All that day there were bangs and explosions. I flinched at every one. Smoke billowed into the sky and joined the clouds. The smell of cordite drifted toward us. At first I assumed it was the scent of our fear. I found I was often sweaty. I thought of my mother on the coast, staying at home and refusing to go to the shelter while shells exploded in the street. This battle was far away, but everything we depended on hung on its outcome.

By that evening we unwound a little to think of contingency plans. One pistol in the hands of two relatively untrained girls would not get very far against a whole German platoon. We decided to move a few essential items to another ruined building we knew about, higher up the mountainside. It was an old shepherd's hut, but at least it meant we could keep a bird's eye view of the camp and we'd have our own bolt-hole. If we were discovered in the camp and had to run we wouldn't have time to gather up any pots or pans or bedding. We wouldn't survive long out on the mountainside without the chance to make a fire, eat and sleep.

'If anything happens, I reckon we go to Tina and Bruno,' I said.

'They'll know of another partisan band perhaps that might hide us for a bit longer.'

'But we can't stay with them for long. The Germans would know we didn't live there. We might bring them trouble.'

Renata picked up the pistol. 'The handle is cold,' she said. 'It's like it's already dead.' She lined the sight up with a tree. I said, 'We'd better not waste any bullets at target practice. Anyway, it might draw attention.' She put the gun down.

I had watched the men adoringly clean their guns. I knew how a barrel would snap open if yanked. I tried it once, making sure it wouldn't send a bullet into any part of my anatomy if I pulled the trigger by mistake. It opened smoothly like a ripe peach and inside I saw the kernel was loaded with three cartridges. Umberto had given us one more pocketful between us before he left, 'Be very careful with them. That's all I can spare right now.' He'd glared at me and cuffed me on the shoulder.

On the fourth day, we heard a twig snap amongst the trees. We looked at each other, held our breaths, listening to the distinct sound of footsteps walking over leaves. We retreated into the barn, peeped round the doorway. A German soldier appeared at the edge of the compound. I don't know how he didn't spot the movement of our heads. He had a gun in his right hand. He glanced around. His shoulder was bloodied. He appeared to be alone. I kept looking beyond him, but could make out no other moving shapes. He advanced slowly towards the building and then he called out in German. I trembled from deep inside. My limbs became uncontrollable. There would only be this one chance. If he saw either of us move he would shoot one and then the other. If he decided to stay on he would endanger our returning comrades.

'Renata, get ready. We'll have to shoot him. We have to,' I hissed. Her eyes were fastened on my face. 'Oh, let me have the gun,' I mouthed. When she gave it to me it was warm from where she'd been keeping it in her pocket.

I grasped the pistol tightly, stretched my arm and looked down the barrel. Then I edged myself round the rotting doorframe. There was less than an instant to lift my arm and aim at the middle of his chest where his heart was beating.

As I pulled the trigger the shattering noise and the jolt through my whole body made me think that I had been hit and I screamed. But it was the German whose legs buckled as he collapsed to the ground.

If any more soldiers were with him they would now come running. I crouched behind the door. 'Stay where you are. Don't move! Sssshush,' Renata whispered. I slumped back against the wall and thought I would faint. Renata was shivering. She crept soundlessly towards me on her hands and knees, stretching out her hand towards mine. The living warmth of her touch reassured me. Her face had altered somehow. We waited for a long time. Listening. It was silent except for the soughing of the breeze in the pine trees and the river. After another minute, I peered out across the clearing. The German lay over there on the ground, in a pool of darkness—a wet darkness that was spreading around him.

Curiosity got the better of me and I stepped out beyond the doorway. Renata started sobbing. I left her and ran over to him. I fell to my knees, hands covering my face. Somebody was whimpering. Renata came up and put her hand on my shoulder and I realised it was me. She hugged me tightly, 'What a great shot you are. You did it,' she said. 'You saved us.'

My arms and legs stopped shaking. 'Hurry,' I said, 'we've got to get rid of him quickly, in case another one comes.'

I picked up his fallen gun, started searching through his pockets, turned my eyes away to avoid looking at his face. I couldn't believe what I was doing. I'd never seen a dead person. But somehow he didn't seem quite dead because he was so big. I thought he must be only wounded and would jump up and grab us at any moment. When I did look him in the face his eyes were open, staring at the sky. His skin was like wax.

'Let's get his things off him. His uniform might be useful,' said Renata. I knew she was right, but nausea rose in my throat. I ran away a few steps as I felt my guts heave. I had nothing to be sick with. Tears were boiling behind my eyes. We dragged his jacket and his boots off and then the trousers. Manhandling his body and touching his clothes disgusted me. Still warm. When I tried to wipe the blood off my hands on the leaf-litter it was sticky. Blood was seeping into the ground and glittered between the dry leaves, like something alive.

His hairy legs made me want to laugh. He was very heavy, but we managed to drag him away from the compound and left him in the woods under a pile of stones. Renata made a cross out of sticks and we went back inside after that and lay down on the straw sacks, two frightened animals trembling in the moonless dark.

By the next evening, some of the men straggled back. We had to boil water, cook up some potatoes and chestnuts. It wasn't exactly home, but they were glad to be back. Fuoco wasn't amongst them. Nor was Stefano. I found myself looking out for them, checking every few minutes. We showed Capitano Umberto where the body of the German lay, but there was only an empty hole.

'You didn't bury it deeply enough,' said Umberto, 'Foxes dug it up. Or wolves. They travel long distances when they're hungry.'

34

'It's not fair,' Petronella cried, 'They've done nothing wrong. They don't deserve to die.'

'Don't be daft, Petronella. If people are in danger we can't leave the bees there.' Alex flapped the newspaper and she couldn't see his face behind it.

'They can go and find a different house to buy, can't they? In any case, the bees have never stung anyone. It's cruel and inhuman.' The house next door was being sold and the purchasers had noticed the bees flying in and out of the wall. Because someone in their family was allergic to bee stings they demanded that the Lamberts remove them.

Petronella thought her head was about to explode. 'If you kill a single bee the other bees will know about it and they'll all come and sting you, too. They give off pheromones, a signal to the others.'

'You're getting emotional about nothing. Be quiet at once.' He looked at her over the top of the newspaper. His reading glasses glinted. He turned the page and continued reading. She picked up a salt cellar and threw it hard against the wall. 'You mustn't let them. Please. You've got to say no.'

'Stop that now, you stupid girl. They're only bees.'

'They're my bees. You can't destroy them. You can't, you can't let this happen.' The anger had reached her heart. She had to put her hand over it to see if she could slow it down.

'Dash it, go to your room, Petronella. I won't have you shouting or throwing property about like this.' He spoke very quietly. 'In any case I've phoned Mr Oldroyd to remove them. He's coming next week.'

She threw the mustard pot against the wall and a brown mark stained the wallpaper. She stamped her foot. 'The bees will curse you if you kill them. And I will never ever forgive you!' The words spewed from her mouth, frightening her as if someone else was saying them.

He stood up and she ran out of the door. She couldn't go upstairs because the bees would be humming in the wall; she already felt like a traitor. She ripped the front door open and fled into the road. She was running away and intended never to come back. She wandered the streets by herself and stared at the ground. Weeds were growing below the garden walls, the drain holes and the culverts. She went to the old bridge and considered throwing herself into the water, but she could see the water was sluggish. She slipped back into the house when the first star or two glowed in the dusk and no one seemed to notice. The bees hummed all night. Hearing that sound made her feel she was being punished for being so young, so ineffectual.

She was at school when the workmen came with veils and leather gloves to kill the bees and by the time she came home a few stray bees were vainly trying to get in their front door. She knew they could not survive without the rest of the colony. They'd starve in a day or two. Miss Brown showed no sympathy. 'It's high time you learned about living in the real world.' Alex never said another word about the bees.

It wasn't long after this that he told Petronella that she was going away to boarding school. She didn't ask him if it was because she was displaying signs of juvenile delinquency. Did it all add up to something in his mind? Was everything connected to everything else?

So it was that she'd virtually left home by the time she was twelve years old—when she first put on that serge grey uniform and got in her father's car with a school trunk on the back seat. Miss Brown didn't wave her off because she was upstairs, packing her own things.

35

Stefano and Carpe carried Fuoco back to the camp, laid him on some sacks and slumped down exhausted. I touched Fuoco's hand, felt some warmth. When I looked at his face, I thought he was about to slip away. I knelt to listen to each intake of Fuoco's breath, but the exhalation made no sound and I watched his chest rise and fall almost imperceptibly.

I didn't know what to do. How on earth was I supposed to know? Renata and I had learned how to cook meals from almost nothing; we'd had to wash the men's tattered clothes crawling with lice; we'd had to rinse their hair in kerosene to kill the bugs and now we were expected to nurse men who had wounds in their bodies we could never have imagined. I thought that I wouldn't want to die by myself, but how should I keep company with the dying? Should I talk to him or remain silent? Suppose he was in pain? Was there anything I could do that would make any difference? Perhaps I should say a prayer. With my finger I smeared a little water on his dry lips. He did not lick it.

I wiped his forehead with a damp cloth but he wasn't feverish. It did not seem right to leave him alone. 'Fuoco,' I said, hoping he'd hear me. I spoke again, but there was no response. I got up to ask Stefano, thinking he might be able to advise me. Renata was fetching fresh water for the two of them. I said, 'Stefano, tell me where he's wounded, can you?'

Stefano murmured, 'It was a bullet... went right through him. The wound must be kept clean; it'll have to be bathed. Can you manage that?'

'And what's his real name? I need to know.'

He lifted himself on to his elbow to look at his friend. 'His name's Vittorio. I think you should use it—yes, he's much more likely to respond to his own name. Keep talking to him, if you can. He might be able to hear you and it might bring him round. If he stays unconscious he could just fade away.'

It occurred to me that Fuoco's body must be exhausted from the general hunger that gnawed at us like rats in the night. He'd been fortunate so far and had avoided the brutal deaths we'd sometimes heard about—faces smashed, arms blown off, ears and fingers hacked off those taken prisoner. Perhaps it would be a kindness to let him escape such a gruesome death.

'Vittorio, can you hear me? Vittorio, are you all right?' Not knowing what else to do I started gabbling to him: 'Do you … remember … the taste of gnocchi? How they crumble softly in your mouth, all buttery and smooth.' I settled myself beside him. 'With pesto, perhaps, or tomatoes in olive oil so strong you could taste the olives, and sugared with grated pecorino cheese? I used to watch them drop into boiling water and then rise to the surface. My mother scoops them out as she counts because they mustn't stay in the water too long. She knows exactly how long, counts out the seconds.'

I stumbled on. 'Vittorio, think of a golden peach straight from the tree, how you bite through the furry skin all that yellow juice runs down your chin. And you slurp it up with your tongue and wipe it off with the back of your hand. If you pick it when it's just right, it breaks open in two halves falling away from the stone—the hollow is red like a flame and tastes the best.'

His eyelids flickered and, for a moment, his eyes looked straight into mine. The lids closed again, but my heart leaped. After thinking he'd gone, then seeing him return, it was like a miracle.

'Vittorio,' I said. 'You're all right now. You're safe.'

After a while he began to mumble. 'If you are captured you must say nothing. If you are tortured you must forget your friends. If you say anything at all you may endanger the whole band.'

'Vittorio, Vittorio, it's all right.' I wiped the cool cloth on his forehead again. Watching him come round was frightening, as if something dead was coming back to life.

'Shoot me. You have to shoot me,' he gabbled, his eyes looking straight at me.

'You're okay now. You're safe. No one is going to hurt you, Vittorio. Not now. It's all over.'

'Don't let them capture me. Shoot me or give me a gun. They've got my name.'

It was their rule; if you are injured, better to shoot yourself than be captured.

'They will put me in prison and shoot me. Better to be dead. Give me a gun.'

I knew what Umberto had instilled in them: if a comrade is injured and asks you to shoot him you must do it. It is your duty to do so. Medical help is a long way away and he may become very ill before he dies. You know that, if captured, he will not be allowed to die easily and he will be tortured to reveal information.

When his eyes opened again he lay still. Relief trickled through my limbs. He tried to shift his position and flinched. That seemed like a good sign. When I folded up a jacket for a pillow it made me feel calm deep inside, as if I only need be myself. Not Florence Nightingale. I leaned over and dabbed some water onto his lips. This time he licked the drops. His eyes watched me. I lifted his neck and held the cup for him while he swallowed.

'Do you want more?'

He nodded. I stood up and he moved his head so that he could keep an eye on me as I went outside to fetch more water in the cup.

'Thank you. I was very thirsty. I thought I'd died and my punishment was to be thirsty forever.' He drank again. 'Tell me, was it you talking to me before?'

'Well, I guessed that talking about food might bring you round. When you started shouting I knew you were getting better.'

'I heard my name. But why did someone not shoot me? They were under instructions to do so.'

'Why would anyone do that? Silly idea.'

'They are meant to shoot me if I was wounded.'

'You won the battle and the Germans were forced to retreat. They wouldn't want to lose you, of all people. Look, you're safe in the camp now. No one is going to interrogate you.'

'Ah! We beat them back, did we?' His head tipped backwards, exposing his throat.

'Yes. But you were wounded and became unconscious for a while. Luckily the bullet went straight through you or you'd be waiting for a doctor to remove it. You'd be on a stretcher. Not here.'

'How did I get here?'

'Stefano and Carpe carried you quite a long way between them. They wouldn't leave you behind.' I wiped his forehead with the damp cloth again. I couldn't think what else to do.

'They carried me?'

'Yes, Vittorio. After the Germans retreated, they carried you back here; sometimes over their shoulders, sometimes one took your legs and one took your arms. It must have hurt you a lot.'

'How did you get my name?'

'Stefano told me. I asked him. We thought you'd respond to the sound of your own name.'

'Ah, my friend, Stefano. Saviour and betrayer. I'll knock his teeth out when I'm up.'

'He only told it to me to help me get through to you. I won't use it again. I won't say it to anyone. It's safe with me.' I was fiddling with the cover, trying to make sure he was warm enough.

'What's done is done now. I'm tied to you, now, aren't I? Tell me something, are you a nurse?'

'No, no, I don't know anything about nursing,' I laughed.

'What's your name? Do I know you?'

'I'm Maddalena, Maddalena. You know me. I'm the one who is always getting cross with you. I'm the one you taught to shoot. Rather well, actually.'

He was staring at my hand that wasn't holding the cup. He stretched out a hand to me, took my fingers in his, held them as if he needed my warmth.

'When I thought I was dying I wanted to tell you something, Maddalena.'

'But you didn't know who I was.'

'I did. I always would.'

'What was it, then?'

'I... I... I'm afraid I can't remember. Wait....'

'Tell me later. I need to go and find you something to eat. Then you must sleep.'

Two or three weeks later, when Vittorio was up and about again, Captain Alex turned up. Renata nudged me, whispered something about his sweet manners and dry humour being just my type. When I was talking with the captain later, Vittorio caught my eye. His glance made me catch my breath.

That evening, the men were assembled round the campfire. The usual clink of Liar Dice fell silent when he approached; everyone was eager to hear what he knew of the progress of the Allies across Italy. I saw, turned towards him, a sea of faces lit by the flames, their eyes gleaming with expectation in the orange glow. He reported that the Allies had ground to a standstill. The men listened to this news in silence. 'How do you read the situation, *Commendatore?*' one of the lads asked him.

'They've reached a stalemate, but there is still a good chance the line will be breached before the winter.' He was staring into the flames.

'And if not? What then?'

'If not... we will have to conserve ammunition and provisions as best we can through the winter. We will wait for new instructions and, until then, keep raiding enemy supply routes as often as possible and take their provisions in order to replenish stocks here.'

It didn't sound like a problem at the time. And even he couldn't have known what was around the corner. We were mainly supplied by the parachute drops from the Allies and some victuals were sent by mule now and then from the towns on the coast. We were dependent on the courage of other people. When a parachute drop was imminent he usually carried the news himself or made use of couriers. The drop-zones had to be changed frequently so as not to alert the enemy.

With increased German troop movements that autumn it became more difficult to move around without being detected. So Renata and I became the couriers. The Germans were unlikely to suspect two young women on bikes and so we were often sent with vital messages to other brigades: new orders, important new contacts, requests for small items of equipment. Sometimes we carried explosives, too. Once, we carried grenades in a shopping basket. Another time, we took cartridges. It worked out all right. We managed to dress ourselves up a bit, put on lipstick. Occasionally, we even came back with chocolate or wine, given to us by the German soldiers. We carried news as carefully as if it, too, were ordnance.

We would move from one camp to another, stopping away overnight sometimes, with regular visits to Bruno and Tina. During this time, I was learning to use their radio equipment and became adept at the Dante code. We sent and received messages to and from other partisan brigades, which could slip through German and British Intelligence. We developed our own lines of communication. Verses from Dante were perfectly suited to this because all of us had learned *La Divina Commedia* at school. My father had taught me particularly well.

It was useful for us to know what was being decided elsewhere before each visit from Captain Alex. Useful, but not always possible. We wanted to be at least one step ahead of the Allies; after all, it was our country. The next time Alex arrived on one of his reconnaissance trips, Umberto asked him to let the British know that without their full support throughout the winter we would not have enough supplies to live on, that it was vital the parachute drops should continue. The Captain's eyes were expressionless when he replied that as far as he knew all troop movements were to be halted and it was considered too dangerous to fly a plane over the high mountains in winter at night. He told us that the Allied commander, General Alexander, had said that all the partisan brigades should stand down for the winter. 'With an order like that, my hands are tied.'

'That's really pig-ignorant. It just isn't possible and they should know it!' shouted Umberto. 'We would all be picked off by the Fascists and transported to Nazi work camps, if not shot first.'

It was generally assumed by everyone that the Allies didn't take us seriously, used us when they needed a spot of sabotage and dropped us when we became inconvenient. When I heard the captain's reply I realised that there was nothing but hope to get us through the winter. But we had precious little of it, not enough even to season the food we prepared.

36

At the end of half-term week Petronella drove home, determined to get everything else removed by a dealer. From the chest she brought the jewellery box, the black Garbo hat with the veil, some scarves and gloves, the old photo albums and the exercise book with the photo of the strange man, the letter and the copy of *La Divina Commedia*. She had her mother's silver hairbrush and mirror that used to sit on the dressing table. She also found the little wooden hat with a feather she had never been allowed to touch, wrapped in a piece of tissue. Maddalena used to breathe on it to make it shine like a conker and then place it back where it belonged. Petronella knew it had been a kind of talisman. She thought Matt would admire the workmanship. He really would need to go to Dale View himself and take whatever he wanted from the house, some keepsakes to remind him of his grandfather: the tools, perhaps, or a vintage wireless.

She knew he'd been upset about his grandfather's death. He had stood between her and Todd at the funeral last month. It was she who had cried, tears concealed by the piped muzak, the plastic flowers and the chrysanthemums her mother would have hated.

'He was a private man,' one of his neighbours said to her later over a plate of vol-au-vents. 'Always kept himself to himself,' he said in a hushed tone as if this might comfort her. 'But I remember when he and your son made rockets out of plastic bottles which they inflated up with a bicycle pump and flew over the garden fence. That was a laugh, by heck.'

Matt was waiting for her when she banged through the door laden with bags. 'Oh, I see... a welcoming committee?'

'Surprise for you,' he said. When she heard what he'd done while she had been away she sank down on a kitchen chair.

'You what? Are you having me on?'

'No, it's true.'

'Oh, come on. You have to be joking, Matt. I don't believe it.'

'No, it is true, Mum. I really have.'

'What the hell are you up to?'

'Look, I'll show you the documents if you want. Prove it to you.'

'Oh shit, Matt. Tell me, what's got into your head? Why now?'

'Well, when I had the idea, I thought I'd go over to the Recruitment Office and find out a bit more about it. They seemed to be offering a good deal so I thought I might just as well sign up there and then. Easy.'

'Without consulting me?' She was hurt he had acted while the coast was clear. 'And so when exactly did you decide this was what you wanted to do?'

'Er, not long after Granddad's funeral actually.'

'But why? Tell me why. Whatever for, Matt?'

'It just came to me. There was a talk at school once and I was interested then, but didn't think you and Dad would ever agree. But then I realised it would have pleased Granddad really. And get me out of your hair.'

'I didn't know it was something you'd considered. Never once occurred to me. You never said anything.'

'I knew you wouldn't be mad keen about it so I decided not to tell you till it was done.

'Too bloody right. But thanks for the vote of confidence.'

'I knew you'd try to persuade me out of it so I decided to go for it...'

'Can you swear to me that you haven't done this just to piss me off as much as you possibly can? I am a committed pacifist, you know.'

'No, it wasn't anything like that. It's something I really want to do. Granddad was in the army after all. I don't see a problem.'

'But it was wartime, Matt. That was different. There was conscription in those days.'

'Look, I don't seem to do anything right in your eyes. I thought you'd be surprised at first and glad after you'd got used to the idea. They'll get my head sorted at any rate.'

'Hopefully before they get you killed.'

'I'll get fit and they'll keep me off the streets, Mum. And they'll pay me while I get trained.'

'Yes, trained to kill people.' Her voice dropped away.

'No Mum, to keep the peace.'

'Oh yes. You've had practice at that here, I suppose. See yourself with a blue beret helping refugees across a mined road, do you?'

'Something like that. It feels, you know… as if I'd be doing something real. I just can't see myself spending my life in front of a computer screen in an office. I'd go mad. It isn't me, is it?'

'Well, I suppose I'll just have to try and come round to the idea. I hope you never get sent to a real war zone.'

'That's the whole point though, isn't it? Look, I'm twenty, Mum. You don't have to be thinking after me.'

'Old enough to make sensible decisions, you'd think.'

'It's only for three years, that's all. Like going away to university.'

'Where they don't happen to teach you how to fucking kill people.'

37

Christmas came and went like any other day. Then New Year. That night there was heavy snowfall. Renata and I had never seen snow before. I caught some flakes and watched them melt from their edges in the warmth of my palm. The snow wrapped us in quietness, as if the rest of the world no longer existed. I thought the snow might not stop and we would be buried in the beautiful, smothering drifts. The dawn light was bewildering.

The compound soon became a mass of slush. Renata and I were glad that timber had been collected and stored or we would have been in trouble. Survival became our priority. It was forbidden to steal, but sometimes desperate men will do anything, even eat strips of bark or chew leather. Sometimes desperate women, too.

We were facing starvation. At an emergency meeting of all the men it was decided that, as a last resort, a party should strike out across the mountains to see if we could get victuals from a well-supplied partisan band further north—they had recently been lucky enough to receive parachute drops from the English. It would be a difficult journey over the passes in the snow. As he knew the routes so well, Vittorio volunteered to lead the group. Capitano Umberto agreed and together they chose five more men, including Vittorio's closest friend, Stefano.

In Umberto's control room, as he called it, they spread a map out on the floor. I crept into the room, pretended to be sorting something out. They took no notice of me. Vittorio was pointing out the route over the mountain to Ordasio, one that would take them along the ridge for a short way and then drop down on to the far side so that they would be less likely to be spotted by someone with binoculars. The path across Monte Ronte and into the Taparello valley was steep. Stefano snorted that it wasn't likely any fool would be bothering to keep watch. Umberto said that they couldn't be too careful. He suggested an overnight stop would be found at Pagra. There was a guerrilla band there, too. They might not have food, but would at least have a roof for shelter.

'I wonder...' I'd had an idea.

Umberto looked annoyed. 'What now?'

'I'd like to be considered to join the party going to Ordasio,' I said.

Umberto looked at me in mock-astonishment. 'And just what do you think you'll contribute to the mission?'

'I think they might find an extra pair of hands helpful. If they need to find refuge, people will be more likely to offer shelter if there is a woman amongst them. And I think that the partisans in Ordasio may be more likely to release some of their supplies if it is for a woman. I can also be a useful scout and go ahead of them. Being a woman no one will suspect me and I can spot the locations of German patrols. And, as you know, I speak English; there may be British soldiers at Ordasio, which would be why they've got supplies.'

'That's a lot of reasons. But you're under my protection and I'm not convinced. Let me discuss it with Fuoco and Stefano. Leave us now. I don't want any more interruptions.'

As I went out of the door they carried on poring over the map. I waited by the door. Umberto stood up and embraced Vittorio and Stefano. 'For all our sakes I wish you every success. We will look forward to your safe return.'

'And what shall we do about the girl?' Stefano asked.

'I think that I will leave that up to you to decide. My fear is that she won't have the stamina for this and that she would slow you down.'

'Right, let's tell her that she can't come. It isn't safe for a woman. We have enough to take care of.' Stefano moved his chair and I vanished into the night.

Since shooting the German and realising that I might never see my brother again, I had decided there was nothing to be feared. I felt careless of my own safety and was determined to make a contribution to the Resistance effort. It made me desperate to go with them. I was much more afraid of the thought of dying slowly of starvation, lying on a straw sack by myself. Doing something dramatic was preferable, even if it meant I was likely to die sooner. It was impossible to imagine how any of us would survive much longer, without a miracle.

I listened all night for the sound of them getting up. At last I heard them waking each other, the sound of buckles, of feet slipping into boots. I had nothing to take except the clothes that I had to wear day and night. Renata had given me a scarf and some gloves, very holey but better than nothing. I slipped outside to wait for them to leave and then followed them at a slight distance. I guessed that six men would never notice another unobtrusive figure in the dark, would think I was one of them, forgetting, when sleepy, to count themselves. By the time we had gone a certain distance, it would be too far to make me turn back on my own.

I'd gathered that their route would take them through the village of Revalla where they were going to borrow some mules and then on up the pass to Passo Guardia. I reckoned that they might discover me when we got to Revalla. But, by then, it would be too late.

In fact, nobody spotted me until after we had left the village. Birds were beginning to sing out as dawn was opening a crack of light over the horizon. I must have stumbled over a stone and grabbed at the man nearest me. He held my shoulder and hand for an instant, felt how it wasn't a man's.

'What the hell do you think you're doing here?' It was Carpe.

He ran on ahead to the others. A dark figure came back down the path towards me and I readied myself for a dressing-down. Vittorio asked me brusquely why I had come. His eyes were bright in the snow-light. I always tried to avoid those eyes. So I looked away, 'If you won't take me with you then my life isn't worth living.' I hadn't meant to say that, didn't know what I meant by it.

Someone shouted up ahead and he ran back. He hadn't heard what I said. He had more important things to think about.

The path was difficult to follow in the snow. The mules knew their way so our only recourse was to trust them. When it wasn't too steep we rode. It began to rain, a heavy, cold drizzle that stung our faces and froze on our eyelids.

We met a group of partisans in the forest between Pagra and Vione. They had some Russians with them, men who had deserted from the Red Army. They were under their own commander and three of them offered to accompany us. We ate a little, the first for some time. We had brought nothing but wild apples and these had given us stomach-aches.

We rested at their camp and set off again at dusk. We passed the Stations of the Cross guiding us along the route in the half-light. We turned a corner and the last shrine was filled with snow; its Madonna was buried. As we headed beyond the tree line our troubles began. Snow and fog blinded us. We could only travel in the dark as our column, silhouetted against the white landscape in the daylight, would have been easy to spot by German look-outs. Vittorio followed the stars as another would read a map. To him the night was just a different code from the day. We depended on him.

Now we had to clamber over icy rock faces, slither round huge boulders. The chill snow cloud exhausted us.

One of the mules was lost over the edge, but if it hadn't been for the strength of the Russians we might have lost more. Everything was silent, except the wind. The snow fell lighter. We found a zigzag path hewn out of the rock face. It twisted between gigantic masses of stone until we arrived in a small hamlet. I went ahead to find out if there were any Germans quartered here, but they had all left. A farmer let us sleep in a disused goat hut where we rested for several hours. Someone gave us some bread. Ahead, we could see that the pass we had to cross in order to reach Ordasio was buried under deep snow.

Again, I volunteered to go forward to check the way was safe, not knowing what I was taking on. For two hours I could not walk and had to crawl over the deep drifts. My fingers were bleeding and my clothes were shredded. I fell, got up, fell again and so it went on. At the pass I found a shepherd's hut to shelter in till the others finally caught up, the mules struggling through the drifts on their thin legs.

We needed to draw on untried depths of resilience to make the descent towards Ordasio, for we soon found that going down was no easier than going up—to achieve every step we staggered through snowdrifts that held our bodyweight momentarily before shattering beneath us. When finally we arrived at a line of trees Vittorio must have known where to go because he called a halt and dived into the forest. When he came back he was accompanied by partisans who led us to their camp where there was shelter and food. We stayed with them for two days, gathering our strength. Miraculously they let us load the exhausted mules with a few sacks containing flour and lentils; riches beyond my dreams.

38

Petronella's plan was to spend most of her summer holiday in Italy. After a few days in a small town called Caraggio, on the coast near Porto Romolo, she arranged to rent an apartment there. 'I shan't be lounging on the beach, well, not all the time,' she told her colleagues. No one knew her real motive. She couldn't actually put it into words. She'd managed to read and translate another chunk of the account each week, but it was a slow process. If she were to hear and speak Italian for a time she knew she'd tap into the spring of the language within herself, the nuances and inflections she'd absorbed through osmosis as a child.

Matt was due to start his Marines training at Lympstone. Todd said he'd look out for him in case of any emergencies and promised to contact her. She was still furious with Matt and had bickered with him. 'Don't rely on me to support your mad idea. I might not come to your passing-out, Matt. Uniforms don't impress me one little bit, you know.'

In the departure lounge she realised her heart was fluttering. This was the first step into the unknown. She'd packed the exercise book and a dictionary, the partisan identity card, the letter and photo. On an impulse she took the little wooden hat that had sat on her mother's dressing table—just in case she found Francesco who wanted it returned. She kept these with her in her hand luggage, wrapped in a silk scarf. She was hoping that she might be able to track down Renata, whom she had met years ago with her mother. These were all the clues she had to start her off on the trail, unless, it was already too late and everyone who might know anything had died.

Would her ability to speak Italian be up to the job just because she'd beavered away with a dictionary and a verb book to translate her mother's account? And even if Renata were still alive, how was she going to set about finding her?

She could be living anywhere. Petronella looked round anxiously to see if anyone else was afraid, but the rest of the passengers were calmly reading or chatting.

She thought a book might distract her wandering thoughts so she reached into her bag. She'd grabbed an emergency one from a pile she kept in her room, and was surprised to find it was a book of poetry that she had given to Todd, for his birthday, the year before he left. As she opened it she spotted her own writing on the fly-leaf: *To Todd, With all my love, Petronella, February 1990.* He hadn't taken it with him when he left her just before his next birthday, and she wondered if he had ever read it, or whether he simply didn't want it because it had her name in it. And he'd left this, her last gift. Todd had never been keen on poetry. It hadn't been a good choice.

Had she ever made a deliberate choice? Her mind went over the past, but she couldn't think of an instance when she had made a conscious decision. Everything she'd done appeared to be the result of aimless drift: teaching, marriage—yes, even Matt.

The plane lurched on the updrafts as they passed over the mountains. Below, the deep valleys were charcoal and the mountains were purple and gold, with bright lakes. In the distance Mont Blanc glowed ghostly white and a single cloud was skewered on the jagged summit. From up here, the landscape was clearly spread out like a map. One could see which way to go, how to skirt each mountain or follow the silver necklaces of the rivers from valley to valley, all the choices of route and direction she would now have to make on her own. As the plane started its descent towards the coast, the buildings and roads looked unnervingly complicated again and she hoped that she would find answers to the puzzles.

39

The way back would be longer. We had to take a more dangerous route as the laden mules would not manage the way we had come. The only choice was the road—also used by German traffic. So we travelled by night to be able to see their lights approaching.

The storm drove snow in our faces and our feet slithered on ice. After two nights we reached Pagra again and the safety of the forest. The three Russians returned to their unit. We decided to rest for a day in a ruined house on the mountainside above the village, while two of the men, Sandro and Nico, acting as scouts, stayed in an outhouse on the edge of the village.

We were woken at dawn. The village was being ransacked by German soldiers and the narrow streets became an inferno of gunfire during which Sandra and Nico were badly wounded. The Germans had not discovered them and swept on to search for Resistance fighters in the next village up the valley. Knowing we could no longer stay in the vicinity of Pagra we were directed by villagers to a ruined church where we laid low for two days and nights. The wounded men were in great pain. No one from the village wanted to help us and I could see why; they had suffered enough. When I glanced across at Vittorio, I saw his despair.

One of the men went on to fetch help from our own partisan brigade, and the two casualties were taken by stretcher back to Revalla where a friendly doctor tended them. We returned to our camp with the mules carrying the food we had brought back with us. Those we had left behind watched our arrival in disbelief. But a cheer went up when Capitano Umberto saluted and embraced each of us, even me. 'You have saved all our lives, I thank you,' he said solemnly. Renata, wrapped in sacking against the cold, wept for joy to see us. Vittorio stood by the mules to ensure the food was unloaded in an orderly manner, while the stove was being cranked up to start cooking the lentils. Eating them uncooked could kill starving people. The men would have ripped open the flour sacks if Stefano had not guarded them. I helped Renata mix some flour with a little water to make some instant, digestible sustenance for the queue of bedraggled men.

But before eating anything more, I needed sleep. I must have slept for hours. When I opened my eyes I saw Vittorio's face next to mine. He was leaning on one elbow, watching over me as I woke. It was a shock to know I was being observed. Had I been snoring or dribbling?

'You should be tucked up in a bed,' he whispered. I smiled, still half-asleep. He asked, 'Have you always been like this?'

'What do you mean?'

'Always assuming you can do whatever you want.'

'I don't know what you're getting at, Vittorio. You're suggesting I'm pig-headed?'

'Perhaps that's what it is. I had another word for it.'

'You didn't want me to come. You thought I'd be a liability.'

'I knew the expedition was a huge gamble. I didn't want to see anything happen to you. That's why I didn't want you to come.'

'I've never been in a situation like this, Vittorio. Perhaps having to live with Fascism every day has just made me a more determined person.'

He fell silent for a while. 'You said something to me just before we left Revalla. What did you mean?'

'Oh, did I? Nothing, I should think.' My heart began to pound. 'Have you noticed how I want you to kiss me?' I said in English.

'If we met somewhere else, say in a café or on a train and I asked you, do you think that you'd let me walk you home?'

'Yes, I might.'

'I'd like that, Maddalena. Then you'd invite me in for coffee perhaps?'

'Hmm, maybe. And you'd come in?'

'When all this is over... we could go dancing... go to the cinema... anything you like. Supposing, after a while, I were to fall in love with you, just a bit...' He was looking down at his hand. Not at me. I felt confused.

'What then?'

'Well, would I stand a chance?' When he looked at me I thought he could read my thoughts. I rolled onto my back but my head turned and my eyes slipped back to his gaze.

'I can't talk hypothetically, Vittorio.'

'It could happen though, could it?'

'...but, Vittorio, we only have the present.' I moved towards him. I felt his breath on my forehead. His lips were so soft when he kissed me. And I thought that now love had begun it would never end. I crept in against his curved body as if he were a sun-warmed stone beside which I could shelter. I could hear his heart beating; the movement of the breath in his throat came and went like the thrum of a bird's wing in the air.

Whatever I was doing I knew if he was near to me; my skin felt his presence before I saw him. If he was away on a mission I was more afraid than if I myself were about to be sent into combat. I felt terror when I heard he was running an ambush. Taut like a stretched elastic band, I would forget what I was doing half-way through doing it and Renata moaned at me or elbowed me out of her way, rolling her eyes up to heaven at my incompetence. I didn't really want to discuss what was happening. But it was obvious, to Renata at least. 'I can tell what you're thinking,' she'd say impatiently, 'but could you just get on with the job?'

While he was away, the day was interminably long. I was always watching for his return. It wasn't just his absence that drained me; it was the fear of losing him. When he did return I had to restrain myself from running to him. It wouldn't do at all. I'd hand him his ration of food like the others. Once I laid a butterfly's wing on the rim of his plate, another time it was a leaf, a blade of grass, once even a red money spider that I found on a rock.

After any length of absence he would come to find me somewhere and bury his head in my hair as if inhaling the scent satisfied his need. And it was enough for us both that we were close to each other—safe.

One night he challenged me that in ordinary circumstances I would not look at him, a bearded man in ragged clothes, stinking, unwashed. I replied that all my so-called education and ability with languages was nothing to do with my inner self, they were only things I had learned. He smiled then and I watched his eyelids close as his lips caressed mine, suppressed laughter still bubbling in his throat.

Not so long before I had thought that I was careless of my life, but at that point I would have done anything to preserve it. I became vicious at the thought of losing hold of my body and would have fought anyone with my bare hands who might destroy either Vittorio or me. We said to each other that the death of either would have meant the slow crumbling of the other.

I loved his arms. The sinewy length of them, the strength of his grasp, the smoothness of the long muscles and the way they twined like a hemp rope. His arms smelt like mineral water, the skin on the underside of his arm was veined like marble.

We often spent the night away from the camp in the empty shepherd's hut further up the mountainside. Vittorio cleared a space and laid two straw sacks to make a nest for our new love.

I remember the depth of my sleep while I lay next to him, the ease of waking, relief from my broken, watchful nights. On several nights lightning flashed and our hovel was lit as if by day. Often the thunder turned down into another valley. More than once he woke with a start, sat up and groped for his gun. When I reached for his arm he flinched like a young horse and then sighed and lay down again, his face nuzzled against my neck. I felt the thumping of his pulse against my breast.

Once the moon lit his body while he was bending over me; later I woke again to find the room was filled with a white glow making me aware that a world of enchantment was following its own life outside. I don't know if I dozed off, but when a bird piped up I thought it was still moonlight frosting the room. As my eyes focussed I recognised the light of early dawn and I left our bed to watch the switchback of mountains grow into shape, the ground turning from grey to green.

'When the war is over where shall we live?' he asked. His voice was tender. I said I didn't mind at all so long as it was with him. His marble arms pressed my face into his neck. Skin was all that lay between us.

'But my parents might need to come and live close to us, or even with us, because Cristiano mightn't be coming home. It depends on what my father wants,' I warned him.

'We could live in Porto Romolo then and I could get a job in a hotel when the English come back. You can teach me how to speak beautiful English.' My toes stroked his soles. 'And what will your mother say to that?' He was kissing my temples.

'She'll be only too glad if I send her some cash from time to time. She'll be able to buy a few things for a change. Vittorio, I still want to go to university, you know.'

His back felt like silk. 'Oh, do you, now?'

'And what do you dream of?'

'Well, I'm going to get the best camera money can buy.'

By dawn we always had to tear ourselves apart if we didn't want tongues to wag or Umberto to appear at the doorway.

I hoped that one day the world would let us be together. I thought a time would come when we could be ourselves —just get up in the morning and live an ordinary day and go to bed at night. But just when you think you're navigating your way through and can see a place to land, the world has moved on again. And every minute that we had together was all there was to have.

40

The street corner was familiar. She hadn't been expecting to recall anything; not having been here since she was a child in 1953. But she was no stranger to the sea light bouncing off the walls, the vistas of the Mediterranean at the end of the palm-lined streets leading down to the bay, the smells of pine tree and coffee. Excited, she realised she must find the central market square; that was where she'd find the first clue. Her feet remembered the way, navigation by instinct. She thought memory must be elastic and live in bone as well as brain cells.

And after the dark little alleyway round the back of the church she found herself standing in a cobbled piazza with a single palm tree, a fountain and market stalls selling bunches of bright flowers. Just as it had been then. A multitude of scooters surged at the traffic lights. The newspaper booths hadn't changed either; same grey metal lock-ups selling Italian and foreign papers. For a moment, she was tempted by the familiar faces of *The Times* and the *Independent*. Catching sight of the headline 'Iraqi forces deny access to Weapons Inspectors' she paused to read further: 'Iraq violates obligations under Security Council resolutions permitting UNSCOM teams immediate and unrestricted access to all sites designated for inspection.' She wondered about the consequences of this sabre-rattling. What were the implications for Matt? She was reminded of how her grandmother described anxiously scanning newspaper headlines on the street vendors' stalls during the lead-up to the Second World War.

La Stampa was the name of the newspaper Renata used to read. She paused, catching sight of the lead article on the front page: Italian voters had voted in three referendums to limit Silvio Berlusconi's media empire, but the ex-premier was fighting back. A picture of him grinning, showing whiter-than-white teeth, made him look more like a celebrity than a devious politician.

She shivered. Looking down at her hand, she spread apart her fingers to check pink ice cream wasn't sliding down the back of her hand. Shadows of the palm tree's fronds flecked the stone fountain. She didn't remember that statue above her. Somali street vendors tried to flog dodgy-looking watches. Swifts screeched and whirled in the sky. She felt a jab of grief under her ribs. Standing on this spot reminded her of Maddalena and the feeling of being very close to her mother. It was in this place she had been happier than anywhere else Petronella had known her.

Perhaps not exactly 'happy'… but not misplaced, as she was at their suburban Wikeley home. More in touch with herself, less constrained—talkative, cheerful and relaxed in the company of Renata, who'd strutted in yellow-shoes-to-die-for.

The thread of her intuition led her into the church of San Pietro. The untypical bareness of the stone walls, more Presbyterian than Roman Catholic, snagged her mind. Petronella sat in a side-chapel and remembered how her mother had sought out a priest to hear her confession. What had that been about? What had possessed her to do such a thing? She didn't recall her mother ever attending church at home. But it was clear to her now that Maddalena had known what to do and where to go. At the time, not being a Catholic, Petronella hadn't known about priests hearing confession. She hadn't had words to interpret what her mother was doing. She remembered how she'd thought the confessional was a wardrobe. Then, just when Petronella had knocked over a chair that made such an embarrassing clatter, Maddalena had burst out of the wardrobe, concealing tear-stained eyes behind dark glasses, and had practically pushed her out of the church into the square. She'd felt guilty, as if her mother had guessed she was on the point of climbing over the rail to touch the plaster baby's hair. They had never talked about her dead baby brother. She had not been told exactly what had happened. She'd tried to broach it with Granny Rose, but even she had clammed up.

Outside San Pietro, it came to her that the thing she must do was to find Renata. Whatever it took she must search till she found her. Renata had been her mother's friend, the only one she remembered, and the two had talked all the time. She was the one person who might be able to give her some confirmation of the account's authenticity. Petronella didn't know who else to turn to for help and no idea where to start looking. Without knowing a surname it would be difficult.

Petronella guessed Renata would be roughly the same age as her mother would have been if she were alive. She was beset by so many questions that almost weakened her recent resolve. She asked herself, how will I introduce myself after all these years? How will I ask what I need to know? Supposing she doesn't remember me? Supposing we don't understand each other? There won't be much time left to find out. It might be too late anyway. She could be dead or too old to remember anything.

41

In March it was still very cold. That particular day had started well enough. After a tip-off through Captain Alex's radio, they had ambushed a German lorry as it crossed the mountains, shot some of the soldiers and taken over two smaller utility vehicles. They also held some German guns and provisions. Our men took a few skin wounds but none had been killed.

But when they came to remove the Germans' uniforms Vittorio said they were all sickened to find that the soldiers were only youngsters, boys. Some were no more than fourteen or fifteen. Many of the partisans had younger brothers at home. Their bullets had maimed the youngsters' heads and chests. One boy had lost his face when they had thrown a grenade at them. Another's skull had been opened, his brain exposed. I couldn't listen to what they said. Bile rose from my belly into my mouth. As they pulled the jackets off the lads, they wept. There had been too much killing.

Vittorio told Alex about the German boys and he said that was a good sign, it meant Germany was running out of men, were forced to use younger conscripts to defend occupied territory. Vittorio said that he thought this war was stinking. The Englishman didn't reply.

There was wine that night and Captain Alex had brought tobacco. The men needed to get drunk, to become oblivious. Sitting on logs around the fire they sang songs:

> *And if I die up there on the mountain*
> *o bella ciao, bella ciao, bella ciao…*
> *and if I die up there on the mountain*
> *you must bury me.*

Bury me on the mountain,
o bella ciao, bella ciao, bella ciao, ciao, ciao,
bury me on the mountain
under the shadow of a beautiful flower.

I heard Stefano's strong bass voice nearby; another lad's beautiful tenor rang out across the night, the cheerful tune and sorrowful words.

The body of a wild goat was hanging from a beam and was going to be roasted for our dinner. Everyone was excited at the thought of a good meal. Across the approach to the camp they had placed a trip-wire attached to some explosive so that they wouldn't be caught unawares by a German patrol. It meant that tonight nobody need be on guard duty and miss out. It felt like a celebration, perhaps because we guessed the war would soon be won. The tobacco and the wine were having an extraordinary effect. All the men were laughing like jackasses. With fresh tobacco, they were all busy rolling up cigarettes. I overheard snatches of conversation.

'How come you want to stay with us in the mountains, Captain Alex?' Vittorio spoke.

'I think I'm of more use to the war effort in my capacity here than if I were posted back to London. I could be sent back behind enemy lines in Southern Italy... wasting time... besides, I like it here.' He was knocking back the rough red wine like a local.

'Ho... some girl you've met?' a voice teased.

'...there might be...'

'Hey, that tobacco is made of rose petals,' snorted Stefano swigging from the wine bottle.

Sparks from the fire and stars revolved around us all. 'No, no, it is tobacco,' Alex giggled.

'Hashish,' Giorgio shouted, 'yes... that's why we're laughing.'

'I warn you she's spoken for.' Vittorio's voice was not slurred.

'Look, here, hang on a minute, I wouldn't dream...' Their eyes glittered in the firelight.'...She's far too cultured for this kind of life up here.'

'...do you mean?'

'Working her fingers to the bone... not the mind.'

'I know her better... none of your business.' The moon was climbing.

'...educated woman...'

The noise level suddenly dropped. 'Look, you may be an English officer. More her sort, or so you might think. But this is not a village dance. We are fighting for our survival and because we want a Republic.'

'Look, my Italian isn't top notch. I sometimes get things wrong.'

I didn't want them to know I was near. I saw Vittorio's eyes searching for me or maybe he was looking round for the bottle. 'Look, if anything ever happened to me, I hope you'd take care of her, my friend. You understand me? But until then...'

At that moment, there was a huge bang and we were all scurrying for cover. Everyone vanished into the forest. There was no sound other than the crackling of twigs on the fire. After several minutes little groups of men emerged again, whispering to each other in the dark. No sudden machine gun fire. No Germans raiding us. Then Renata groaned, 'Oh, no! The goat has disappeared!' Everyone squeezed into the hut to see what she meant and there really was no goat hanging from the beam. We were all disappointed and some of the men ran round the clearing trying to find it. Who could have taken it?

All we could hear was a mysterious growling sound. Someone lit a flare and by its light we saw an enormous shaggy dog with our goat's head in its mouth. We shooed him away and rescued what was left of the goat. The dog must have walked into the wire and set off the explosion, calmly taking the opportunity to help himself to our goat in our absence. It was as if he had worked out the whole strategy.

The next day we heard that a party of Germans had stormed into the nearby village. A group of soldiers jumped down from the tailgate of the first lorry. The back of the other lorry was empty. They were searching for partisans, they said. Every house was raided, turned upside down and all the men of any age, including teenage boys and bent old men on walking sticks, were rounded up and sent to stand in the piazza. While they stood there the soldiers demanded to see everyone's identity papers.

'You people will be taught a lesson,' shouted the officer. 'We are searching for the criminals who are responsible for the ambush on our troops yesterday. We think you are hiding them or their arms.' The houses had been torn apart, furniture ripped and cupboards emptied. Children were frightened and weeping. Women were standing outside in the street looking defiant. The priest was amongst them. 'You'll find that no one who was responsible for the ambush yesterday is here', he told the German officer in charge. 'These people are innocent.'

The officer demanded to be given information about the perpetrators. He issued the usual threats to the assembled crowd.

'Then punish me, if you must, but leave these village people out of it. They know nothing. They are victims, too.'

'You know the rules. For every German who is murdered we will shoot ten of you. The murdering and pilfering must stop. We will tolerate it no longer.'

Everyone heard the crackling of flames, the smell of petrol fumes. Smoke was soon billowing out from the houses huddled together in the narrow streets. It would not be long before many of the houses would be burnt down.

The people stood silently and impassively. A baby set up a keening, the only sound above the seething, hungry fire. The Germans pushed fifteen men into the back of the lorries. They took the ones who happened to be standing nearest to it, regardless of age or physical fitness. 'These people are to be questioned,' the officer said to the priest as he climbed back into his jeep. A woman stepped into the road to stand in the way of the departing lorry. She was not driven over because another woman dragged her away.

We heard that three old men were released after a few days, but had to find their own way back to the village by themselves. They said that the others had been accused of colluding with rebels and were shot. The church became a home for many families while makeshift homes were built out of the charred remains of the houses. Umberto sent a message offering the partisans' help, which was refused. The village remained under surveillance for days, but we weren't aware of this.

42

The only clue she had about the partisans was the worn black leather wallet containing her mother's identity card, so Petronella started the search by looking for a history of the Italian Resistance. From a bookshop in a narrow alleyway near the market she bought a couple of Italian books on the subject. The man in the shop gave her directions to the *Istituto Storico della Resistenza*.

She wandered around the town centre trying to find the street. She passed the marble Casino, awash with red geraniums. A poster outside announced that a man called Mussolini would be playing jazz on the roof garden later that week. He might be a grandson of the jazz-loving Fascist dictator, she supposed. It seemed incongruous.

The Institute was in a poky side street. She rang the bell, spoke into an intercom, then the door buzzed open and she went up some dark stairs. Excusing her Italian, she explained to the man at the desk who she was looking for and asked if he had any record of her. He replied in good English, 'Excuse me, but women were not in the partisans.' She showed him her mother's card to prove that there had been one, at least. He studied it carefully, sucked his teeth and vanished into an office. He came back a few minutes later and said that he would make some enquiries himself. The president of the Institute was away just then; if anyone knew anything, he would. The president had been a partisan too and if this woman was to be found he might be able to locate her—unless she had died or moved away from the area. He shook his head and muttered under his breath, 'Women in the partisan brigades?'

He wrote down Petronella's phone number and smiled cautiously, stretching out his hand towards hers. His grasp was firm and his palm cool. She liked the shape of his animal-brown eyes. About sixty-something she thought, nice face, Roman nose, aristocratic forehead, distinguished greying hair, casually dressed. He said his name was Nando —'short for Ferdinando,' he explained.

She assumed that nothing would come of it. But though he hadn't appeared to believe her, the man at the Institute contacted her a couple of days later. She had spent her time trying to read the new book on the Resistance, which contained lists of names of volunteer fighters from this area in all the different brigades.

She was searching fruitlessly through the columns of names when the man from the Institute rang her on her mobile. He spoke so rapidly she had to ask him to speak more slowly. He said that Renata was now living in a town a few kilometres further along the coast and he had phoned her to ask her permission to give Petronella her address. 'I'm sorry I was a bit dismissive about your question— women in the partisan brigades. It appears I was wrongly informed. I'm only a part time volunteer at the *Istituto*, you see.

'I'd like to know more, one day. I wonder if you'd let me know what you find out, Signora. Would you be so kind, perhaps? I'm retired now. I was a history professor, although this period wasn't my specialism. Where? Oh, the university of Milan. I ought to know better at my age, not jump to conclusions.'

43

The last thing I heard was a twig cracking underfoot. I knew it couldn't be Vittorio for he trod as lightly as a wild creature. I watched the two of them disappear into the trees—Vittorio leading Captain Alex to another brigade headquarters high up above the village of Darnita, the path rising steeply up to a narrow ledge along a cliff. Unless you were familiar with the way you might find the ground crumbling beneath your feet. Vittorio knew this route, but no stranger would. As the sky was clear he would be using the stars to navigate—Aldebaran, Sirius, Arcturus.

No news of them—not that I was expecting any for three or four days—but, all the same, I remained on the alert for the sound of his voice. My heart leaped with anticipation and fell with disappointment a hundred times a day. After a week passed anxiety grew inside like a tumour. The words that had blurted out of my mouth when he discovered me following him haunted me—'If you won't take me with you then my life isn't worth living.' Whatever he was going through now I wished I were there, too. What I had said to him went through my mind like a chant, changing slightly each time, 'If you can't take me with you then my life isn't worth living, you haven't taken me with you so my life isn't worth living, unless you take me with you my life isn't worth...'

On the morning of the tenth day a silence fell on the camp. It was emanating from Umberto's control room where a crowd of men stood in a huddle. I saw Sandro, still recovering from his wounds, peel away and cross himself. Renata's arms were round Stefano's shoulders. When he saw I was watching he came towards me with outstretched arms. His eyes were red and he didn't speak. Behind him Renata was sheet-white. The look on her face confirmed what Stefano couldn't say.

'They've captured Vittorio. He's been taken, but nobody knows where. He might have been wounded.' I knew what this meant, that they would torture him to get information.

'I'm afraid they've shot Bruno and Tina.' Renata took my hand. 'Vittorio and Captain Alex were hiding there. When they tried to escape Vittorio was wounded. That's how they got him.'

Tears were running down my face, but I couldn't cry out loud. I thought my insides were going to be vomited out of me. My limbs became too heavy to move and my joints locked tight so that I couldn't move from the hut. I lay on the straw mat. When Stefano told me that Vittorio was dead and that he had taken the body back to his own village to be buried, I roused myself.

'What about Francesco?' I asked. 'Is he all right?'

'Yes, he's safe. He escaped with Captain Alex. They got away, hid in a cave till the coast was clear.'

Captain Alex arrived with Francesco that evening looking sodden, as if he had lain in a river for hours. I limped over to the boy and hugged him. 'He wants to be with you and Renata,' Alex said. Francesco was in shock, not speaking. The three of us managed to persuade Umberto to allow him to stay with us provided he remained in the camp to assist. 'It's too dangerous for him, a boy of his age. And he's too upset and angry to engage in combat until he's older. Maybe the war will be over soon. He can stay safely here with us till then.' Umberto agreed and Francesco was given the honour of being one of the youngest partisans in the Resistance.

Before leaving Alex described what had happened to him and Vittorio after they set off that night. But he had difficulty remembering what happened after his wound became infected as he was often only semi-conscious. This is what I have put together from his story.

Vittorio and Captain Alex set off together as the moon rose over the ridge, giving them visibility for the precipitous path. On such a night they ran the danger of being seen. They walked in silence, listening for footfalls. Shadows moved on the stone steps as they passed beneath the church. An owl screeched as if the night was being slit open.

A light was switched on in their faces. German voices shouted. A shot was fired. Alex dived into the trees. A machine gun strafed the forest and pain seared his leg. He slithered into a ditch and was making his way like a snake through the undergrowth. He was hoping that Vittorio would follow. The Germans must have thought they were an advance party and had run up the path to see to the rest of the band, which was lucky. He lay still, listening. His leg was running wet. He stuffed some leaves and moss over the wound, hoping to staunch the bleeding.

After some time, he pulled himself out of the ditch. Vittorio appeared and supported him on a path leading up the mountainside. After what had happened in the village a few days ago they couldn't risk knocking on anyone's door. Alex was shivering, but kept going until they reached an open-fronted shepherd's shelter. Alex said he must have fallen asleep for a while. He was roused when he became aware of a man standing over them. Vittorio pulled out his gun. It was Bruno.

'Are you all right? How did you get here?' Vittorio explained what had happened. Bruno tut-tutted. 'Yes, I heard the shooting in the night. There are still Germans watching the village. It isn't safe to move far.' He led the fugitives to the byre attached to the house.

Bruno brought them blankets. Tina put a poultice on Alex's wound with leaves and herbs, which she bound with bandages made of old sheets. 'You will be safe now. No one comes along this path any more,' she said as she left them for the night. 'Bruno will be along in the morning, see how you both are. Get some sleep.'

Alex must have been running a fever because he remembered little of what happened in the next couple of days. In the morning, realising how ill he was, Bruno left to find a doctor who would tend a British soldier. 'You do realise how dangerous this is for you?' Vittorio asked more than once. Bruno and Tina's older sons had been killed on the Russian front and they'd always hoped that someone had taken pity on them in their hour of need. For this reason they would never turn away anyone who needed help. It was why they had welcomed Renata and me. While Alex was laid up, the kindly Tina tended him as if he were her own son. I knew she would do this for anyone who needed help—Italian, Russian, Jew or German. It always felt civilised there, in that house.

Vittorio passed the time playing noughts and crosses with the boy. Francesco asked him to show him his gun and teach him how to look after and clean it. Vittorio was perhaps reminded of his own brother, Eduardo, at that age. The two men slept in the mangers used by the goats, but at mealtimes came into the kitchen. Sequestered with the goats most of the rest of the time they were glad of Francesco's company. He kept saying that he wanted to join the partisans, but Vittorio shook his head, saying he was too young and that his parents needed him.

Alex couldn't stay alert for long so Vittorio listened for sounds of footsteps and watched the light between the cracks in the door; he would know if anyone approached. Alex said he had the hearing or sixth sense of a mountain deer. It was unlikely that the Germans would find them, but they were aware of the risk.

Alex began to recover and when he took a little minestrone he quickly regained some strength. It was a long way down the mountain, but he was determined to leave as soon as possible. He and Vittorio began discussing the day of departure the moment he could walk well enough. Vittorio was capable of making his getaway back to his brigade, but chose to stay and protect everyone. It was just like him. Inside the house, time must have run backwards, as if there was no war going on further down the valley.

They had just finished eating one evening when there came a hammering on the door. A boy of Francesco's age rushed in, out of breath, his eyes wild with terror. He gasped that the Germans knew about the men hiding there: 'Some soldiers are on their way up the hill, to arrest you.' He turned tail and vanished into the dark. Bruno grabbed a few things and hid them in a cavity beneath the hearth. Alex squeezed through a window at the back of the house, followed closely by Vittorio. They scrambled up the terraced hillside towards the larch forest.

On reaching the comparative safety of the tree-line, Alex turned to look back. At that moment a beam of light raked the hillside, followed by machine gun fire. Below him Alex saw Vittorio topple over. A few moments later Francesco dived into the undergrowth next to Alex. They kept stock still while the light swept the terraces; they knew a small movement or even a sniff could give their position away. The soldiers fired a few shots into the forest, but then went into the house.

Minutes later the Germans roughly pushed Bruno and Tina outside the door, before marching them with the wounded Vittorio in a line down the hill; Bruno and Vittorio had their hands on their heads. Francesco jumped up and Alex grabbed him. The boy squirmed and Alex pressed a hand over his mouth, holding him back with his other arm. After a minute Francesco stopped struggling and when they thought the prisoners must have arrived in the village he told Alex to follow him. The two of them spent the night and most of the next day in a cave. They didn't know what was happening to the others till later.

When Alex arrived back at the camp he looked as if the life had been sucked out of him. He talked for some time with Umberto. 'I completely trust him, he would not give them any information, whatever they do to him,' Umberto reassured him. Renata and I knew from Stefano what had happened to Bruno and Tina; they had been shot on the bridge in front of all the villagers. Their mutilated bodies were eventually recovered from the river.

Vittorio had been taken away for interrogation by the SS. Nobody spoke of the tortures they inflicted on him before they shot him. The litres of castor oil they'd have made him swallow; the *manganello* on his back or legs. Their brutality was made more ferocious by the prospect of imminent defeat. To frighten potential renegades amongst the villagers, his twisted body was strung up on a tree for all to see. It was Stefano who cut it down and carried it back to his village for burial.

Io non piangea, si dentro impetrai. L'Inferno XXXI

(I was not weeping for I had turned to stone inside.)

44

She felt like an intruder in her mother's life. She knew too much now to go back. Just where was it all leading? It was a roller-coaster ride to the past. And the account wasn't finished yet.

She decided to ring Nando. 'Ciao, Nando, it's Petronella here. Do you remember me? You do? Well, I've been doing this private research, as you know, and I wondered if perhaps you could explain something. Yes? I was wondering why the British army placed officers to work with the partisans. I mean, was it normal? I see… escaped prisoners of war… supply drops… did you say, exploited? By whom? By the Allies? They wanted control, but what for? Oh, I see, I see.'

She hired a car to drive to the small town of Aureglia where Renata now lived. The old harbour area was bordered by stately warehouses, turned into fashionable restaurants, hotels and offices.

It took time to find a place to park in the busy streets, blue with exhaust fumes. She didn't understand the meaning of the painted lines on the road and asked a man where it was legal to park. She bought a ticket from a newsagent and put it on the dashboard. The tall houses along the streets were painted a dusky yellow and the shutters were green. There was no apparent logic to the numbering system, but eventually she found the door she was looking for in a large old palazzo near the centre, with three labelled bells beside it. Renata's was the top one. A voice echoed through the intercom, asking who was there. When she replied 'Petronella', a buzzer spluttered and the door swung open. She was anxious. How would Renata react to her? When she was half way up the stairs, a figure appeared over the rail and then started coming down towards her, stretched her arms out, calling, 'E tu?

Petronella, Petronella, mia cara, ben venuta,' and then flung her arms round her.

Renata's face was creased like the bark of a cork tree. She was elegantly dressed, with her hair permed in tight curls like a helmet over which she wore a thin hair net studded with tiny beads. Her lipstick was bright red. She had animated lines around her mouth.

She told Petronella how she had moved to this flat with her husband when they got married several years after the war. They had no children. Her husband was from an old Jewish Turinese family; he had died a few years ago. They preferred living near the coast instead of enduring Turin's summer heat and winter cold.

As Renata led Petronella through to her sitting room, she gestured towards an old photo of Maddalena and herself posing beside cannon by the harbour walls of Porto Romolo. Petronella remembered sitting on that cannon, as if straddling an iron horse.

Renata made Earl Grey tea in a china teapot, served in matching teacups on saucers with tiny silver spoons. 'I like an excuse to drink tea the English way,' she said in heavily accented English. There were sugar lumps in a bowl, complete with silver sugar tongs.

'Oh, you speak English well, I see.'

'Yes, I can speak some English. I learned it when I worked in the hotel as we had a lot of English guests. I think being with your mother inspired me and, after the war, it seemed important to me to know this language.' They sat there smiling at each other for a few moments. Petronella watched Renata scrutinising her face.

'I'll show you some things.' Renata drew a photo album from a shelf. The photos had white borders and deckled edges, little slices of the past. She was sifting through the pages, looking for something in particular, and then she stopped and pushed the book towards her. The photo had no border or decorative edging and was of herself and a young Maddalena preparing food in the open air, surrounded by a group of men. Some of these had turned to look at the camera as if it had stolen up on them unawares while one of them was in the middle of telling a joke. One man looked familiar. Someone she had met... oh, what was his name? Was it Stefano perhaps? His name had cropped up in the account, written of with affection.

Renata lapsed into Italian and was speaking so fast it was hard to keep up, to keep concentrating. When she asserted that the war had been lovely, Petronella was sure she must have misheard. There was another photo of the two of them, Maddalena and Renata, looking skeletal and wearing carnations and carrying a flag through a Porto Romolo street on Liberation Day in April 1945.

'Were there lots of women in the Resistance?'

'Oh yes, but not many fighters. Most of them were involved with cooking or cleaning clothes or nursing the wounded. Often women were used as couriers; they took messages from one place to another because the Nazis were less likely to suspect an innocent-looking young woman.'

'It must have been very dangerous for you.'

'Yes, it was. But it was such fun. Sometimes we had to carry munitions.'

'Goodness! You mean grenades? Guns?'

'Yes, things like that. And your mother, she had to run away from the Fascist police when she was caught carrying grenades. It was a capital offence. That was why she had to leave her home.'

'Would they have shot a girl?'

'And maybe worse than that beforehand. But not many were caught. Italian girls are so pretty they can get away with anything.'

Petronella asked Renata about herself and she replied, 'Ah, well, I was also caught red-handed. And, of course, as I was Jewish there was no hope at all for me.'

'And what about your family, Renata?'

She said that her parents ended up in a camp called Fossoli and from there they went to Auschwitz. After she left Porto Romolo she never saw or heard from them again. It wasn't until after the war that she found out their fate. Petronella didn't know what to say. She wanted to ask her more, but wasn't sure if she should continue.

'Yes, it seems unreal now, *mia cara*. Once they were leading a normal life and chatting with friends, too. But when you look around, you realise that it happens to people all over the world. Look what happened at Srebrenica only last summer. We aren't very far distant from Bosnia and Serbia where barbarity has been an everyday occurrence.' She was right, Petronella thought; only the width of the Adriatic Sea and a few mountains lay between them drinking tea and people suffering in the recent conflict.

Renata sighed, smiled at her. 'Now, dear, would you like more tea?'

Was this the moment to ask Renata the most burning question? How to lead up to it? Petronella found herself shuffling towards her in the chair. 'I found this identity card of my mother's in her wardrobe after my father died last year.'

'Oh yes, we all had to have one of those. I don't know what's happened to mine.'

Petronella held out the photo. 'And there was this, too.'

Renata took the photo and looked at it. 'You don't know who he is?'

'No, I don't know. I suppose he was someone my mother knew during the war.' Petronella realised the colour was draining from underneath the powder on Renata's cheeks. It was alarming and fascinating to watch.

'*Ma insomma, poverina!* I can't believe you don't know.' Renata looked at the younger woman over her glasses. She wasn't smiling.

Petronella shook her head. 'Don't know what exactly?' She could see Renata hesitating, having to choose her words.

'You were entitled to be told the truth. I don't understand. But there we are – nothing to do with me. So, now, after all this time, you have only me to ask.'

Petronella's heart was beating hard and she thought Renata must be able to hear it. 'Yes, well, you had better have it from me, Petronella. This is actually a photograph of Vittorio, your father, your birth father.'

For a long moment Petronella couldn't speak. Her mouth half opened, but no words came out. She wondered if it was a joke. Had she misunderstood?

'My father? Really? But he... Vittorio... died...' Petronella's voice became a whisper.

'Yes, the Germans arrested and shot him.'

'What... what... was he like?'

'He looked very like you, Petronella. Same nose, same eyes, same chin!'

'I've been wondering about this photo ever since I found it in my mother's things. She wrote about him being killed... really horribly...' She couldn't carry on, clasping her hands together as if to check she was awake and alive. Intakes of breath felt sharp-edged as if she had been winded. She felt a hand on her shoulder.

Renata perched beside her, on the arm of the chair. 'He and your mother had very little time together. He was very proud, but kind and so in love with your mother. And she with him. But really they hardly knew each other before he was killed. So little time.'

Petronella looked towards the window. She heard a voice, 'My ... my father... Alex, kept some of her things in a chest in his bedroom.' So how come Alex was so involved? The question was forming slowly out of the confusion, like a groan. 'There's a book, a sort of memoir. I've been reading what she wrote about that time.'

'A memoir? You know, I think your stepfather wanted you to discover the truth. He left everything like that so that you would find out eventually. Maybe he couldn't tell you himself because your mother had told him not to.'

It was as though a sharp piece of grit was lodged in Petronella's throat. She coughed, but it jibbed harder. She hoped she wasn't about to cry. 'I didn't put two and two together. It means I know more than I was supposed to.'

'But from what you tell me, Petronella, I am quite certain that Alex did want you to know.'

'Do you think so? I wondered why Alex kept her old stuff for so long.'

'I am sure of it, *mia cara*. Why else would he keep her things? I expect he wanted you to find out, but only after his own death. He was a man of principle and wouldn't break a promise even when he disagreed.'

'I'm sorry that you have to be the person with the job of explaining to me.'

'Ah, but I never promised that I wouldn't, you see. I would have told her anyway that I thought it quite wrong. Alex could never stand up to her.'

'And I've not asked before now.' It was beginning to make sense. Petronella could understand how Alex wanted to keep faith with Maddalena and yet also make it possible for the truth to come out when he wasn't around any longer. He wouldn't necessarily have known about the photo and the letter, but he did know about what had happened during the war. He was there. 'But why? Why the secrecy? It can't just have been shame, can it?'

'I think... I think your mother... would have explained to you when you were older. You were perhaps too young to be told.' Her hand moved round Petronella's back, fingers softly kneading her neck. The touch allowed silence between them. Cars hooted in the distance. Then Renata rose and shut the window. The noise startled Petronella.

Renata remained facing the window and said, 'You know, if you really want to, I think you could find out the rest.'

'The rest? You mean, there's more? This is quite enough for now.' Petronella tried to laugh.

'There is a bit more, but you know the main part. There's someone you should meet, *mia cara*.'

Petronella barely took in what Renata was saying. Her body felt numb, but her mind was oscillating between feeling sad for her mother and angry that she wasn't told before—she thought that Alex had betrayed her, that Maddalena had deceived her. Too late now. All too late.

Renata said, 'Sometimes, my dear, it can be dangerous to know too much. You may want to think about this.' Petronella couldn't frame any more questions, didn't feel up to asking what she meant by that.

'You've had a big shock, Petronella, *mia cara*. You've gone quite pale, you know. Are you all right?' She heard Renata speaking to her as if she were an invalid.

'Thanks, I'm fine. You're right, it's been a thunderbolt— I don't think I understand who I am any longer. But obviously I never have known.'

She felt a lump of something welling in her chest, which might come out as a howl or a shout. Holding it back made her feel queasy. She must get away as fast as she could to be on her own. She tottered towards the door, 'I'll be okay. Thanks so much for telling me, Renata. I'd better be off now, let you get on with things.'

'Oh, but you must wait a moment! I'll just see if I can find an address for you, *mia cara*.' She went to her bureau and rummaged through a small drawer. It was so quiet in the room; her immaculate nails tapped on the wood. She wrote something quickly on a piece of writing paper and handed it to Petronella. 'Go and find this man,' she said. 'He was a good friend to us both. He knows everything. He knows the whole story, because he was there.'

'Now, are you absolutely sure you'll be all right to drive?' She smiled at Petronella, then kissed her on both cheeks, *'Arrivederci, mia cara.'*

In the evening air Petronella walked around the town. In a few moments she was lost. To get to the sea she had to cross a road. She stepped off the pavement, slipping between the parked cars. Brakes squealed, a man shouted. She walked beside the low wall that cradled the harbour and a lighthouse was winking in the dusk, a gem-star holding her position. Voices and laughter floated across the water.

She needed time to think through the revelation. Alex wasn't her father. He wasn't! The unarticulated question had been so strong. It was a kind of relief. Instead her father was this man Vittorio. And who was he? What did this mean for her? She looked across to where the last light was draining out of the sky. Now it was too late to retrieve anything—Alex was dead, her own father and mother long gone. The waves hauled themselves onto the rocks at the base of the wall, but they were lazy as if the sea was sleeping, dormant.

45

Fede portai al glorioso offizo
Tanto ch'io ne perde li sonni e' polsi
    (L'Inferno, Canto XIII)

(I did my job so faithfully
that I lost my peace and my life)

The image of Vittorio's body lurked behind my eyes even when I slept, broken like a puppet and dangling from a tree. I was withering from inside out. All that held me together was skin, like a suit of armour. The spaces inside were hungry for the truth.

I knew that speaking with him would incriminate me. When I knocked on his door my limbs shook, an uncontrollable trembling deep in the muscles, as though my body knew something my mind wasn't aware of yet. The door was pulled open and the man I was seeking stood in front of me.

'Yes? What do you want?'

'Could you spare a moment? I'd like to ask your advice,' I said.

He jerked his chin. Peering past him into the house I saw an outline of a woman in a patterned dress, heard a child crying. He pulled the door to behind him, slouched against the corner of the wall. His eyes stared at something beyond me.

He was bone thin, his features sharp as the skull underneath. He smirked, 'Do I know you? Why have you come to my house?' He looked down at his feet as if I wasn't worth looking at.

'I wanted to ask you why you told the Germans about Bruno and Tina.'

'What are you talking about? Who are you?' His eyes flickered at my face.

'Tell me, please… what did they pay you?'

'I don't know who you are or what you're on about. Get away from me.'

I knew he wasn't about to admit anything. 'What made you tell them that there were fighters at Gribonita?' I had the bit between my teeth.

He shrugged. 'Fighters? Huh, rebels, you mean.'

'Why did you do that to such harmless people?' I persisted.

'Harmless? Look, I don't know what you're talking about and I'm busy, I have things to do. You're speaking to the wrong person. It could have been anyone round here.'

'Just explain to me, please… so that I can understand. I know it was you. I have been told it was you by more than one person. I just want to know why you did that.'

'Oh, nothing to do with me, I can assure you. Probably some child's tittle-tattle. After all, everyone here knew what they were up to. It could have been anyone… anyone in this village. Why pick on me?' He jerked himself upright as he prepared to slouch back indoors.

'But it was you, wasn't it?'

'What's it to do with you? Look, I won't be interrogated by a filthy whore like you any longer. You should go home and take care of your own parents. Stop dabbling in what is not your business. I know your sort. Bitch.' He snarled me away, shutting the door in my face.

I knew what I had to do. Everything I had experienced so far had led me to that moment—arriving there, learning how to use a gun, getting to know people and even loving them. I had no care for the consequences. If I was caught and shot, it no longer mattered; I would have done my duty.

The next evening I hid myself in a niche in the side wall of the church to wait. Everybody else had finished their work for the day and gone home. He came out of the house and set off to his plot of land to shut away his few hens.

I ran ahead of him to the bridge near the mill, which he had to cross. I had learned how to move quietly between the trees and remain unseen. I had spent the day figuring out where was the best place to be within range and yet be concealed.

The river was flowing fast with the first snow-melt waters. Gushing water seethed noisily in the narrow channels between the smooth rocks. I clambered along the bank beside the bridge between the trees just coming into leaf. Difficult to see through the branches. He was about to come down the path in a minute or two. A mist was rising from the rushing water. The path shone pale in the twilight.

When he appeared round the corner and crossed the bridge, I took aim—my arm was steady and straight—and fired at him just as he reached the apex of the arched bridge. His body slumped against the low parapet and he toppled slowly into the river. I slipped over to the bridge to check he was really dead. He lay face down in the deep pool below the arch, his blood clouding the water. After a minute, I climbed my way through the tangle of trees and away from the river. I didn't even have his blood on my hands.

Less than three weeks later the war was declared officially over. Italy was freed from the German occupation on April 25th. Only days before the declaration, the Fascist militias fled the mountains. We weren't sure—even then—that they wouldn't come back, because they had done this before. We marched down from the still icy mountains, the chestnut forests giving way to olive and eucalyptus trees. These evergreen trees would provide a better chance of survival in the event of an ambush. We would be camouflaged amongst the leaves during enemy fire. Our eyes searched everywhere for snipers.

So it was a surprise to find lines of people waiting for us on the pavements in the outskirts of Porto Romolo. They were wearing carnations in their lapels. They made us think that ordinary life might one day be possible. We were the conquering heroes. The partisans sang in unison as they entered the town, marched down the main street, lined with onlookers:

The wind ceases, the storm calms
The proud partisan returns home
waving the red flag
at last we are victorious and free.

Afterwards came marches and long speeches. The streets were packed with people waving flags, embracing each other, wearing those red carnations. Everyone was laughing as if they had become hysterical. I felt only numbness. We had won the war, but I had lost everything.

46

Some things were too dangerous to know. But it served the collaborating bastard right. Of course, Maddalena had to shoot him. Well, somebody had to. They didn't know it was the end of the war and he might have put more people at risk. Good for her.

In the space of a couple of days Petronella felt she had become someone else—she loved the same people, experienced the same likes and dislikes, looked at the world through her own eyes, spoke in her own voice— yet everything was changed. She began to see that the imaginings of her childhood had not been far removed from the truth. The past was being reconstructed piece by piece, a past in which she had played no part, but which had made her what she was.

In all this flux she needed some handholds. She decided to make a mental list of facts. She had been born and brought up in a house in Wikeley called Dale View; her mother was Maddalena and she had died when Petronella was eight years old; her grandmother was Rose and she had lived at Middleton Villas; she had a son called Matt who was training to be a marine; once she had been married to a man called Todd and they had lived in a house called Lane End; she was a teacher and now lived on her own in another house.

She liked the solid feel of this information, but didn't feel certain how to believe in it. She never had. At the least it provided an anchoring point, but it was what it didn't tell you that mattered most. Just as she discovered who her real father was, she read about how he was killed. And now this.

Petronella wanted to know more about collaborators. In an occupied country there must have been so many of them. Perhaps Nando would know. She decided to make a point of asking him later.

Her car moved hesitantly along the corkscrew road to the village where the Valettis lived. On the steep slopes the sun's rays kindled the grey of the eucalyptus, the jewelled glow of the birches, the darkness of the oak, the blue-green of the hornbeam. As she approached the village Petronella noticed that the walls were plastered with posters of electoral candidates. Someone had inscribed *Viva Il Duce* in black paint on a metal crash barrier. Petronella followed signs to the church, passing beside neat terraces full of vegetables where the olive leaves fluttered in the wind like prayer-flags, to a little bridge over the river. Butterflies flew about like winged flower petals.

When she knocked on the door of a house with blue window-frames a woman's face peered down at her from between the red begonias on the first floor balcony. Her expression was bewildered and her face slightly creased, as if she had just woken up. By the time the woman reached the door she had composed herself and was welcoming, but surprised by the arrival of a stranger.

'I am sorry to bother you. My name is Petronella. I'm looking for Signor Valletti. Is this the right house?'

'Yes, this is it. You're in the right place. Signor Valletti is my husband. How may I help you?'

'Your address was given to me by a friend of mine called Renata. I think perhaps you know of her?' She nodded, but with no expression.

'Please come in, signora,' she beckoned Petronella.

'Renata was an old friend of my mother's. She suggested that you might be able to tell me something about my parents... Signor Valletti knew them many years ago, in the war.'

She was a short, wiry woman in her mid sixties and introduced herself as Maria. 'The war? I'm afraid I don't know much about what happened and my husband was only a boy. I'll call him and you can ask. Make yourself comfortable.'

Petronella said she hoped she wasn't intruding, but the woman told her it was nothing and offered her coffee. 'Then we can sit and talk. I will just go and find him.' She disappeared into the kitchen, closing the door behind her. Petronella heard her voice in the other room and that of a man responding. She asked herself why she had come here. Her courage was beginning to unwind.

The latch on the door squeaked and the woman brought in a tray. Close behind her was a sinewy, short, dark man of about the same age. *'Buon giorno, piacere,'* they shook hands. In her grip, his hand felt rough and honest. He hovered behind his wife while she set out coffee cups on the table, one by one, poured the coffee and offered sugar. His face was gnarled like a peach stone. As they both sat down Maria said, 'I think Renata meant you to speak with my husband. His name is Francesco.'

'Francesco!' Petronella shrilled, nearly spilling the sugar she was spooning into her coffee. 'My God, I never dreamed it possible. I didn't think I was really going to find you.' She was so excited she wanted to get up and hug him. At the same time she was afraid she was blundering about in alien territory. 'I have something… something I brought with me… here, to show you, Francesco. My mother kept it in her room.' She had wrapped the wooden hat from her mother's dressing table in tissue and put it in her bag, like a message that was waiting to be delivered: *If found, return to Francesco.* She had rescued it and was returning it to its rightful owner. Petronella watched him unwrap the tissue, fumbling with his knotted fingers.

'I wonder if you'll recognise it. It has your name on. I think it might be yours. It must be, mustn't it?'

Out fell the small wooden hat, the feather so skilfully fashioned out of the same piece of wood. His face crumpled as if the air had been let out of him. He placed the hat on the palm of his hand and held it up, trembling.

Petronella murmured, 'She never forgot you. She kept it near her all her life'.

Maria shuffled on her chair and poured more coffee as he lurched out of the room, returning after a moment with another identical one.

'I gave that hat to her, they were a pair, you see. They're models of hats worn by the Alpini regiments, precious to me because they were made in the First World War by my father. I gave your mother one of them, to seal our pact.' He wiped his eyes with his rough hands and then fiddled in his pocket for a handkerchief.

Maria handed Petronella a plate of almond biscuits as if nothing much had happened. Nobody said anything for a few moments. Petronella was nervous, unsure where this meeting was going to lead or how the two of them were reacting. Aware that many people disliked talking about the war, she knew that the role of the partisans was often contentious. Francesco took out a packet of cigarettes, offered her one and lit one for himself. 'So, Maddalena is your mother?' and he looked her in the eyes. She could not guess what he was thinking because his face was as creased as a quilt and his eyes were watery.

'Yes. She was, she died a long time ago, I'm afraid to say. In England. You knew her?'

'I did know her. She used to come to our house during those last months of the war. My mother was fond of her, treated her like a daughter, you know. She loved her as if she were her own.' The cigarette smoke soothed him. He asked Petronella when and why Maddalena had died and Petronella reflected how sad it was that she wasn't alive when some of her old friends were still going strong.

'So young. What a tragedy for you. And you were only little.' Maria touched Petronella's hand. Another pause.

'You want to know about what happened in the war, do you?' Francesco almost sighed. Hunching his shoulders he looked at the floor, as if looking for something he'd lost. 'Many terrible things happened in the war, Petronella, many terrible things.'

'Hmm, I don't know that much about it, you see. My father met my mother during the war, but he was killed by the Germans, so I understand.' Petronella explained how Maddalena went to live in England and married the English captain. 'This was where they met, up here in the mountains. My mother was with the partisans, wasn't she?' She spoke methodically, trying to remember the grammar and the correct conjugation of the verbs.

'Yes, that's right. I remember your father very well.' Francesco astounded her. She doesn't know which of the two men he might mean. 'Also Renata, of course.'

'So… you knew them all?'

'The English officer was wounded and had to stay somewhere safe till he was better. My parents hid him and Vittorio in our house.'

'Oh, and so who was Vittorio?' Maria asked.

'Oh, Vittorio… *che bravo*! He knew the mountains almost as well as my father. He was the son of Eduardo, the Bee Man. They came from a village called Carano.' He waved his hand at the window as if to show Carano wasn't very far away from where they were. 'It was set alight by the Germans in reprisal for what some fool partisans did,' he continued.

'So what happened to the villagers, to Vittorio's father?'

'A lot of the villagers there were killed. They were rounded up and taken away. That's the sort of thing that happened at that time. Excuse me, one moment.' He pulled a handkerchief out of his pocket and blew his nose noisily.

'We were worried about the English officer who was wounded, the one Maddalena later married; he was very ill for a while.' Francesco explained that Captain Alex was another of their visitors. One time he handed over a new radio he had procured for Bruno, who was a vital link in the Allied lines of communication. Bruno had been a radio operator and could make a workable wireless out of old bits. He had been an expert at Morse code and had an uncanny habit of knowing what was going to happen in advance. He informed the Italian Secret Service about the movements of various paramilitary units so the Allies could keep a panoramic eye on the critical border area behind enemy lines. Bruno's information was apparently used to double-check other intelligence reports.

'What he did for the Allies was dangerous to him personally because, from time to time, he also picked up German radio messages and sent them through. His transmissions could easily have been intercepted by German operators.'

'Wasn't that risky to give them shelter, in the circumstances, Francesco?' Petronella asked.

'I should say so—in any circumstances. But my parents were willing to take that chance.' He offered her a cigarette again and lit another for himself. 'And your mother, Maddalena... she and her friend, Renata... it was dangerous for them, too. Excuse me please.' His wrists were resting on the edge of the table and Petronella saw the trembling of his hands.

Maria said, 'People here, we tend not to talk about that time. It is best to try and forget and get on with our lives, but memories do not fade. We've had to live with the past.' Francesco stood and looked out of the window. 'There is a lot more you need to know. There are things I have not even told my wife. I owe my life to Vittorio. After the war, I had to try to forgive myself for what happened to him. It is hard, very hard. But now I must tell you.'

He went out to the kitchen and returned with a bottle of wine. His eyes had turned bloodshot. He explained that during the last two years of the war, the whole area had been occupied by Germans who were always raiding the houses to steal food or livestock. Nothing was safe. The partisans were all over the mountains hiding in caves and mines and old houses. They were a mixture of Italians and escapees of one kind or another: Russians, Jews, lots of people on the run from the Germans and the Fascists, basically. Some of them were bad people—brigands, in fact, thieving what little the peasants had. When the weather was cold and snowy and if people had spare food, it was left out for the partisans to collect, for example by the cross at the edge of the village.

He said people couldn't trust anyone except their own family; there had been informers, Fascists and spies but they knew roughly who they were because they had supported the Fascist regime before the war. But no one could ever be sure because the Germans would bribe people with food and false promises. Everyone was in a desperate plight. The Germans put up posters saying it was a capital offence to aid and abet the partisans. It was even an offence to remove the posters. But the posters were removed and most people helped the partisans, hoping that someone somewhere would be looking after our brothers and sons in the same way. Everyone in need was seen as a member of someone else's family.

Francesco added, 'My two older brothers had been killed in the early years of the war in Russia. So it was just my parents and me on the farm. Excuse me. One moment.' He swallowed some more wine, rolled a cigarette. He explained that there had been some action in the next village, some houses were set alight and there were explosions. The usual thing. A German vehicle was blown up. They'd watched the flames from their house and smelt the cordite in the smoke, too. The next day, because of the danger, Francesco's father had not worked in the fields as usual. He went out to check the animals before night fell. When he arrived back, Francesco and his mother were anxiously waiting for him as he had been out longer than expected.

He'd found two men in the sheep shed. They had blood on their faces and clothes. The English officer, Captain Alex, had been there before; couldn't walk, was wounded and trembling with cold. The other was a local man, Vittorio. Francesco's mother washed the Englishman's wounds and gave them clothes. She fed them 'our supper, as I recall' and they had to sleep in the cattle mangers. 'Not in the house, you see, so that, if there was a search party, we could, at least, try to pretend we knew nothing about them. They were with us for some days, as it was too dangerous to leave and the Englishman was so ill. Excuse me. One moment.'

Francesco coughed. He took out a handkerchief again and blew his nose. His cigarette burned out in the ashtray. He drank some wine and Petronella heard him swallow as if it hurt.

'Then one evening, after quite some time—I forget how long, but it might have been about a week later—one of my friends from the village ran as fast as he could to warn us that the Germans were already on the way to our house, searching for partisans or munitions.'

Alex and Vittorio, who happened to be in the house at the time, clambered out of the window. They rushed away up the mountainside. Bruno flew around trying to hide any incriminating evidence. Then Tina pushed Francesco out of the window, instructing him to escape with the two men. 'And don't come back' were her last words to him. Moments later, the Germans were at the door.

He made a dash for the shelter of the forest above. In the light from the moon he spotted a stumbling figure, just below the line of trees. A movement through the undergrowth caught his eye. He paused and saw that it was Vittorio veering diagonally across the slope. He reckoned later that, from his vantage point, Vittorio must have seen that the Germans' searchlight was about to catch Francesco in its beam, and hoped to divert their attention. A rifle cracked out and Vittorio fell sideways. By then Francesco had reached the first trees. The lamp didn't find him.

'Excuse me. One moment.' Francesco took out his handkerchief and wiped his eyes, swelling with tears. They spilled down his cheeks. It went through Petronella's mind that this bit of the story was not in the account. Or had she missed something? Alex can't have described the order of events to Maddalena. She wondered why he had omitted that.

Francesco blew his nose again, 'Excuse me. I have not talked of this since it happened.'

Maria laid a hand on his shoulder. Francesco described how he and Captain Alex had watched from the edge of the forest. The soldiers marched his parents at gunpoint out of the house and down to the village. Vittorio was with them, limping. 'It was the worst moment of my whole life, watching the soldiers push them along that path.' He stopped, took a deep breath and continued. 'I wanted to run to them, but Captain Alex... he held me back. I struggled, but he was stronger than me. We couldn't see what happened except the lights that were moving in the village and there was the sound of commands. Shots were being fired. We spent the night in a cave that my family knew about. It was cold and we had to keep each other warm, but my father had stashed some emergency supplies for just such an eventuality.'

Later they heard that Vittorio was in prison. His parents had been shot on the bridge in front of everyone. As an example. The force of the bullets made their bodies fall over the bridge and into the swirling current below. The villagers found the bodies some way down the river. They were buried in the cemetery.

Francesco continued. 'After that, I joined the partisans because I wanted to revenge my parents and to fight for my country, to rid ourselves of the German occupation—I was only fourteen years old, but that was what I wanted. I was frustrated because they said I was too young to get involved in any fighting. I stayed with Renata and Maddalena in that partisan group until the war ended only a few short weeks later and then I lodged with my aunt in the village. The two of them went home when the war was over and—though I have kept in touch with Renata—I never saw Maddalena again. I knew she had gone to England.'

Tears were running crookedly down the lines on his face. Maria had covered her eyes with her hands. Petronella's throat was so tight she felt sick.

'And… you lived with my mother for a while, with the partisans?'

'Yes, the war was coming to an end. But we didn't know that for sure. The Germans began to retreat, but slowly. They looted houses, burnt the homes of anyone who stood up to them. People fled into the mountains to save themselves. And Maddalena made herself scarce after that. And with good reason. Before she left, she did what I was too young to do. She found out the name of the informant —she loved my parents, you see. She saved me the job of having to kill him. But we were in it together. She couldn't have done it without my father's gun. Not even she could know where he kept it.'

47

He had little faith in words; he knew how easily they distorted. He trusted stars. He followed them as they revolved round him through the night—Cygnus, Cetus, Orion. He knew their positions at different times of the year and understood the weather conditions foretold by cloud formations. That was the language he understood. He didn't say as much, but he thought words formed experience into a false shape and colour. Once, to my astonishment, he asked if I liked moonlight or sunshine best. He really wanted to know what I thought.

All I had to guide me was rows of words. It was my nature to wrestle with sentences, to line up the phrases so that they followed one another, as if this might order life. I looked for connections, thinking that one event must lead from and to another. I liked to smooth and flatten the fabric of a story and fold it away. But so many things happened for which there were no words. Sentences fit like bones in a body. They are held together by the grammar of cartilage, muscle, sinew; but when the body has died the bones dry out and fall apart.

He had no ordinary concept of time; all things happened at once. One event did not lead to another. He had other means of navigation. He'd run his finger over a map as if feeling for a pulse. He knew the script of land better than any cartographer, estimated the possibilities of the ground described by the data in the geometric grid. He could visualise moving through a map as if he was already familiar with the terrain. He understood a bend in the river, a rocky outcrop, a line of trees and what he would expect to find if he went there. This was why he was always valuable, in most demand for dangerous missions.

48

The next day Francesco led Petronella along a path that twisted along the forested side of the mountain. The last few dwellings in the village were roofless ruins. The early morning sun was burnishing trees, rocks and open ground as it rose above the ridge. Soon the valleys would be butter yellow. Low-growing ferns, wild thyme and lavender sparkled with dew.

They were alone on the wooded path, following the contour alongside old terracing. Pine cones scrunched under their feet. Francesco said that the terraces were once all worked. The people who lived there had mainly been subsistence farmers with little or no cash. A few cows and goats, some rabbits and guinea pigs. They grew everything they needed and picked mushrooms and berries from the forest. They had little use for money because they bartered for anything else.

The sound of water filled the air. The river composed its own stories along the valley, inscribing the banks with new lines of loose stones. Close up, its voice was like chattering people. Occasionally, as if it was following them, there were glimmers of water between the figures of ancient chestnut trees. Their twisted, lightning-struck bodies were like stone statues from prehistory.

Round a bend loomed a house. Looking as if it had grown out of the ground, its slate roof was still intact and its fissured chestnut door was barricaded by an old beam. The windowpanes were long gone and the frames had become warped. The door needed to be barged, then scraped across the flagstone. A jay squawked in alarm.

Francesco stepped in first and she heard his exclamation. 'It's just as I remember,' he said. 'It is all exactly the same.'

Her eyes adjusted to the dark. A passageway lay ahead, with a staircase at the far end.

'Do we dare go up there?' she murmured in the silence. 'Do you think the stairs are safe?'

'They've been here long enough and haven't fallen down yet.' He was half way up before she followed. It felt as if there might be someone waiting upstairs. Francesco must have had the same thought because he called out, *'Buon giorno? Siamo qui!'*

The downstairs utility room was organised and neat, but the upstairs was chaos. The furniture was in disarray, some items had been turned right over and there were empty drawers strewn about. There was a jumble of rusted kitchen utensils and old shoes on the floor. Petronella spotted a pair of boots in the corner. They had survived longer than the man who had worn them. They were moulded to the shape of his feet and had the marks of where he walked, at work on the terraces or tending his animals. The laces were undone and the tongue flopped forward from when he had last taken them off. Perhaps he had given them a rub of polish to keep them pliable before carefully placing them there in the corner of the kitchen to wait for the morning's duties.

The next room was empty apart from some pictures that had smashed when they fell from the wall—the only sound in many decades. She turned the frames around but they were empty. The bare wooden floor was almost undamaged and there was an attractive skirting of slate. There were also two old chairs by a large open fireplace. The upholstery was ripped and the straw stuffing had practically gone. Wisps lay scattered on the floor.

'We'll look at that hearth in a minute. But I just want to see something in here first,' he said. In the next room there was a huge bed with a torn mattress, concave and improbable. An ash tree was growing so close to the house its leaves burst through the window space. The light was almost green. She remembered sleeping in a bed like that at her grandmother's house, how she had to clamber in. It felt like being in a boat. There had been a tree outside the window and twigs tapped the glass when it was windy.

Francesco was studying the depths of an old wardrobe. She peered over his shoulder, clutching his elbow. Inside it there were two floral print dresses with buttons down the front and an old tweed jacket with a greenish herringbone weave. Francesco didn't speak. The clothes did not look grubby, but she thought the dresses seemed forlorn. By comparison the jacket looked as if it could be pulled off the hanger and worn again. 'It might have happened only last year,' he whispered. He crossed himself and turned away.

He marched from the room and said, 'We need something to prise up the hearthstone. Hey!' he shouted. 'You'd better come down here.'

She ran downstairs and out into the glare of the sun.

'You'll want to see this. It was where your father and the English captain slept. It's here.' Outside, there was another door leading into what was once a shelter or byre with two wooden mangers suspended along the length of the back wall.

As they stood there the rushing sound of the river rose towards them and a buzzard mewed in the sky.

'Bruno and Tina must have been good people,' she said. 'I feel full of gratitude. I keep thinking, without the help they gave my mother I would probably never have been born.'

'Yes, they were always generous to everyone. It was their nature.'

In the cellar they found an iron crowbar. The wood ash in the hearth had turned to dust. Petronella imagined the fire of fragrant chestnut wood that had been burning on that last night.

One of the hearthstones was uneven so Francesco tried to get a purchase on it by scrabbling at the edges with his fingertips and attempting to slide first a finger or two and then a hand beneath. After a while he found one of the corners that had a hole beneath it. After much levering with the crowbar the slab shifted. There was a flash of something in the darkness.

She peered down into the cavity and gasped. There was a suitcase and an old shirt. When the leather lid was lifted Petronella saw it wasn't a suitcase at all. It was entirely filled with a wireless set: a canister with some wires, knobs and switches and a radio headset.

'My God, Francesco! Your father's radio. What a clever disguise. So small. And nobody has found it.' They squatted, looking at the knobs and switches. Francesco flicked a switch and then, as if it had stung him, he flicked it off.

'I don't see the gun,' she said after a moment.

She tugged the shirt, half expecting a mouse or a scorpion to jump out. A revolver clanged on the slate. It lay on the floor. When she picked it up the handle fitted comfortably in her hand and her finger automatically stretched towards the trigger. There was a scrap of something white poking out of the barrel. She pulled out a roll of paper. She unravelled it and smoothed it on her lap as if stroking a cat. It was faded and almost illegible because it was written in pencil, but she recognised her mother's writing. Petronella thought, the last person to touch this weapon was my mother, the day she put it back under the stone. She looked at the writing in the light of the window and saw it was a poem. She recognised a word or two here and there, 'shadow', 'indelible.' She wondered if it was the same poem that she'd read in the exercise book.

Francesco sat down in one of the small armchairs and looked across at her. 'I helped your mother. We were in this together. I gave her this gun and we made a pact between us. After we got out of the cave the only thing I wanted to do was join the partisans. I wanted my revenge. The English officer took me to your mother's brigade and I stayed there with her and Renata.

'I was glad of your mother's company because we both understood what each other was going through. I told her about my plan, but no one else. She argued me out of it, saying that she would do the shooting for the two of us. I agreed to let her use their revolver.

'I led her up the path to my home late one evening, when there was no moon. She wouldn't have found the way without my hand guiding her. The air was alive with the sound of owls hooting from one side of the river to the other. We were both equally determined to carry this out and I don't think I would have changed my mind had her will failed at any point.

'The door of our house was still half open. Inside we decided it was safe enough to light a candle so long as we kept it well away from the windows. The house was horrible in its emptiness, with no fire in the hearth and no welcoming smile to greet us.

'I showed her this loose slate in the hearth. In the sputtering candle flame it was difficult to see inside the hole, but on the top, wrapped in this old shirt, was my father's British-made revolver. It shone in the glow of the light. I kissed the gun and placed it in her hand: there you are. Do it. Do it for them. I started crying then, completely uncontrollably, and she held on to me tightly as we sat there on the cold floor. We wept together for what seemed like a long time.

'Then I pulled myself away, to go and fetch something I wanted to give her. I took the candle with me and left her in the dark. I was exhausted from all that weeping, feeling weak as if I had poured myself out. A moth followed the candle flame. I heard her voice call to me from the room next door.

'When I came back I slumped on the floor beside her. Little shudders were running through her body.

'Here, I said. This is for you to keep. In her hand I placed the little wooden hat. The one you now have.

'Thank you, Francesco, she said. It's beautiful.

'It's one of a pair, I told her. My father made them. They're models of the hats worn by the soldiers of the Alpini regiment. He and his brother were Alpini soldiers in the last war. His brother was killed.

'She understood its significance, said: I'll treasure this.

'This one is yours, I repeated. I'll keep one and you keep one and that way we'll know that we will always be friends because we've both done this thing together.

'Just one more thing, I said, taking a penknife from my pocket. I took the hat from her and scratched those words on its base: *If found, return to Francesco*. This is a token. Now you'll never forget our pact.

'And then we got up from the cold floor and, at the door, we blew out the candle and came down the steep slope in the dark. I remember there were many stars that night and I held her hand because she was nervous about falling and I knew every step of the way.

'So, Petronella, you see we were in it together. I was just as responsible as she. But she was the one who happened to pull the trigger. If you want to know, your mother did absolutely the right thing to shoot the informant. And I was quite prepared to do it if she hadn't.'

'Francesco, she took it all on herself. She didn't mention anything of your pact in the account she wrote. As time went on, she became convinced she'd done something terrible.'

'Yes, I can see how it might have haunted her. In the end, it wasn't me who pulled the trigger. It was her. But it could have been me.' He took out his cigarettes and offered Petronella one. She shook her head and he flicked on his cigarette lighter, bending towards it with the cigarette between his lips. He added, 'The Germans made an example of them—my parents, your father. For nothing! It's terrible to think that the war was soon over after that and they wouldn't have had to hang on for much longer.' He was looking exhausted and she could see it had been too much. For her, too.

'But we only know that in hindsight.'

'Nobody knew what was happening, Petronella, especially not up here where communications were poor... you never knew... how things were going to pan out. The world was a mad dangerous place.'

Before putting the radio away he pulled it towards him and twiddled the knobs to see if he could make it work. In amongst the wires, lying on the top, she noticed a booklet. She shook the dust off it. She was thinking of that terrible night, of how terrified Francesco must have been; the risk Vittorio took; the awful responsibility Alex must have felt; the way everyone must have hoped the German search party wouldn't react with its full force.

He said the book contained their codes. His father had known them all by heart. It wouldn't normally have been left with the radio, but was probably put in there that night for safekeeping. He lowered his voice as if someone else might be listening, 'Your mother made use of this radio, too. She came here and sent messages to other partisan brigades. She used another code—it was called the Dante code, but it was a mystery to me.'

'Maddalena was sending the radio messages from here? She never mentioned where. But she did write about the Dante code.' Petronella was able to explain to him that Resistance groups had sometimes wanted to communicate to each other, bypassing the Allies. Lines from Dante were encoded and if the messages had been intercepted they would not be understood. Because the Italians knew chunks of *La Divina Commedia* by heart there was no book of codes.

'It can't ever have been written down, then; you had to know it, as she did.'

'So there must have been lots of communicating by radio taking place here, Francesco. I wonder why the Germans didn't stop them earlier.' The reality was becoming obvious to her now and she blurted, 'I suppose they shot Bruno and Tina because of Vittorio and Alex staying here, Francesco. The reason wasn't the radio and the secret messages because they found no evidence of that. It's still here.' The thought came out of her mouth before she had time to think what was coming.

He didn't react as she had feared. 'It wasn't possible for them to turn anyone in need away. It was in their nature to help anyone and everyone.'

'I'm so sorry, Francesco. Perhaps you have every reason to hate me now if that is true.'

'It's nobody's fault—except for the enemy, of course.'

'Don't you see, it makes everything much worse? It's both my fathers' responsibilities.'

'Look, it was a war. And war is always horrible beyond comprehension. The Germans could have known about my father sending radio messages—they might have picked up his signal through their own systems. They might just have been after fugitive partisans. Perhaps this or perhaps that. We could go on forever.'

She felt that the events that had happened had never left the place..

'Francesco, if only Captain Alex hadn't… hadn't…'

'Hadn't what?'

'I can't help feeling he was like a catalyst. He made everything that happened here so much worse than it needed to be. Providing radios, putting people in danger, getting himself shot and needing to be looked after... '

'He was doing a job, Petronella.'

'Did he really have to go round making use of people?'

They put the radio, the codebook and the revolver back in their hiding place. When they stepped outside Francesco closed the door and then they walked back down the mountain path in silence. The old house had been the scene of momentous happenings in both their families and the mountains towered above it, indifferent. Bees were humming in the bright yellow broom flowers. Petronella had the sensation of being watched.

They crossed the arched bridge over the river and lingered for a moment. Petronella placed a pine cone on the parapet while Francesco leaned over and looked down into the dappled water. The shadow of a branch swayed over the pool below.

They took a path that climbed through the trees and up to a shrine. From there they could see the river glinting as it snaked through the deep valley. Francesco turned to her. 'All I can be certain about is that first Vittorio and then Alex saved my life. I wouldn't have survived if it hadn't been for their both being there. You know, it's very probable that my whole family and I would not have existed. I owe my life and my children to that. And Vittorio, your father, made a great sacrifice.' She was grateful for what he said. She had concluded that he was entitled to hate her. 'Come back to my house for lunch and I'll show you all the photos of my grandchildren.'

After seeing the pictures of seven-year-old Cesare, six-year-old Corrado and little Maria, Petronella felt happier. Before she left Francesco held out his hand towards her and dropped the little wooden hat into her palm. 'You should take care of this, now. For the both of us.'

Back at the holiday apartment in Caraggio she unrolled the scrap of paper that she'd found in the barrel of the revolver. She also took out Maddalena's flimsy exercise book, handling it carefully. She tried again to read the second poem Maddalena had scrawled on the back cover, the one Petronella hadn't been able to decipher last year.

She compared the two columns of writing. Maddalena had composed the poem in the exercise book, and written it out neatly on to the piece of paper that she'd poked into the revolver. Petronella treasured the crossings-out because she felt they let her see into her mother's mind. She said the words to herself out loud and imagined Maddalena mouthing it with her, as she used to do when Petronella was a child trying to speak Italian phrases:

A Fury

Because the pillow still held your scent
I thought the shapes of winter trees were you.

A shadow stood weeping in the corner
of the room. Its tears bled me.

Attached to me like the indelible
feel of my hand in yours. Over time,

its tears ran dry. I tried running away
but it hid beneath my feet.

When I closed it in a cupboard
it squeezed out through a crack.

I buried it under the soil but it wouldn't
stay put. Once I threw it on a fire

but, being a shadow, it didn't burn.
It watched me while I slept,

entered my skull so that I couldn't tell
who was doing the dreaming.

Once when I cut myself on a knife, I trembled
when it licked my drops of blood. It hungered

for a blood-price. All I have to offer is myself.

Her mother had written these words. Maybe she thought
leaving the poem with the weapon would bury all the
horrors. Petronella thought about what Maddalena had
gone through to arrive at the only possible conclusion.

Was it really murder? She tried to imagine how it felt.
She willed herself to see how things looked from her
mother's eyes. A weight of anguish had crushed the breath
out of her: losing Vittorio, her friends Bruno and Tina and
then the decision to revenge their deaths on the man who'd
informed on them. And shadowing these thoughts was the
fact that she had shot someone in cold blood.

Then there was the question—why had she married
Alex? He couldn't have deliberately put Vittorio in harm's
way, could he? Alex was not the sort to have been driven by
jealousy.

She met Nando in a cafe in the town centre. He was
pleased to see her, shook her hand warmly. He listened to
her story.

'It was a difficult balancing act for everyone,' he said. '*I
sconosciuti*, the unknown, the disappeared. There were a very
few cases came to court after the end of the war, but there
were, of course, many demobbed partisans who had scores
to settle with people who'd collaborated. You can
understand it, of course, but after the end of war the
violence is meant to end.

'Still, it must have been an agonising decision for her to
shoot the collaborator, even in war-time. It's there in the
poem she wrote, about how the desperate need for revenge
dogged her. The spy was responsible for destroying
everything your mother held dear, and so she felt duty
bound to stop the man from destroying others. And then

she couldn't leave the boy to commit murder, could she? In any case, he might well have fouled it up, got himself caught and been arrested and shot.

'I would like to have met your mother. What do you think you have inherited from her?'

'Nothing much. I wouldn't have had a clue what to do, in her situation.'

'I don't expect she thought she would either. Conflicts push people to their limits, into situations they'd never want to find themselves.'

Petronella said, 'You know something… no one would ever have believed her capable of it.' She thought, is that the woman who brushed my hair so tenderly; the woman whose lips formed the words of her mother tongue which she was willing me to speak; the woman who cooked unusual recipes for me and my incredulous friends? Rosa and Gianni's daughter?

She examined her feelings towards this revelation as though it were some esoteric object that had landed in the garden from outer space.

And another thought came to her—that she just might be getting interested in Nando. It was not something she'd been looking for—romance. It would be nice if it did happen but she wouldn't want to take her clothes off. No —nothing like that. Anyway, she supposed he must be married.

49

Every day I waited for my father's return at the station. After the fighting was over, trains started to arrive from the border disgorging displaced men and women. All of them were emaciated, feeble-minded, barely alive. The local hospital soon filled. The Red Cross set up soup kitchens outside the station. The queues of famished, bedraggled men grew longer. I watched them standing in silence as if just sniffing the smell of soup brought them relief.

I carried a photo of my father, asking these hopeless men if they had seen him or if anyone remembered him. Inside the station building the walls of the concourse were covered with photos. It was a gallery of faint hope. Someone had inscribed the word 'Remember' in red paint across the smoke-stained slabs. The paint dripped from the corners. Another sign said 'Welcome Home.'

At first I was convinced that every train approaching would be the one. The catalogue of lost people grew longer every week. The photos on the walls carried men's names or announced new addresses because the streets been shelled or families had moved.

Then stories filtered back from the Italian office in Berlin about the dreadful conditions in which the Italian workers had lived: starvation rations, the brutal treatment of those too weak to work, TB and other diseases. The dead lay unburied. If he had managed to survive those months away how would he find the strength to get home?

One day Captain Alex arrived at our door. At first I didn't recognise him without his uniform. I introduced him to my mother and she shook his hand and invited him in. He had a tonic effect on her, talking in English about the places and the countryside she remembered from her childhood. The war was barely mentioned. He told me how he had promised Vittorio that he would take care of me if anything happened. But I did not want him to care for me; I wanted him to find my father. He said he knew who to contact to get Gianni traced. He promised my father would be found if he were still alive.

Alex was also able to help my mother. My Aunt Margery had written to urge her sister and myself to go and live with her in Wikeley, a more comfortable life after the privations of the war. My mother wouldn't hear of leaving our house in Porto Romolo until Gianni returned. I knew it would be good for her health to have a fresh start somewhere familiar and I wanted to make use of Alex to motivate her. I had no intention of staying away myself for very long, though I had to let my mother think that I would remain with her at my aunt's or else she would never have made the long train journey by herself. I wanted to get her away to England and return home in time for the birth.

What I hadn't realised was that my mother had her own plans. Alex married me before my baby was born, so that it would not be illegitimate. But my belly never grew very large and nobody even noticed until I was about eight months pregnant. Even then, I could have been putting on weight.

I have never believed in my own marriage. I somehow haven't been involved. Alex asks so little of me, as if he doesn't really want me. Curious, these English. We have always slept in separate beds. When we were first married he came across to me in the night and held himself above me so as not to squash the baby. I lay there until he finished bobbing up and down.

I had to spend the last few weeks of my pregnancy in hospital. They said I was debilitated after living on nothing but mountain air and the doctor was concerned about my health and the baby's size. But the baby arrived safely. Tiny, but beautiful, a replica of her father—a fact nobody ever mentioned. I called her Petronella.

50

She showed the sketch map to Nando. He had a different military map of the area and suggested they could take a trip there together before she returned home to start the new school year. He could also take her to meet some people from the partisans, to form an idea of what it might have been like.

'How come you know so much about the partisans?'

'I'm writing a book about the local brigades in this part of Liguria. I've been researching it for the *Istituto della Resistenza* since I retired.'

So he was not interested in her. It was the new narrative she was giving to his book.

'I… I was thinking of adding a chapter on women's involvement, now I've heard your parents' story. What do you think?'

'But, what about your…family, your wife? Won't she mind you going away so suddenly?'

'My wife's dead, Petronella. Some years ago. A car accident.'

A few days later they set off from Caraggio carrying small rucksacks. On the coast the sky was clear, but dark clouds lurked in the distant mountain range. There was only Nando's map to follow, which showed the routes connecting one village to another. Sometimes the map was wrong and a path shown on it no longer existed. She was willing to let any well-trodden path be their guide—stretching ahead of them it offered a route to somewhere. She felt confident in its twists and turns because she was following the footsteps of others—a boot print in the mud, a crushed clover flower, a stone recently dislodged, a rock placed for a toe-hold to skip across a stream—like lines of a script belonging to forgotten narratives.

Each night Nando found them somewhere to stay without difficulty, even though it was a tourist area. Everyone was friendly. They were fascinated by the reason for Petronella's journey, asking questions and recalling events. It wasn't clear what was true and what was embellished.

In one village she heard a tale about partisans who were hidden inside a hollow oak tree for two days while Germans came and went along the path. At one time they had even sat below the tree to have a smoke. She also heard about a man who could read the future in the stars. Sometimes he gave the partisans accurate information about the whereabouts of German soldiers when their own intelligence told them something different. He would say to the incredulous, *'Chi non crede all stelle e fa di sua testa, paga di sua pella'* (Anyone who does not believe the stars and uses only his mind pays with his skin). People believed he was a magician and travelled long distances to hear his predictions. When the Nazis eventually shot him and stole the family's goats, his grief-stricken wife sat on the roof every night to watch constellations and to listen to the owls. From the tones of the owls hooting and the appearance of the moon she affirmed there would be a dire end for the occupying forces. She would shout curses into the night: *'Un diluvio sui mostri del sangue, del terrore e del morte ai Teutonici'* (A downpour of blood, terror and death to the Germans).

In another village they met an old man who had once been a couturier in Florence. He had retired to the mountains so that he could grow vegetables, flowers and fruit trees. Despite his age, he was still chivalrous and it was easy to imagine his fingers charmingly organising the folds of women's dresses and gowns. He declared that there never were any partisans, that it was fabricated by young men to get themselves girlfriends. 'Your mother was a prime example,' he said, 'falling for a man who claimed he was a hero.' Nando's hand squeezed hers. The old Fascist filled up their glasses again. 'Mussolini did a great job for Italy—a dictator who was only slightly pink like a perfumed rose.' He said that Italy needed a dictator or else the Communists would have taken over. 'And then where would we have been?' She appreciated the brief but encouraging handhold.

Sometimes, people shook their heads at the mention of partisans. 'Don't talk about that lot!' An old countryman explained, 'They were just brigands, brought us nothing but trouble. My parents gave them everything we had.' Petronella wondered why his parents were so generous to people who apparently behaved so badly. 'Yes, my father took food every day to a whole group of them hiding in the cave over there.' From where she was standing, looking up at a sheer cliff face partly covered in scrub and scree, she saw that getting to the caves must have been perilous. He told her one thing, but his father's voluntary and courageous actions told her something else. She wondered where the truth lay, if anywhere. And why did it always slip and slide around? So many people had willed themselves into forgetting.

They walked higher and higher into the Maritime Alps, the forested slopes giving way to rock and cliff. Beside the river, there were fertile meadows where goat bells still rang. Stone-bordered terraces were carved out of the slopes, rippling down every mountainside and overgrown with trees or shrubs and wild flowers. Many of the slate-roofed houses stood empty and boarded up. The nights were cooler up there, but the afternoon sun was hot and they were glad to be walking through the shade of pine and chestnut woods. The trunks of the ancient chestnut trees were twisted into gargoyle shapes.

On the afternoon of the third day, they reached Meraldo where her Grandfather Gianni had been born. They scooped cool water in their hands from the fountain in the little square beside the cemetery and then sat on a wooden bench, where Nando opened the map to show her exactly where they were.

Walking through the wrought iron door to the cemetery at Meraldo she felt as though the dead people had been talking until the moment she arrived. She wished everyone 'Good afternoon,' out loud, to her own amusement.

The dead kept their secrets to themselves, but she imagined eyes watching every move. On each gravestone there was a photograph. Gianni was born and brought up in this village, but until now she had no idea that so many of his family came from here. There were generations of the same huge extended clan buried in that place. His family stretched in all directions: grandparents, aunts and uncles, cousins of cousins. And here they were, all together, as if she'd arrived at a surprise family reunion.

Amongst the family's names there was another Maddalena, a young woman in her twenties whose beautiful face had been photographed in profile. She read her inscription:

Il nostro caro piccolo fiore.
I tuoi desolate genitori e fratelli piangono della tua partite

(Our dear little flower,
Your desolated parents and brothers weep for your leaving)

In these words she felt a frightening sorrow open up. Was this all that was left of the terrible loss they suffered when she had unaccountably died so young—as had her namesake, her own mother?

Nando explained that names are often used again and again to honour the elders and to bless the baby. Young people following in the footsteps of a previous generation.

She could see that there were plenty of Giannis, great uncles perhaps or second cousins, all of whom lived into ripe old age, their faces wrinkled like withered apples or tree bark. The war had denied her grandfather smiling old age. These Giannis looked as if they were optimists by nature, resilient enough to cope with whatever life had thrown at them.

When she left she murmured 'Goodbye.' She visualised them all talking about her, asking each other, 'Where did that one come from? Whose granddaughter is she?'

Above Meraldo a mountain soared. It looked as if it was still heaving itself out of the earth and rushing upwards. She found it hard to believe how these human dramas could unfold while the land remained unscarred. Blood flowing over the rocks, bombings and fire were all forgotten. What had happened to all that violence and fear? Does it vanish like a smell of cordite in the air?

There was a connection between the landscape with its rock falls, screes, hidden footpaths and streams, and the old people whose photographs were looking out from their gravestones. She knew that the past had marked the futures of the people in all those families. They had passed their histories to her—in the shape of their fingers, the texture or colouring of their skin, their attributes of patience or resilience.

51

When Johnnie was born without drawing a breath, I realised things could no longer go on as before. At first I was left in the hospital feeling like a lump of flesh on a butcher's slab. At home the colours of the world hurt my eyes as if I saw them for the first time. Then the consultant told me that there was nothing he could do. He couldn't say how long the cancer might let me live. Pregnancy had speeded it up.

I had only a short time left to deal with the past. My priority was to find a way to make amends. I would gladly suffer the consequences of what I had done and confess to the police. I thought prison would be freedom. While I still had strength I decided to go back to my home town.

I didn't discuss this with Alex. I wrote him a note and left it on the hall table so that he would find when he came home. I said there had been an urgent call to return to Porto Romolo. Someone in the family needed me and I would be back before long. Another lie wouldn't matter.

I didn't want him to know what I was intending until it was done. He might dissuade me, afraid of what other people would think. I wasn't going to let him or my mother know. They would find out later. I could already visualise the local paper headline: 'Local Woman Confesses to Cold-blooded Murder of Wartime Collaborator.'

I had written to Renata to tell her we would be coming. But I didn't tell her the exact date of our arrival as I didn't want to be met at the station. I needed time to revisit the town of my childhood on my own. I would phone her later from the hotel room. Renata with her wavy black hair, her quizzical eyes and her pointed questions. I wanted to keep things to myself. I asked her not to tell any of our old friends that I was coming back. Not until I had done what I came to do.

The journey across France was slow. I relaxed, feeling I could be a foreigner in a foreign land. I once thought the future was inside a box we could open and take out what we wanted. And the past was something that could be put away in another box. On that train journey I realised that it never goes away.

At Marseilles, we boarded another train for the journey along the south coast into Italy. The air was balmy. I had forgotten the shifting colour of the Mediterranean—one minute deep blue gentian and the next, the paler blue of plumbago. The train thrummed in and out of tunnels, the mountains in cloud, sunlight glittering on the waves.

When Petronella and I stepped off the train the air was syrupy with the scent of mandarins. I felt raw. The sound of my language filled me with sweetness. The things I had wanted to forget came back to me on every street corner. But now I wanted to savour every memory. Petronella carried her toy poodle and held my hand tightly in the busy street. Did she notice the change in me?

Eight years after the war had ended traffic flowed along streets that had been full of rubble, people promenaded near the harbour that had been too dangerous to approach, flowers were sold in the market again. But I saw some old people begging for a few coins; young men who had been disabled or maimed loitered in the piazzas. The ruin of war hidden beneath a thin veneer. It looked like a stage set. I stepped into a bar for a coffee before looking for a hotel, and the tinkle of cups was like recollecting a favourite tune.

'What did you come back for? And where is your husband? Do tell me, are you up to something?' Renata was standing at the window of the hotel room, a cigarette in her hand, its smoke curling round her. The room was cramped—not what she expected of her English friend—but there was a view of the sea and the walls were rinsed with sunlight. There was an adjoining room for Petronella, who was reading a book. Renata observed that Petronella was short for her age, untidy in her smart clothes, in the way of the English.

'Yes, you're right, this isn't a holiday.' I was sitting across the room from her and perhaps something in my voice drew Renata to sit on the arm of my chair. I spoke in a deliberate low voice about the stillbirth, how I'd hoped the baby would be the chance of a new start for Alex and me and help me to forget. 'I've been having terrible dreams since then, Renata. You know, about what happened, what I did. All that.'

'You poor girl.'

'Renata, I'm going to have to tell the authorities about it, make a formal statement and face the consequences.'

'Why? Will it do any good, do you think?' Renata lit another cigarette and inhaled deeply. She crossed her legs and flicked off a yellow stiletto.

'I have to do something to get this out of my mind. It won't let me rest. You've heard of the ancient Greek idea of the Furies who avenged all crimes that upset the natural order of things? What I did was part of the war machine of killing and suffering and now the Furies want retribution. Admitting openly to what I did is the only thing I can think of. I have to do this to protect Petronella from the consequences... she mustn't be affected by what I did— she mustn't even know.'

'Isn't that what your Catholic confession is for?'

'I don't believe in prayer or absolution. It's never done me any good.'

'Perhaps you could try it. You could rend your clothes as well if you wanted.'

Renata could be so infuriating.

'I haven't been to church since Petronella was christened. I don't even consider myself a Catholic any longer.'

'But it's still there inside you, Maddalena, a part of you. Being brought up as a Catholic never leaves you, even if you think it has. And I know all about that, with my background.' I remembered how Renata had once claimed that she would never let being born a Jew affect her. 'And what about Alex? Doesn't he know how you feel?'

I said that Alex didn't know anything.

'Maybe it's time you tried telling him. It isn't too late.'

'I can't do that. It wouldn't help at all.'

'How can you be so sure? And he does know the circumstances, after all.'

'It's got beyond talking. Renata, don't you see? I am paying for it every day of my life and then there was Johnnie. Maybe... maybe, he was a... blood-price.' I hadn't wanted to express my worst fear; saying it aloud made it seem possible, but not credible. She would never take it seriously now. But she didn't know there was no hope. 'Anyway, he doesn't like talking about things, you see, Renata. That's part of the problem.'

'Do you ever give him a chance? He is your husband and I know he loves you.'

'I'm not so sure it's called love. More like bound together.'

Renata was certain that the *carabinieri* wouldn't show any interest. They'd need evidence. There had been cases of Fascist sympathisers murdered after the war was over and some of those came to court, but this was different. 'It was during war-time, for heaven's sake. All's fair in love and war, as they say.'

'But it doesn't excuse me, does it? It doesn't mean there were no rights or wrongs, Renata. And what about the family of that man? What about them? Nothing at all is fair in love or war, that's not right.'

'But it is in the eyes of a court. Anyone would understand, you poor dear. Crime of passion!'

'Oh, Renata, do you really think they won't listen? I'll write a statement about it. A long account. I'll account fully for it and give reasons.'

'No, it won't make any difference.' She said they'd need corroborative evidence for their paperwork or they wouldn't be bothered. They'd politely show me the door. 'You'll only feel an absolute fool.' Renata clasped me to her for a while in an awkward embrace and then said that she would like to take me somewhere.

She led us through the old quarter of the city, past the flower stalls in the market, to the place where her parents had lived. The medieval streets were cobbled and narrow, veining the steep hillside. Children played in the streets and washing was strung above their heads. A canary was singing from a cage in a window, a woman was ranting from deep inside a house and a man was painting a door. In a small, sunny piazza she indicated her parents' house . The house was still beautiful, the sort with ornate patterns on the ceilings and a decorated cornice. A bright purple bougainvillea grew against the wall.

She said it had taken months after the war had ended to get official confirmation about what had befallen her parents. After Renata had escaped from the town and joined the partisans in 1944 they had been taken one night to an internment camp in central Italy. Later, they were crammed in a freight train with many other Italian Jews and, without food or water, conveyed to Auschwitz. They were separated on arrival and neither survived. Renata said the knowledge that she could never revenge their deaths made her sick. Her only consolation was the thought that fate might cause their murderers to suffer as a result of their actions. She said, 'When something like that happens I know how you want to kill them. At the very least hurt them. I can tell you that doing nothing might be just as bad as acting in the way you did.'

As I tucked Petronella up in bed that night it came to me that my life had been lived. Now there was nothing left to do but make the journey back to Alex and whatever future was left. I didn't doubt that he would be glad at my return, but it was a love that merely brushed against my skin. Domestic chores and motherhood would have to content me after all those dramas. What little remained of my life was in England. Yet the ceremonies of everyday living had no significance any more. I couldn't help it. Alex was always a kind man and there was no reason not to love him. But I even resented him because it was he who had married me.

And once I'd had the dreadful thought that if Alex had reacted quicker things could have been different, it was impossible to get rid of it. Yet I could see my task was to find a way to forgive him, not expect someone else to do it for me.

On the train home to England I sat with my back to the engine, looking back at what I was leaving. As I watched the landscape stream away I listened to my own voice reading out Italian fairy tales to Petronella. I didn't know how much she understood.

While I read my mind was elsewhere. I decided to write it all down—and maybe I would see the connections, understand what was driving me. Reckoning up the costs would help me estimate how much more there was still to pay.

At home when I wake I still don't always remember where I am, or which language I should be speaking. As my eyes open I wait for my mind to catch up with the present. Sometimes I feel like a child waking out of a nightmare in a strange bed. Other times I could be back in the mountains next to Renata, alert to danger. I can't call out in case I am still in the Resistance. There is always a crease in the consciousness between waking and sleeping. Then, as my eyes focus on the furniture, I orientate myself: 'There's the wardrobe and the dressing table, so I must be married to Alex and living in England.' Or is it sleep-waking? If you dream you've woken, have you really woken?

Late one night, roused by the sound of a footstep on the garden path, a familiar panic flickered in my mind. The street lights had been turned off by then so I realised it must be after midnight. Moonlight was shining through the chinks in the curtains. I was sure I heard the sound again. Alex didn't stir. Sliding from under the bedclothes I moved to the window. There was a shadow, darker than the night, moving on the front lawn—a space like a negative: blank, not black.

Grabbing a cardigan I hurried downstairs to open the door, but there was nobody on the threshold. I stood on the porch in bare feet. The darkness was transparent like the beginning of dawn. There were no footprints across the frosted grass.

My skin prickled. I called to him, but knew there would be no answer. I stood for a while longer at the front door, the chill night air swirling into the hallway. I went back to bed, but my feet were too cold to let me sleep. Alex continued to breathe deeply. Petronella slept on in the room down the landing. The baby's cot had been dismantled.

A phrase crept into my mind—*Io non mori e non rimasi vivo* (I did not die and I did not stay alive). I chased the words down a corridor and caught up with the line in a school classroom with sunlight pouring in through a window so high up I could not see out of it. The teacher pointed at me to recite those particular lines and I read the words aloud, but didn't understand them. Dante's *Inferno*, Canto thirty-something, came to me, as if a voice was calling from somewhere in the distance.

52

A wooden finger post pointed the way to Carano along a narrow path that zig-zagged up through the forest to a point where a stream tumbled down a fold of the mountain. An hour later Nando and Petronella emerged out of the pine trees into the sunshine and crossed a field dotted with ox-eye daisies, valerian and vetch. They reached the dusty road that led to the village and passed a row of eucalyptus trees whose leaves were fluttering like bunting strung across a street for a village party. Behind the smooth tree trunks stood a wall with a fissured oak door into the cemetery. Beside it lay spent red plastic votive candle-holders in a messy heap. Petronella fumbled the iron bolt open and entered. She thought she would find Vittorio's grave, but she couldn't.

Leaving the cemetery she stood still, feeling disappointed and bewildered about to what to do next. An eagle was wheeling above. After the steep climb through the forest, distances and angles were disorientating. Looking down on the valley, places seemed far closer to each other than when you were there—the shining road a connecting strand between the villages and scattered farms, slate roofs glowing in the light, window panes dark where the sun couldn't reach, birch and fir trees growing on scree while larch forests spread like a shadow up the craggy mountain sides. Difficult to know which perspective was accurate.

She and Nando sat on a rock and shared a sandwich. It was a new experience for her to be looked at in the way that he did, without feeling judged or self-conscious. When he spoke he concentrated on her, gauging her interest. When she spoke he listened with attention, not as if he had to park his eyes somewhere.

As they ate they watched an old man on a grassy terrace below them. He was wearing a veil and was bending over a blue beehive. He'd taken off the roof and was sifting through the first of the boxes stacked on top of the hive. Bees were humming round the old man's head. They weren't threatened, only keeping an eye on him. He wore no gloves and had no smoke to quell them.

When he finished his work he came up the path, waving his crooked hand. '*Salve!*' He was about to go by.

'*Buon giorno*! A good year for honey?' Petronella felt she must engage him in conversation.

'Yes,' he replied. 'It'll be a good harvest this autumn.'

'Aren't the winters very cold for bees up here?'

'The chestnut and hawthorn blossom has been full of nectar. It got them off to a fine start and there'll be plenty for them for winter and some left for us.' He made a little whistling noise through pursed lips while his head nodded in agreement with himself.

'You haven't had them swarming, then?'

'No! No, I don't let them,' he paused, looking at her curiously. 'You know something about bees, do you?

'Only a bit. I used to have a couple of hives, but I wasn't very competent. Since then I've rather hankered after keeping bees again.' She liked the old man.

Nando pointed at his hands, 'You don't seem to mind about being stung?'

'No, not at all. I am immune to bee stings. Because of my father, you see. You inherit immunity. He kept bees, too. And it's good for you, being stung a bit, prevents arthritis and rheumatism.' He whistled again.

'Really, I never knew that!' said Petronella.

'It's true. And it promotes longevity.' He was lean and tough. All that walking up and down steep hillsides.

'So, where are you from?' he asked. 'I don't think I've seen you here before, have I?'

'We're trying to find out about my family. I was born in England, but my grandparents came from here. Nando is from Porto Romolo.'

'So, *la signora* is English? Pleased to meet you both.' He stretched his hand out towards them. Her hand felt the shapes of his splayed, misshapen thumb, his twisted fingers, and the power of his grip. While their hands were joined they both smiled.

'Did you, by any chance, ever know Eduardo, the Bee Man?' Francesco had told Petronella that this was how Vittorio's father was known.

'That was my father.' He whistled, his head nodding.

She shaded her eyes with a hand to look at him. 'Really? Your father... was Eduardo, the Bee Man?'

'Yes, he was. We had the same name. I am called Eduardo, too.' A pause of inquisitiveness. Finally, he asked, 'How do you know about him?'

'This must sound very odd... but I am the Bee Man's granddaughter.' She smiled uncertainly.

'What do you mean? It's not possible! You're English, you said.' His whistle was staccato.

'She's more Italian than English, actually,' Nando chipped in.

'If you are Eduardo, the Bee Man's son, then your brother was Vittorio?'

'Yes, he was called Vittorio. But how...?'

'Then, I am your niece, your... your brother's daughter.' The words echoed in her head and she heard herself speaking as if from a distance.

'What are you saying? My brother had no children.' His shrug made her think he was going to refuse to believe her.

'My mother was called Maddalena.'

He glanced anxiously at Nando for help and then his eyes fixed on hers as if trying to find a way to fathom her mind. She looked back at him, biting her lip, waiting.

'Looking at you, I do see something in your features,' he said as though his whistle was delivering a sentence.

She fished Vittorio's photo from the rucksack and handed it to him. 'Here, this is a picture of my father.'

He peered at it, holding it away from him, and shook his head. 'I can't see it properly. I'll have to go and get my glasses. Come to my house and we'll have a glass of wine. It's too hot out here now anyway.'

They followed the old man between banks of mauve vetch and pale blue scabious down to the centre of the village. The path became an alleyway between houses and the sunlight slanted straight down in a bright sliver between the tall buildings. There were sounds of voices from inside the houses, but everyone had gone indoors during the heat of the day. A radio gabbled away by an open window. Pots of bright flowers stood beside dark doorways.

His house was on the other side of the village, standing by itself on the edge of the woods. He unlatched the door, beckoned them in, Nando ducking his head, into the dark interior. Eduardo put down his veil and hive tool and gestured for them to sit by a table laden with books and jars and various other tools. He cleared a space with his elbow and took down a bottle of wine from the shelf. He poured the blood-red liquid into cracked glasses, which they clinked together.

Petronella noticed the skin round his eyes was nearly transparent, as if he was made of beeswax. It reminded her of a baby's skin, it made her trust him. His hands and face were like a map of this landscape, fissured and craggy. His eyes, grey and veined like marble, barely left her face. 'Now,' he said, 'let me see that picture again.' His intake of breath was piercing.

He hooked his glasses onto his nose to study the picture in the light from the window; as he did this he swayed a little. Nando jumped up to grab him and lowered him into a chair. Eduardo put his head in his hand. 'Ha, my head is spinning. Whew! *Scusate.*' He took out a handkerchief to wipe his nose and then lifted his gaze to look straight at Petronella again. She was squatting beside his chair and he grabbed hold of her hand, in both of his.

'It's a shock! This really is my brother. It really is. Tell me, please, where did this come from?' She explained about how she found it, what she knew about her mother and how she hadn't known any of this herself until recently.

'A miracle,' he said spreading his arms wide, 'it's a miracle. That you should arrive here and find me. You know, I once heard my brother loved a woman. But I never heard her name. Maddalena, you say? A beautiful name.' Petronella told him about her mother's marriage to Alex and her early death.

'I need time to recover, my friends. So do you, judging by your faces. Look, young man, let my niece sit here, will you, so we can see each other properly? You can sit by the window perhaps.' Eduardo again seized Petronella's hand, pressing it so she felt as though something he kept in the palm of his hand passed into hers. 'In a while I promise, *principessa,* I will show you where my brother—your father —was buried.' He tipped more wine into their glasses and after passing round the packet he lit himself a cigarette. His cheeks flushed brightly as he told his own story. Petronella silently hoped he wasn't about to have a heart attack. She got up to fetch him water, but he shook his head disdainfully, gulped the wine in his glass like a thirsty man. He explained how during the war nearly all the villagers were taken away.

'And you, how did you escape?' asked Nando.

'My father had already sent me away. I was lucky. Just before the Germans invaded I went to stay with an aunt in a town on the other side of the mountains. My father asked his sister to keep me for a while. When I came home all my family had vanished so my aunt took me back. I spent much of my life in Vica. Do you know it?'

245

'Yes, I've seen the name on a map. It must be quite a long way from here. What happened to your parents?' Nando was following his own line of questions.

'They were taken prisoner and shot along with several others for something they didn't do.'

His head shook, the whistle was like a distant cry.

'That's awful. How did that come about?' Nando offered Eduardo another cigarette.

'It was in reprisal for something the partisans did.' He lit the cigarette and watched the flame travel along the matchstick till it reached his finger ends, then shook it out.

'Something the partisans did?' Petronella's skin prickled all over as if ants were biting her.

'I don't know what, exactly. I wasn't here, of course. There were always ambushes and so on. The Germans were completely indiscriminate about whom they punished. You couldn't easily sit on the fence.'

'Your father? Had he been involved in some way?' Petronella asked.

'No, not directly. I don't think so. Can't be sure. He just got caught up in it all. It was like a tidal wave you couldn't escape from and everyone was swept up in it somehow or other.'

'Did your family always live in this house, Eduardo?' she continued. Had this been Vittorio's home?

'No, not this place, ours was just up the hill. When my father and mother disappeared our house was torched by the Germans, but this building was untouched. When I came back, it was convenient to live here while I rebuilt my family home. But I haven't finished doing it up and I've stayed here ever since. Kept bees, like my father.'

'You know something, Eduardo,' Petronella said, 'I've always had this thing about bees—right from when I was a child they've kept me company.'

'Ah, of course, they're in our blood, *principessa*. They take hold and never let go.'

Nando persisted. 'And so when did you come back here, Eduardo?'

'Oh, I spent most of my life in Vica and didn't return again until my wife died. I came here to fix things up while I still could. It would be all right to die here, you see, in the place where I was born.'

'I'm sorry about your wife. What was she called?'

'Emilia. We have a daughter, Lilla. She's married and now lives in Milan. They have a son, Vittorio.'

Late in the afternoon Eduardo led them back through the village where a group of old people were sitting on wooden chairs in the shady piazza. It was their regular meeting time, but they fell silent and watched as the two strangers approached. Eduardo greeted them and spoke in Caranese dialect. Their faces lit up when they realised who Petronella was and they all gripped her hand.

When they entered the cemetery he led Petronella to the farthest corner and pointed out her father's gravestone, behind other more monumental stones. 'The villagers said they put him here because they wanted him to feel safely hidden away after what had happened to him. Leave him to rest in peace after his terrible end.'

He never told the Germans anything, you see, *principessa*. Not even when they tortured him. It was too dangerous to know as much as he did.'

On the stone was written simply *Vittorio Liriani 1922-1945. He died for Liberty and Justice.* Eduardo and Nando moved away and left her alone. There was a small photo next to the inscription: a young man wearing a suit and looking beyond the photographer as if he could see something in the far distance. 'My eyes, my nose,' she murmured.

Her insides trembled as if Vittorio had just brushed past her, and a sense of what was lost welled up. She longed for what she had never had, a happy family. It unsteadied her. How could she grieve for what she'd never known?

Something was illuminated. She could see a crack that was only the size of a bee-space—it was the crack between what her mother wrote and what Francesco told her had taken place. Such a tiny thing, but it could make a difference. It was that moment when Vittorio realised the Germans' searchlight was about to pick out Francesco on the mountainside. In order to deflect attention from the boy he ran back down the hillside, putting himself at risk.

Vittorio had acted in a flash. He wouldn't have stood by and let the young boy be caught. As a result he was wounded, captured, tortured, killed. And because of that her mother, broken-hearted, took revenge on the informant, the action that caused her to feel consumed with guilt for the rest of her short life.

Alex didn't spot what was unfolding down below him on that mountainside. It was a struggle for him to climb the steep terrace banks because the pain in his leg was holding him up. The mountains weren't Alex's natural environment – he wouldn't have been able to distinguish the small movement of a person from a rustle of leaves in a gust of wind – while Vittorio, born and bred in the mountains, would have known what every sound meant.

If only Captain Alex, the senior officer, had ordered Vittorio to leave Bruno and Tina's house earlier. If only he had managed to limp away a day or two before it all happened. If only he had noticed that Francesco had followed them through the window. If only he had been the one captured—the Germans wouldn't have tortured and shot a British officer: under the rules of war they would have had to imprison an enemy combatant. But Vittorio had been considered a terrorist.

How could Alex know that this would end up unleashing a train of events that ruined the lives of both Maddalena and himself? And when Maddalena gleaned (from Francesco perhaps?) this tiny bit of the story, she couldn't stop herself blaming him for Vittorio's death. But it hadn't been Alex's fault. None of it had. And he probably never stopped blaming himself.

She stood for a while on her own, listening to the wind in the trees as if it might have something to tell her. A few dry leaves scattered across the ground. From somewhere in the sky she heard a young buzzard whining like a kitten. Here were his name and image in this quiet corner of the graveyard and her stomach was being gnawed by an unfamiliar sorrow.

Looking around she saw other graves with the same family name. Nearby she was startled to see her own name, Petronella, inscribed on one of the stones. Judging by the dates this would be Vittorio's mother's generation. This woman gave nothing away in her photo. It was not possible to decipher the lines engrained on her inscrutable face, whether they were due to habitual smiling or to a pursing of her lips. Petronella liked the kindly and patient look of her.

From her rucksack she took out the exercise book and the photo of her father. She looked at the picture of the unkempt but handsome warrior in a tattered uniform. This was the man who had handed down to her the shape of his eyes, nose and chin, a love of bees, and of mountains, as well as curiosity and impatience with anything less than the whole truth. She understood herself a little better.

Something of huge importance had appeared—out of the feeling of loss itself. Deeper than words, she recognised how she had been born of her parents' love.

Eduardo and Nando walked back towards her. Petronella felt awkward in front of the old man now she knew he was her uncle.

'Eduardo, do you suppose I could have been named after your mother, Petronella?'

'Of course you were. It's quite usual. A mark of respect, young Petronella. Look around you.' He gesticulated at many of the plaques in the cemetery and walked over to his mother's grave.

Petronella had often wondered where her name had sprung from. Maddalena had left a message concealed in the choice, like a code linking her life to a generation she'd never been able to meet. But the link between them had been clearly signed in the same way as her father's name had been linked to a whole line of ancestors before him. Her own origins grew from this rocky landscape, from the two villages joined by a footpath she had walked along, from the sharp-edged mountains which cast long shadows in the short days of winter and which pulsed with the lights of fireflies in summer.

Petronella flushed so hot that her tears burnt up. The blueness of the sky against the jagged rocks made her feel exposed, on the edge of panic. She was feeling light-headed and it wasn't the effect of altitude. 'Thank you,' she said, unable to think what else to say. 'Thank you.' She thought her voice would break if she said anything more.

Eduardo's hand landed on her shoulder, the same grip holding her. 'When you leave here don't forget to come back. I would like to meet your son before too long, Petronella. My brother's grandson. We all move on in the end, but we leave good things behind. It would mean a lot to me and, maybe, to him in time. He will need to know where his bones come from. Bring him back with you, my dear niece. Bring him back before too long. You know where to find me.' He leaned towards her to kiss her on one cheek and then the other, and flung his arms round her, patting her back, as if passing across his physical strength.

'Yes,' she said, swallowing. 'I had better go back home, Eduardo. I do need to talk to my son. We had an argument before I left so I must go back and sort it out with him now I know about Vittorio… and you. All of this. I'm sorry, Nando, but I've got to head back now. Is there a bus from somewhere round here, do you think?'

And, without waiting for an answer, she sped down the hill, waving back, 'I'll return soon, I promise. *Grazie, Zio Eduardo, grazie.*'

Two hours later they stood together at a bus-stop. There were several other people gathered there and, when the squeaky doors of the bus opened, they all crowded on board gossiping with the bus driver. Inside, it smelled of diesel and cigarette smoke. She sat by a right-hand window, leaving Nando with the extra leg room of the aisle seat.

The road followed the coils of the river which, after the rains, ran white before plunging into pools of green. Where the water broke, small clouds of mist formed like ghosts materialising. The klaxon blared as the bus swerved round bends above the precipice. Her stomach lurched and she visualised the bus wheels teetering on the edge and tipping over, how it might feel to be falling into that chasm. She looked at Nando's face, but he and the other passengers swayed in their seats impassively. His eyes seemed glued on the road ahead through the driver's window but, at that moment, he glanced down and reached for her hand, his thumb firm inside her palm.

'It's really good of not you to mind leaving, Nando. But, you see, Matt has a week's leave from his training and I must tell him what I've discovered—about Alex…and where we come from…Matt and I…'

'It's okay. That's not a problem.' His fingers squeezed hers a little.

She looked down at his hand, realising that its blue veins and the lines across his knuckles looked already familiar. She hesitated, thinking how to phrase what was in her mind. 'I don't know what you must be thinking, my strange behaviour…rushing away so suddenly…'

'We don't know much about each other, do we? You have let me in on so many things, let me know things you yourself didn't know. And that's the only part I do know…'

'I'm beginning to think that sometimes I don't listen to what I hear. For instance, Nando, I don't even know the name of your poor wife.'

'And would that do you any good? Knowing things about me?'

'Yes, it would.'

'Then, that's a start, isn't it?' he said, drawing her arm through his. He didn't say anything else but leaned across and looked through her window, smiling at her view of the rocks below but then his eyes swung upwards, scanning the spine of the mountains. Her heart was in her mouth again. Supposing she misunderstood this moment, read too much or too little into it? She was feeling frightened. 'Yes,' she said, 'a start…not an ending, I think.'

He murmured, 'Do not be afraid; our fate cannot be taken from us; it is a gift.'

'Who said that, Nando?'

'Guess.'

'Oh… Dante?' She laid her head down on his shoulder–but only for a moment, because the bus was careering round the hair-pin bends and almost banged their heads together. Between the hum and whirr of the engine noise and her own speeding thoughts, she forgot about the steep drop. Outside, grey-leaved eucalyptus trees flapped crazily in the wind.

They sat in silence for a while. In this lull she was trying to recollect a scene that his words had brought to mind. What was it exactly?

53

A man had come towards them through the dark, that last night in Porto Romolo. Her mother and Renata were sitting on the sea wall—no one else about. A globed street light above their heads. Petronella could not tell what was the dark of the night or the dark of the water. She was running up and down the stone steps to the beach in the safety of the pool of light.

Out of habit, absent-mindedly, Maddalena fumbled a cigarette from her bag. The lighter was running out and she could not thumb a flame. The failed clunk sounded like a bad throw of the dice.

An orange glow materialised out of the dark. 'Would you like a light?'

Maddalena gasped as a big man enfolded her in his arms. Then, he held her out to examine her and, as his face split into a gap-toothed grin, Maddalena giggled.

He said, 'I'm so glad to see you – I thought we might have lost you, Maddalena.'

Petronella wasn't sure if her mother was laughing or weeping.

His face drew towards Maddalena's, his head held on one side. The two cigarettes winked in the dark while the reflection of the lights floated like jelly on the water.

'So, Stefano, how are you these days?' she asked after a pause.

Petronella didn't catch all that he said—asthma... trying to stop smoking... after the end of the war... afraid of his dreams. He began talking about his own children and he leaned across to Petronella to chuck her under the chin. A whiff of wine on his breath. His eyes looked straight into hers. Petronella wondered why he was peering at her face.

'So like your father.' He chuckled, '*Carina*', pinching her cheek.

He looked down at the ground, touched Maddalena's elbow. 'More to the point though… how are you?'

'I'm all right, thanks.'

'Are you? Are you really, Maddalena?'

'Oh, Stefano, I don't know what I'm doing here any more.'

'Perhaps it would help if I told you something. It's something you ought to know. Renata told me what was tormenting you. Alex had nothing to do with it. I hope you're certain of that.'

His eyes glittered in the light from the lamp-post. Nobody said anything. The silence was like the darkness, filled with secrets.

'But I think you do know that, don't you? There's something else I want to say.'

'You were always such a help, *caro mio*. Tell me.'

'This is more difficult to say. I was friends with him, as you know. The greatest friend I've ever had. Because of that I have always been grateful that you did what you did. It has made my own survival more bearable. It could so easily have been me that was killed and not him. I don't know why I survived and he did not.

'What you did was like… oh, I don't know… a symbolic act. Yes, that's it. At the time, that is how it felt. I've always wanted to thank you although it… it must seem strange now. I don't know if that's any good to you. I just thought it might help you.'

Maddalena shot the smoke to the back of her throat, swallowed as though it was a splinter. He took her hand, squeezed her fingers. 'So I'm rambling. You may feel differently now. Looking back at that time, perhaps you find it hard to be at peace with yourself. But, you see, I know the reason you had to do it. I'd have done the same.'

He stretched across to her, wrapped his arms round her. Renata got up and called to Petronella to join her in the darkness of the beach. Together they threw stones at the gentle waves until Petronella grew tired and ran back up the steps to fling herself against her mother. Maddalena lifted her on to her lap. 'I think it's time for bed.'

Renata said, 'And time for a last little drink at my place, first? To wish you good-bye, my friend. Petronella can rest on my bed, if she likes.'

The man stubbed out his cigarette under his shoe and swept Petronella up in his arms to carry her back to Renata's apartment. As he settled her down on the bed he spoke in her ear. 'Your father was a very special man. We loved him. We would have done anything not to lose him.' He kissed her on each cheek, his stubbly face prickling her.

He left the door open and Maddalena lingered behind.

'Who is that man, Mummy?'

'His name is Stefano.'

'He says he loved Daddy.'

'Yes, they were good friends.'

'But why does he say he loved Daddy? Does he still love him? Why doesn't he come and see him? What does he mean?'

'Oh, he loved your father because… Your father… He…' Maddalena's eyes filled with tears that stuck behind her lids. Petronella watched her mother's lip quiver, but no sound came out of her mouth.

'What does it feel like? Love? How do you know you've got it?'

A record was playing down the corridor. 'You just know… I suppose it feels… as if you are falling into somewhere new.'

Maddalena leaned down and kissed Petronella's forehead, cupping her face in her hands. 'Go to sleep. You're tired. We have a long journey tomorrow. Let's talk about it on the train. I'll tell you what happened then. No.

Not now, *carissima*. Too late for a long story. And the others are waiting. Tomorrow, we'll have all day.'

Lying in bed with the door slightly ajar Petronella watched the furniture in Renata's bedroom take shape as she grew accustomed to the dark, listening to the voices of the three adults down the passageway. She could hear another familiar sound, punctuated now and then by laughter and gasps. It reminded her of home, playing Alex's favourite game, the one he'd taught her. But her mother never used to join in. So she had known how to play after all. The chink of dice being shaken in the hand, the clatter as they were thrown, rolling into positions on their flat impassive faces. She listened to her mother laughing, to Stefano's low voice rumbling beneath the murmurs of the two women. Finally lulled to sleep by the ivory sound of Liar Dice.